Welcome home to Springwater, Montana. . . .

In five marvelous novels, best-selling author Linda Lael Miller has masterfully crafted the wonderful world of Springwater, the dusty stagecoach stop that grew to a bustling frontier town.

This wonderful series began with *Springwater*, the breathtaking novel of a young widow who stepped off a stagecoach in Montana Territory only to find the love of her life—and a place to call home. Next came the Springwater Seasons—four intertwined novels, each a delightful tale on its own: *Rachel, Savannah, Miranda,* and *Jessica.* Now, come home for an old-fashioned holiday in Springwater—with a heartwarming story of love's redeeming powers and the gift of forgiveness.

A Springwater Christmas

Praise for *SPRINGWATER*

"Heartwarming. . . . Linda Lael Miller captures not only the ambiance of a small Western town, but the need for love, companionship, and kindness that is within all of us. . . . *Springwater* is what Americana romance is all about."
                                                                          —*Romantic Times*

. . . and the *Springwater Seasons* novels

"A delightful and delicious miniseries . . . The first volume of *Springwater Seasons* will charm you, enchant you, delight you, and quite simply hook you." —*Romantic Times*

Praise for Linda Lael Miller's Irresistible Western Romance

THE VOW

"The wild west comes alive through the loving touch of Linda Lael Miller's gifted words. . . . Breathtaking. . . . A romantic masterpiece. This one is a keeper you'll want to take down and read again and again."

—*Rendezvous*

"*The Vow* is a beautiful tale of love lost and regained. . . . The talented Linda Lael Miller provides a magical Western romance . . . that would be a masterpiece in any era."

—*Amazon.com*

"Linda Lael Miller's belief that we can have new starts is evident in *The Vow*. Everyone with the courage to try has a second chance to mend fences, reclaim dreams, uncover the past and move into a bright new future. Thus, *The Vow* is a romance that inspires not only to rekindle passion, but to reclaim the love between a child and parent and to never be afraid to challenge ourselves to change for the better. Brava, Ms. Miller!"

—*Romantic Times*

"A beautiful tale. . . . *The Vow* is a heartwarming love story that is a combination of smoldering passion and sweet romance that uplifts readers to new heights. . . . FIVE STARS."

—*Affaire de Coeur*

Praise for
MY OUTLAW

"Ms. Miller's time travel novels are always precious but this one surpasses them all. The premise is incredibly invigorating, the passion hot and spicy. Memorable characters link it all together to create a keeper."

—*Rendezvous*

"Miller's reasoning is brilliant and will fascinate time-travel aficionados.... This sexy, smart, heart-stirring love story fulfills romance readers' dreams. This is destined to be a favorite."

—*Romantic Times*

"In one thousand years, a panel of twentieth-century experts discussing time travel novels will first talk about the works of H. G. Wells and Linda Lael Miller. [This] time travel romance has everything a reader could want in a novel. The story line is exciting and action-packed, with an incredible heroine who will do anything to save her beloved's life. *My Outlaw* is a keeper that will stand the test of time.... FIVE STARS."

—*Affaire de Coeur*

"Exhilarating.... Linda Lael Miller still reigns supreme in the time-travel romance universe."

—*Amazon.com*

Books by Linda Lael Miller

Linda Lael Miller

A Springwater Christmas

POCKET BOOKS
New York London Toronto Sydney Tokyo Singapore

An Original Publication of POCKET BOOKS

 POCKET BOOKS, a division of Simon & Schuster Inc.
1230 Avenue of the Americas, New York, NY 10020

ISBN: 0-671-02752-2

First Pocket Books printing October 1999

10 9 8 7 6 5 4 3 2 1

POCKET and colophon are registered trademarks of
Simon & Schuster Inc.

Cover art by Robert Hunt

Printed in the U.S.A.

For John and June,
with love,
gratitude,
and the greatest admiration

And he said, What hast thou done?
The voice of thy brother's blood crieth unto me
from the ground.
And now thou art cursed from the earth,
which hast opened her mouth to receive
thy brother's blood from thy hand:
When thou tillest the ground, it
shall not henceforth yield unto thee her strength;
A fugitive and a vagabond shalt
thou be in the earth . . .

—Genesis 4:10–12

❧ Prologue ❧

Tennessee,
Spring 1863

IT WAS JUST AFTER DAWN, but Wes McCaffrey was already striding down the road, for all the world like he knew what he was doing, a bedroll strapped to his back, his prized squirrel gun dangling from one hand. When Will overtook him—he hadn't wanted to alarm their folks by calling out—he grasped his twin brother by the lapels of his coat and flung him backward against the trunk of a live oak.

Wes let out a grunt, glared at Will, and bent to snatch up his cap, which had tumbled to the ground in the skirmish. "You can't keep me here," he said, and sick as the fact made him, Will knew it was true as gospel. "If you want to stand on the porch and wave to the Yanks when they come to burn us out, that's your choice. Me, I'm gonna fight."

Will's jawline tightened, but he held his temper. Oh, he wanted to explode, right enough, but when you were dealing with Wes, you had to keep your wits about you. Beating the hell out of him, which Will yearned to do at the moment, would only make him dig in his heels. When that happened, he was about as easy to reason with as a bee-stung mule knee-deep in a mud hole.

"You can't stop them, Wes," he said quietly, after a long time. "Nobody can. There's too damn many of them, and they've got more of every-thing—horses, guns, food, everything. It's a fool's cause."

Wes's blue eyes flashed, and his face went red as a whore's petticoat. He dragged a hand across his mouth, as though it were all he could do to keep from spitting in Will's face. Maybe it was. "I never thought my own brother would turn out to be a coward," he fumed, breathing the words like fire. He came over to Will, stabbed at his chest with an index finger. "General Lee heard you talkin' like that, he'd see you hanged before the sun went down."

Will folded his arms, stood his ground. Wes wasn't the only obstinate person in the McCaffrey family. He was, as it happened, just one of four. "Well, General Lee ain't here, is he?" he taunted. "Damn it, Wes, if you didn't have a head full of tall tales and visions of glory, you'd know I'm talk-ing sense. What the devil are you so eager to defend? Slavery, maybe? The interests of a lot of fat plantation owners and aristocrats who'd sooner take a horsewhip to you than see you dance with their daughters? You know what they call people like us, don't you, Wes? White trash, that's what."

"Shut up!" Wes yelled. If there had ever been any hope at all that the folks wouldn't hear this row, that must have put an end to it. "It ain't that, and you know it! It's them coming down here, them blue-bellies, burning and looting and killing. I won't stand for that."

"You talk like you can stop them all by yourself. You're seventeen years old, Wes, and barely that. You're a kid, off to play soldier, and you're going to get yourself killed if you don't watch your step!"

Wes moved toward him again, thought better of the idea, and came to a grudging halt. "I'm goin'," he said, low and serious. When Wes got his back up about something, he forgot all about the grammar lessons he'd learned at school. "That's that. You got any guts, Will McCaffrey, you'll go with me."

Will shoved splayed fingers through his hair, let his hands rest on his hips to keep from throttling his only brother. "You'd leave," he marveled, in a raspy voice hardly above a whisper, "without so much as a fare-thee-well to Mama and Daddy? Wes, that'll kill them."

At last, Wes backed down, but only a little. "I plan on writin' a letter home soon as I've joined up with a proper outfit," he said.

Will's eyes burned all of the sudden; pure frustration blurred his vision.

"You say good-bye to them for me," Wes said, when Will didn't speak. Couldn't speak.

At some length, Will drew a deep breath, heaved it out. "I'm going with you," he replied slowly. "But I won't leave without speaking to Mama and Daddy first. They deserve better than this from you, Wes, and you damn well know it." Privately, he didn't figure they'd be all that surprised, not about Wes, anyway. All around them, men and boys alike were marching off to war, and nobody talked about much else these days.

Wes looked away, wouldn't meet Will's gaze after that. "I'll wait for you," he said, quietly stubborn now. "Down the road a ways."

"No, damn it," Will growled. "I'll tan you right here in the road, Wes—I swear to God I will— before I'll let you do this to them."

There was a short silence, during which everything hung in the balance. Then, in that quicksilver way he had, Wes relented. Even grinned, if somewhat sheepishly. With his free hand, he slapped Will's shoulder.

"All right," he said. "All right."

They went back, along the familiar road, neither of them speaking. Will took in the hills and hollows of the land as he walked, storing the sight of it, the sound and the smell of it, up in his memory, so it would always be there, right inside him, when he needed it to draw upon. Wes whistled some tuneless ditty, through his front teeth; if anything, he was impatient to be gone.

Their mother was at the stove when they entered their house, their father in his customary place next to the fireplace. June-bug set aside the spatula in her hand and left the fried eggs to burn; the knowledge was in her eyes: the day she'd dreaded since the first shot had been fired on Fort Sumter had finally come. Jacob folded his arms, his countenance solemn, and waited.

"I guess we'll be leavin' this mornin'," Wes said, when Will refused to make it easier for him by speaking first. "For the war."

June-bug groped for a chair and sank into it, but Jacob crossed the room and stood facing his sons. Will was nearly as tall as he was, but Wes had some growing to do.

"This what you want to do, Will?" Jacob asked, his voice low and resonant.

Will swallowed. "No, sir," he said.

Jacob's dark gaze slid to Wesley's face. "It's all your idea, then?"

Wes's neck and jawline went red. "It's what's right," he said.

Jacob merely shook his head. Then his eyes clashed with Will's. "All your life, you've been lookin' out for your brother, here," he said. "I reckon you see this as your duty."

"Yes, sir," Will said. He was about to break down and cry, and he figured if he did that, he'd just about die of shame, right then and there.

Jacob laid a hand to Will's shoulder. He looked at Wes with an expression of angry sorrow, then walked out of the house. Will guessed his father needed a few minutes alone; it was something he understood.

June-bug had gathered her composure by then, though she looked to Will like someone clutching the pieces of some irretrievably broken treasure. She put her arms around Wes, held him tightly for a long moment, watched with her heart in her eyes as her second-born twin turned from her embrace and fled, overcome by emotions of his own.

Will came to stand before her, and she laid her hands on his upper arms, stood on tiptoe, and kissed him lightly on the cheek. "Your daddy's right; you always did look after Wes," she said. There were tears gleaming in her eyes, and she sniffled, tried to smile. "I hate to think how much hide you've lost, growin' up, on account of your brother."

"I'll see to him, Mama." The promise came out rusty-sounding, like a hinge on a weathered door.

She nodded, touched his face with her fingertips. "Mind you don't forget to look after yourself," she said.

He kissed her forehead, turned to leave, but she held on, made him face her again.

"Don't let anything happen to him," she said.

Will didn't trust himself to speak; he merely inclined his head. Then he pulled away, once and for all, and made for the door. He saw his father, striding toward the cotton fields, back straight, head high, powerful arms swinging at his sides. Wes was already headed for the road; the fury of his pace was indication enough that he and Jacob had had words of their own, while Will had been saying good-bye to their mother.

Will hurried to catch up.

CHAPTER

✤ 1 ✤

Springwater, Montana Territory, Fall of 1882

THE DISTANT HILLS were skirted in every shade of crimson, yellow, and brown, the sky a blue so deep that it caused something to twist softly in the depths of Olivia Wilcott Darling's spinsterly heart, the air crisp with the promise of an early frost, perhaps even of snow.

Olivia, busy throughout that October morning burning dry branches pruned a month earlier from the trees, shrubs, and lilac bushes growing in her yard, stopped to touch the back of one hand to her brow. The acrid, autumny scent of woodsmoke roused within her an odd but familiar feeling of sorrowful festivity. Though she mourned the summer, vibrant early on with peonies and lilacs and sleepy bees, and then later with roses, the fall was still her favorite time of year. She loved its vivid colors and strange, chilly promise and, at moments like this one, with the fragrant fire crackling cheerfully nearby, with her fine, spot-

less white house rising behind her, solid and very
nearly grand, she felt expectant, as if something
were about to happen. Something out of the ordinary, something wonderful.

A friendly female voice interrupted her revery.
"Olivia? Aren't you planning to join us at Rachel's
for the quilting bee?"

She managed a smile for Savannah Parrish, who
lived with her husband and several children across
the road, then approached the neatly painted
fence. She'd hired young Toby McCaffrey to white-
wash the pickets in the spring, and he'd done a fine
job.

Savannah, a lovely woman with hair the color
of copper and eyes that shone with happiness, was
married to the town's only physician. She'd told
Olivia herself, right off, that she'd once been a
saloon owner and singer, news that had amazed
Olivia at the time, since those were not things
most women would have admitted to a close
friend, let alone a mere acquaintance. Now, clad
in a gray cloak and a practical, lightweight
woolen dress, roughly the color of cornflowers,
she stood beaming at Olivia, her basket of sewing
supplies over one arm, and waited expectantly for
a reply.

Olivia shook her head, looked away for a
moment, looked back. The women of Springwater
couldn't be accused of shunning her—she was
invited to every tea party, every church social,
every quilting bee. Once or twice, she had actually

attended, but she had felt so painfully out of place in the swirling midst of all that joyous chatter that it seemed easier just to stay away.

"We'll be finishing up Cornucopia's quilt today," Savannah prompted, smiling. "Who would have thought that trail boss would just ride into town one day, buy a pouch of tobacco from her over at the general store, and ask her to marry him, just like that?"

Olivia's effort at a responding smile simply wouldn't stick to her mouth. At thirty-two, she had long since given up on marriage and a family of her own—she'd been passed over and that was that, as her late aunt had so often reminded her—but that didn't mean she didn't still pine sometimes. While she liked Cornucopia just fine—indeed, she liked them all, Mrs. McCaffrey, Mrs. Wainwright, Mrs. Hargreaves, Mrs. Kildare, Mrs. Calloway and, of course, Savannah and all the others—secretly, she'd been bruised by the tidings of the store mistress's good fortune. It only served to reinforce what Aunt Eloise had always said: she, Olivia, was too tall, too plain, too thin, too smart, and far too contentious to attract a good man. She might just as well accept the fact and move on. The trouble was, it wasn't always such an easy thing to do.

"I've—I've got to tend this fire," Olivia said, finding her tongue at last. "I'm all sooty and my clothes smell of smoke—doubtless my hair does, as well. By the time I finished making myself presentable, you'd have that quilt finished up and tied with a bow."

Savannah shook her head, but her expression remained kindly. "Nonsense," she said. "Everyone will be disappointed if you're not there."

Olivia glanced back at the fire, already settling down to embers, then met Savannah's gaze straight on. "I'm sorry. I'm just—too busy."

Savannah looked at her in silence for a long moment, then nodded and gave a small sigh. "Maybe next time," she said.

"Maybe," Olivia replied. She would have another excuse at the ready when another social occasion arose, and Savannah plainly knew that. She hesitated briefly, nodded once more, and hastened away toward the home of Rachel and Trey Hargreaves.

Olivia watched until the other woman had disappeared around the corner of the Springwater stagecoach station, and felt even lonelier than usual.

Springwater.

He reined in the strawberry roan and leaned forward to rest an arm on the saddle horn, surveying the valley, the springs, the tight cluster of buildings in the midst of an ocean of grass, bustling with enterprise despite the first purple shadows of twilight creeping across the landscape.

A long sigh escaped him. He ought to rein that roan around and ride off for parts unknown. Put the whole matter behind him, once and for all.

On the other hand, he'd be thirty-seven years old, come the spring, and he'd been living under an assumed name for so long that he had to think twice sometimes to recall who he really was. Damn, but he was tired of running. Tired of telling lies, tired of waking up in the middle of the night, drenched in sweat, with his guts wrung into a ropy knot and his heart thundering fit to crash right through his rib cage.

He'd go right on calling himself Jack McLaughlin for the time being, he reckoned; no sense in shocking folks right off. They'd be getting on in years now, the people he'd come to see, and one or both of them might be in failing health. He'd keep a careful distance, take things slow. Once he'd reasoned out what was what, he'd either tip his hand or get back on that roan and take to the road again.

He didn't much cotton to the latter prospect, yearning the way he did for a roof over his head, regular woman-cooked meals, and real beds with clean sheets on them, but if he'd learned one thing in his life, it was that only fools expected an easy path.

He waited another few moments, watching smoke curl, blue-gray, from the chimneys of that little town, then pressed his heels lightly against the roan's sides and loosened his hold on the reins. As though anxious for gentle company himself, the gelding obeyed instantly.

* * *

It was nearly dark when he showed up at her front door, that hulking, shaggy stranger, hat in hand, blue eyes meeting her questioning gaze straight on.

"They told me over at the Brimstone that this is a rooming house," he said.

Olivia's back straightened slightly. Most travelers slept at the Springwater Station, where they could indulge in June-bug McCaffrey's legendary cooking, if they were the sort to seek indoor sleeping quarters. Therefore, the request caught her slightly off guard.

"Yes," she answered, but primly. She couldn't afford to be too cool, though; after all, she'd spent Aunt Eloise's entire bequest buying this house, she was down to her last few dollars, and she needed paying guests. In truth, she hadn't had any guests at all, paying or otherwise, as of yet. Still, she made no effort to open the screened door between them.

His mouth tilted upward at one side, in a semblance of a quizzical grin, and Olivia was thunderstruck by his resemblance to—to *someone*. She couldn't for the life of her think whom it was he looked like, but she relaxed a little all the same, if for no other reason than that sense of benign familiarity.

"I'm sorry I bothered you, ma'am," he said, and started to turn away. He was tall and powerfully built, especially through the shoulders, and his clothes, dungarees, a colorless woolen shirt, battered buckskin chaps, and a long gunslinger's coat, had all seen better days, as had his boots.

"Wait," Olivia said, and bit her lip.

He stopped, turned back.

"I charge two dollars a week, without meals," she told him, well aware that she was falling over her own tongue and there wasn't a thing she could do about it. "Four if you want breakfast and supper. I do laundry, too, but I charge by the piece for that." She paused, cleared her throat. "You'll have to pay in advance. The two dollars, I mean."

He might have chuckled; the sound was so low, she couldn't be sure. "Fair enough," he said. He'd been about to don his hat again, but now he held it loosely in the fingers of his right hand. "Name's Jack McLaughlin, if that's important."

Praying she would not be murdered in her bed— or worse—Olivia unlatched the hook and opened the screened door. "It is. Come inside, Mr. McLaughlin," she said. "I'll show you your room, and put on some supper, if you're hungry."

"Do you have one?" he asked, standing there in the foyer, taller than the long-case clock ticking against the wall.

Olivia hesitated, hoping her voice wasn't trembling, the way the pit of her stomach was. She had the most peculiar sensation of dizzy exhilaration, as though she'd just stepped over a precipice in the dark, trusting that she would survive the fall. "A room?" she asked.

He smiled. "A name," he prompted.

She raised her chin. "Miss Olivia Wilcott Darling," she said. "Miss Darling will do, when you have occasion to address me." She had never wanted to barber a man in her life, wouldn't even have *thought* of such an intimate thing, but just looking at Mr. McLaughlin brought up a fierce desire to take her sewing shears to all that light brown hair, that dreadful beard that hid so much of his face.

" 'Miss Darling' it is, then," he responded, with ease, still holding his hat.

Olivia took up her skirts, just high enough to keep from getting her feet tangled in the hems, and started up the broad center stairway. She did not dare look back at Mr. McLaughlin, for fear he'd have sprouted horns and a pointed tail while her back was turned. What, she wondered, had possessed her to buy this house, sight unseen, from an advertisement in a newspaper, using up practically every penny she had, and travel to this remote and rustic community, where she had known not a single soul? It had been the first impulsive thing she'd ever done, in the whole of her dull and sheltered life, lighting out for the wild west barely a week after Aunt Eloise had been buried in the family plot back in Simonsonburg, Ohio.

What had made her think she was suited to the demands of running a rooming house? Why, given her reputation for being unsociable, she might lie dead in this house for a considerable length of time before anyone missed her . . .

"I may not look it, ma'am," Mr. McLaughlin

said, from a pace behind her as they mounted the stairs, "but I'm a gentleman. Never laid a hand on a woman—not against her wishes, anyway—in my life."

He'd read her mind. Olivia did not dare allow him to see her face, which was surely flaming with color, so hot did it feel. "I am not afraid of you or any other man," she said, falling back, in her desperation, on bravado. "Besides, I keep a thirty-eight in the drawer beside my bed, and I know how to use it."

An eloquent and perhaps slightly amused silence followed, and Olivia had ample time to regret mentioning her bed, let alone the little pistol she had purchased upon her arrival and never once fired.

Gratefully, she reached the door of the best of her three guest chambers, turned the knob, and stepped aside.

Mr. McLaughlin passed her, lingering there in the hallway, and stepped over the threshold. The room was dark, and Olivia was forced to go in and light the lamp on the table just to her left, revealing the plain iron bedstead and its coverlet, one of the many she had crocheted during Aunt Eloise's declining years. There was a bureau, too, and a small washstand, but little else.

"This'll do just fine," Mr. McLaughlin announced.

He shed his coat, and Olivia, frankly disturbed by the simple but innate masculinity of the gesture, felt her breath quicken and her face color up again. His presence seemed to fill the room, to push at the very walls, and she would have sworn he was using up more than his fair portion of the air.

She remained near the door, one hand on the knob. "I'll bring up some water, so you can wash before supper."

He was standing with his hands on his hips, and Olivia noticed for the first time that he was armed. He carried the pistol—a .44, she suspected—in a shoulder holster, just under his left armpit and within easy reach of his right hand.

"There are a few rules," she said, raising her chin a notch.

Mr. McLaughlin thrust a hand through his hair. "I reckoned there would be," he replied, with a smile in his voice. He removed the pistol—he noted she'd been staring at it—and laid it aside on the bureau top, though he didn't bother to unbuckle the holster. "No smoking, I'll wager. No drinking, either. And no visitors above the first floor, the female sort in particular. Anything else?"

Although he had spoken in a polite, even friendly fashion, Mr. McLaughlin's words made Olivia feel like a fussy old maid, and she was irritated, though she could not have said whether with herself or with him. "No swearing," she added. "No spitting, and no animals of any kind."

He very nearly laughed out loud; she could see that he wanted to, and she turned and fled like a coward, scurrying along the back corridor and down the narrow rear stairway leading to the kitchen. There, she immediately set herself to the tasks of heating the promised wash water and planning supper, but staying busy didn't help the way it usually did. Her thoughts trailed behind, lingering upstairs, with Mr. McLaughlin. She heard his boot heels echo on the hard wood floor as he crossed the room, probably to the window, and marveled at the effect he had on her.

Like most men traveling alone in the west, her new boarder almost certainly had a *past*; no doubt he was dangerous, too, though in an entirely different way than an outlaw or a drunk or any other sort of rascal would have been. He hadn't done anything wrong, had treated her cordially and with quiet respect from the very first, and yet—and yet, she was troubled. He'd had an instant and profound effect on her, one she didn't begin to comprehend, and her virtue, always firm around her like a corset pulled to the point of bursting its laces, suddenly seemed slightly, well, *loose*.

"Preposterous," she murmured, and banged down the lid on the hot water reservoir, at one side of the stove.

"Beg your pardon, ma'am!"

She nearly started out of her skin; had the man removed his boots and sneaked down the stairs in his stockinged feet? She whirled, the blue spatterware ladle in one hand.

He grinned in a way that could only have been described as boyish, though there was no denying he was a full-grown man. "Sorry if I scared you," he said. "I figured on sparing you a trip up the stairs with that hot water, that's all."

She stared at him mutely for a few moments, wondering why just looking at him, just hearing the timbre of his voice, should quicken her heartbeat the way it did, and cause her breath to come with ever-so-slightly more effort. "You'll—you'll be wanting supper?"

He nodded. "Please," he said. Then, after reaching into a pocket of his dungarees—he'd removed the buckskin chaps—he drew out a gleaming twenty-dollar gold piece and laid it on the table. "I'll be here a month or two, I reckon."

It was all Olivia could do not to bolt over to the table and snatch up that substantial coin before he changed his mind, decided he'd stay at the Springwater Station after all, and took back his rent money. She indicated a bucket hanging tidily on a nearby peg, and he took it and the ladle and began drawing steaming water out of the reservoir.

He smelled of horse and man and fresh October air, and of something else that was quite indefinable, and Olivia was profoundly aware of the heat and power of his body, even though they weren't touching.

"Do you have a trade, Mr. McLaughlin?" she asked, because if she hadn't said something, she would have bolted like a shy bride confronted with a naked husband.

His eyes twinkled when he looked at her, his

large, callused hands still busy with the bucket and ladle. "Well, ma'am, I've done a lot of different sorts of work in my time. Helped build a railroad or two. Did some blacksmithing once or twice—I'm a fair hand with a hammer and saw, too. And like just about every other man west of the wide Missouri, I've herded my share of cattle." He paused. "You?"

Olivia did not quite know how to answer. Indeed, she did not quite know how to *breathe*. Not for the first time, she wished she were closer to Savannah Parrish and Rachel Hargreaves and the others. It would have been a comfort to have someone, a married woman with a working knowledge of such phenomena, to ask about the strange impact this man had upon her nerves and senses.

"Have I herded cattle?" she stalled.

He laughed, replaced the chrome lid on the reservoir, steam from the bucket of hot water a mist floating between them. "I guess I was asking how you came to be way out here in Springwater, all by yourself, running a rooming house."

"How do you know I'm alone?" Olivia demanded.

"That's pretty obvious, given the fact that you're scared to death of me, but willing to have me under your roof and at your table, all the same. Besides, you introduced yourself as 'Miss' Darling, remember?"

She wanted, inexplicably, to tell him everything about herself, that was the odd thing. Wanted him to understand that she'd had fine dreams once, and high hopes, just like every other woman, explain how she'd been orphaned at fifteen and subsequently spent her best years looking after a crotchety aunt. But it simply wouldn't do, spilling out such personal details.

"Your question is a bit too familiar, Mr. McLaughlin," she said.

He grinned, shrugged those massive shoulders, and turned away to head up the stairway again. Why did he seem so very familiar when he was unquestionably a stranger?

"Supper will be served in an hour," she called after him.

"I'll be here," he replied.

Jack stood in front of the wavy mirror over Miss Olivia Wilcott Darling's spare-room bureau, assessing himself. He looked like one of those old codgers who lived off in the tucks and folds of nowhere, and all of the sudden his beard itched fit to set him to scratching like a hound dog. A shave would have been just the thing.

No, he thought, with a long sigh. No sense getting reckless. He wasn't ready to be recognized, not just yet, anyhow.

So he washed at the basin, with the hot water Miss Olivia had provided, and put on his spare shirt. After supper, he would have to go out again and find shelter for the roan, as he'd left the poor critter tethered in front of the Brimstone Saloon, but for now he meant to enjoy the rare and singular pleasure of taking a meal with a handsome woman.

Miss Olivia was tall, lithe as the willows that had once grown alongside the creek back home. Her hair was a rich reddish brown color, like fine rosewood polished with beeswax, and her eyes put him in mind of the kind of sherry genteel folks drank, when they had cause to celebrate.

He leaned forward, his hands braced against the edges of the bureau, and once again gazed at himself in the mirror.

"You've been on the trail too long," he muttered. "She's a lady, Miss Olivia is, and a Yankee at that. Not interested in the likes of you, Jack McLaughlin."

He frowned. The name felt threadbare all of the sudden, grayed by time and worn through, like an old pair of long johns, and he wished he could discard it, square his shoulders, hold up his head, and set the truth right out there in plain sight.

Yet he didn't dare, he knew that. His backbone curved, and his shoulders sagged. He was a coward, pure and simple, a yellow-belly. He'd been trying to escape that one, horrible, irretrievable, cast-in-stone day for better than half his life, and he was likely to continue, futile as it was.

He shouldn't have come to Springwater in the first place.

The thing to do, he decided, was eat supper with Miss Olivia, leave her with the gold piece for her trouble, and get out. Ride all night, and all the next day, and never so much as think about coming back.

He raised his head and this time saw contempt in his eyes. Contempt for himself. "You're not going anywhere," he said fiercely, and then he turned his back on his own image.

Olivia went outside, lantern in hand, cornered one of the hens in the chicken house, wrung its neck, and prepared it for the soup kettle with dispatch, a talent she had developed only after her arrival in Springwater. The first few times, she'd nearly retched, but now she could swing an ax, clean a carcass, and pluck feathers as ably as any farmwife in the territory.

By the time Mr. McLaughlin appeared, looking brushed and scrubbed and wearing, she couldn't help noticing, a fairly fresh shirt, that bird was boiling on the stove, steaming up the window over the sink and filling the house with a delicious aroma.

"I've made dumplings," she said, feeling only slightly less rattled than before, "and I could put on a pot of coffee. If it wouldn't keep you awake, that is."

"I'd enjoy drinking somebody's coffee besides my own," he said. He didn't take a seat at the table, although it was set. Somewhere along the line, Jack McLaughlin, drifter, had learned at least a modicum of good manners. It was a heartening thing to know. "Thank you very much."

Olivia inclined her head to indicate the table.

"Go ahead and sit down, Mr. McLaughlin. I don't mind serving your food. This isn't a social occasion, after all."

He hesitated briefly, then drew back one of the chairs and sat. "You get many boarders?" he asked, sounding as shy and awkward as she felt.

She shook her head. Might as well be honest, since she had a choice in the matter. She had Mr. McLaughlin's twenty-dollar gold piece, and she wasn't about to give it back, not without a fight anyhow. "Not many," she said, lifting the lid off the chicken and dumplings and blinking away a rush of steam. "Most people stay down at the Springwater Station."

He arched an eyebrow, watching as she pumped water into the blue enamel coffeepot at the sink. "Oh? Why's that?"

She set the pot on the stove, took a glass jar down from the shelf, and scooped coffee beans, ground by Cornucopia at the general store just the day before, into the small metal basket. "Mrs. McCaffrey— June-bug—is a fine cook. Folks just seem to take to her, and to her husband, too."

He was quiet for so long that Olivia finally broke down and glanced his way. "Mr. McLaughlin?"

He smiled, but it seemed like an effort. With a sinking heart, Olivia began to suspect that her precious boarder already regretted staying in her establishment instead of at the station.

"Must be hard to make a living," he said, after a long time.

It took Olivia a moment to sort out what he meant: he wasn't referring to the McCaffreys and their thriving business, but to her own pitiful efforts at supporting herself. Aunt Eloise had been right, she thought, with an inward sigh. She hadn't the stalwart nature for running a frontier rooming house; she should have stayed in Ohio, crocheting and teaching Sunday school, given a few piano lessons perhaps, and lived in dignified poverty, off the interest on her modest inheritance.

"Yes," she admitted, softly. A little reflectively. "Yes, it's hard. I guess that makes me a bona-fide member of the human race."

He chuckled. "You're not much given to self-pity are you, Miss Darling?"

Using two crumpled dish towels for pot holders, Olivia hoisted the kettle of simmering chicken off the stove and carried it across the room. "What good would that do?" she countered, setting the meal down on the table with a thump and going back to fetch a ladle and give the coffeepot a little shake. "Feeling sorry for myself, I mean?"

"Not much, I guess," he allowed, resting his hands on the table, fingers interlaced. "Still, sometimes that's the only way a body can get any sympathy."

She realized he was teasing and might have smiled, except that the coffee started to boil and she had to hurry back to the stove and take the pot off the heat.

"Sympathy," she said, upon her return to the table, "weakens the character."

He watched as she pulled back her own chair and sat down across from him. He had not touched the food, although she could see that he was ravenously hungry. In fact, in the spill of shadowy lamplight, he looked downright gaunt, as though he'd been wandering the face of the earth for a long time, with nowhere to settle in.

"Maybe," he allowed, after some thought. "But it does make the world seem a little warmer, doesn't it?"

She didn't know how to answer, and so reached for Mr. McLaughlin's dish and the ladle, simultaneously. Though she would normally have offered a brief blessing before eating, she was so distracted that she forgot entirely. Instead, she served up her boarder's supper and set the food before him. "It seems to me that there's no profit in pretending the world is anything *other* than cold," she said, realizing only after the words were out of her mouth how embittered they must have made her sound.

Well, perhaps she *was* a little bitter. As a child, she'd envisioned herself as a smiling and balanced adult, with a loving husband and several lively offspring. Instead, she'd wound up nursing Aunt Eloise through a series of illnesses, some real and just as many others imagined, and after a few years, she'd begun to abandon her dreams, one by one. Now, they were all gone.

A silence fell between them then, broken only

by the usual sounds from the Brimstone Saloon,
down at the corner. Olivia held that particular
establishment in very low esteem.

Mr. McLaughlin ate with gratifying appreciation. "You sit right there," he said, when Olivia
would have gone to the stove for the coffee. "Finish your supper. You take sugar or cream?"

Olivia was, for a moment, too startled to
respond. No one, but for June-bug McCaffrey, during her brief stay at the station, when she'd first
arrived in Springwater the winter before, had
served her anything in as long as she could recall.
If she'd had her wits about her, she would have
told him that she didn't take coffee at night.
Instead, she replied, "With sugar, thank you. It's
there on the shelf next to the stove."

He brought the sugar bowl to the table, along
with two fragrant cups brimming with fresh, stoutly
brewed coffee. She wouldn't get a wink of sleep,
Olivia thought ruefully, but she didn't care. It was
a treat, having someone in the house, even if he
was only a drifter, badly in need of barbering.

"What brings you to Springwater, Mr. McLaughlin?" she asked.

Just like that, his face lost all expression. It was
as though he'd pulled a set of wooden shutters
closed with a decisive snap.

She waited.

"I don't reckon on staying long," he said, when
he saw that she wasn't going to back off from the
question. It had been a reasonable thing to ask,

after all, given that he would be spending the night—perhaps many nights—under her roof. "I've got some business to attend to, when the time's right. Then I'll be moving on."

She sat a little nearer the edge of her chair, concerned. He sounded so mysterious, almost secretive, as though his "business" in Springwater might be less than honorable. "It takes an effort to get to this town," she persisted. "Folks don't come here by accident, or just for something to do."

He took a sip of his coffee, eyeing her over the rim of his mug. Perhaps, she thought, she'd been foolhardy, renting a room to someone she didn't know. On the other hand, if she wasn't going to cater to strangers, she might as well move into the nearest poorhouse and be done with it.

"I'm looking for a place to winter over," he said, at long last. "When I heard about Springwater, back in Choteau, I figured it would do as well as anywhere else. The Jupiter and Zeus silver mine is here, isn't it? I reckon I might find work there."

Olivia rose from her chair and began to clear the table. "I imagine there's work in Choteau, too," she observed, without looking at him. Why, she wondered yet again, was she trying to drive away the only customer she'd had since she'd come to Springwater herself? Was it because he'd stirred her emotions and senses, without apparent effort?

She heard his chair scrape lightly against the floorboards as he stood.

"I'll just see to my horse," he said quietly, and then he was gone.

Olivia held her breath, figuratively at least, until much later when, reading in her room, she heard him enter the house and climb the stairs.

He paused outside her door. "Good night, Miss Olivia," he said.

Olivia's heart was thumping; had she lost her mind? For all she knew, the man could be a rounder and a rascal. An outlaw. Even a murderer, bent on vengeance.

"Good night," she replied, all the same.

CHAPTER

2

TREY HARGREAVES ASSESSED the stranger filling the doorway of his office at the back of the Brimstone Saloon. He couldn't get past the feeling that he'd seen him someplace, doubtful as that seemed. He had a good memory for names and faces, Trey did, and if he'd run into this man before, he'd likely remember it plain.

He tamped out the cheroot he'd been smoking—his wife Rachel, whom he adored, didn't favor the use of tobacco—stood up behind his desk, and held out one hand. Springwater was, after all, a friendly place, a place eager to grow and prosper. For that, of course, you needed people. "Come in," he said.

The visitor stepped over the threshold—except for Jacob McCaffrey, he was the biggest galoot Trey had ever slapped eyes on—ducking a little to keep from smacking his head on the lintel over the door, shook hands with Trey, and cleared his throat.

"Name's Jack McLaughlin," he said. "I heard there might be work to be had, up at the Jupiter and Zeus, and that you'd be the man to see about it."

"Sit down," Trey replied. He didn't see the need to offer his own name, since it was plain that McLaughlin already knew it. Just like everybody else knew the newcomer had taken a room over at Miss Darling's place the night before. She'd finally landed herself a customer.

McLaughlin took a creaky wooden chair facing Trey's desk and leaned back a little, interlacing his fingers. There was a calmness about him, something in his manner and in his movements, that continued to tug at the edges of Trey's memory.

"You ever done any digging? Down in a hole, I mean?" he asked, taking a second cheroot from the silver case he carried in his breast pocket and then offering the box to McLaughlin.

The other man declined, waited politely while Trey lit up. Then, at long last, he said, "I've panned for gold a time or two, but I can't say I've ever been too far underground." The shadow of a smile touched his mouth. "I was sort of saving that particular experience for last."

Trey snorted slightly at the joke, then drew thoughtfully on the thin cigar, regarding McLaughlin through an acrid, blue-gray cloud of smoke once he'd exhaled. "Some men can't abide it. The notion of all those tons of dirt and rock suspended over their heads, I mean."

"I do what I get paid to do," McLaughlin answered simply. "I learn fast, I work hard, and I can use the money. Seems like that makes me a likely bet, from your point of view, anyway."

Trey smiled. Whoever Jack McLaughlin was— Trey'd developed an instinct where people were concerned, dealing with cowboys, drifters, and the like, at the mine and at the Brimstone Saloon, and he'd have bet the name was a false one—the man had a good head on his shoulders. "Forty dollars a month if you're willing to set dynamite charges, thirty if you aren't. My men work ten hours a day, six days a week, and the first time I catch a whiff of liquor on you, I'll show you the road. Fair enough?"

McLaughlin grinned and Trey's curiosity quickened once again. Damn it, he *knew* this man— didn't he? And if he didn't, he damn well should.

"Put me down for forty a month," McLaughlin said, rising and offering a hand to seal the bargain.

"We ever met before?" Trey asked, frowning a little.

McLaughlin's good humor held, though his eyes were watchful and solemn. "No, sir," he said. "I reckon I'd recall it if we had."

Trey nodded, but he was still struck by the other man's resemblance to somebody he knew. Best concentrate on the business at hand, he thought, and that was hiring a fuse man. "You can start tomorrow. You'll need a heavy coat and a better pair of boots than those you've got on." Trey reached for the desk drawer where he kept the store of petty cash. "I can advance you a few dollars on your wages—"

"No need," McLaughlin said. "I've got a little money yet. I'll be at the mine by sunup. Anybody I ought to check in with?"

Trey shook his head. The foreman was a man named Smiley Beckett, but McLaughlin didn't seem like the type who needed watching over. In fact, unless Trey missed his guess, and he seldom did, this down-on-his-luck drifter was somebody to be contended with. McLaughlin would make a place for himself soon enough, and probably never feel the need to take orders from anyone.

"I'm obliged," McLaughlin said, and then he was gone.

It was about then that the bartender, Charlie, poked his balding head through the office door and said, "You told me to warn you, Boss. Mrs. Hargreaves is headed this way."

Rachel.

"Thanks," Trey said hastily. Then he grabbed up a newspaper and started waving it around in a vain attempt to dispel some of the lingering cheroot smoke.

All of the sudden, she was there. He must have looked like a fool, for Rachel's eyes were bright with laughter as she stood on the threshold, head tilted to one side, a hand resting on each hip.

"Flies?" she asked, knowing full well what he'd been doing.

He couldn't lie to her; never had, never would.

It would have been like lying to his own soul. "Smoke," he said, sounding a little forlorn, even to himself.

She laughed, crossed the room to put her arms around him, and raised herself on tiptoe to kiss his chin. "You looked like a naughty little boy just now, trying to hide the pieces of a broken cookie jar."

He pulled her against him; being anywhere near her always made him want to do that. Dear God, she felt good, soft and warm and curvy in all the right places.

She blushed. "Well, maybe not a *little* boy," she conceded, in a purr, and ran a finger tip down the edge of his lapel.

He kissed the end of her nose and then, very leisurely, her mouth.

"Not a boy, either, then," she gasped, when, at some length, he withdrew. "But quite *definitely* naughty."

"Guilty," he confessed. Then he chuckled and, however reluctantly, put her gently away from him. A back room at the Brimstone Saloon was no place to make love to a fine lady like Rachel—was it?—but he was bound to break down and seduce her if he didn't get a grip. "What brings you to this unworthy place, Mrs. Hargreaves?" She always set his senses to galloping like a herd of scared mustangs.

She hooked a finger under his belt buckle, just long enough to let him know who was boss, went over and closed the door, then drew up the chair McLaughlin had just left and sat herself down. Resting her elbows on the edge of the desk, she cupped her chin in both palms and looked up at Trey, her expression frankly inquisitive.

It was harder and harder to resist her.

"So? Who is he?" she asked, in a confidential tone, barely higher than a whisper.

He sank into his own chair, shifted a bit in a useless attempt to get comfortable. He wouldn't be comfortable for hours, maybe not until supper was over and the kids had been bathed, read to, prayed with, and put to bed. "Who is who?" he countered, though he knew.

"Who is *whom?*" she corrected, ever the schoolmarm, though it had been a good long while since she'd taught. He'd kept her busy over the years since she'd come to Springwater, and so had their growing tribe of children. "And darn it, Trey, you know who I mean, so stop stalling. It isn't every night that a man stays at Olivia Wilcott Darling's house, after all."

Little wonder, Trey thought, given that woman's prickly nature. He and Miss Darling were sworn adversaries, her feeling the way she did about the Brimstone Saloon and him feeling the way he did about nosy spinsters with too much free time on their hands. "He calls himself Jack McLaughlin."

Rachel didn't miss much. She leaned forward, her beautiful eyes narrowed in racy speculation. " 'Calls himself Jack McLaughlin'? You think he's somebody else, don't you? Why do you suppose he's staying at Olivia's, when they've got plenty of open rooms over at the station?"

Trey held up a hand to stem the tide. "Rachel, if you want answers, you're going to have to hold your fire till I get a word out. Sure, the man's probably got a secret or two, but there aren't many out here who don't. He's all right, though—if I didn't think so, I wouldn't have given him a job. As for his choosing Olivia's place, well, maybe he's taken with her. June-bug might be a better cook, but she's old enough to be his mother."

Rachel laid a hand to her bosom—how he loved that bosom—plainly stunned. "Do you think she'll marry him?"

Trey lived to tease his wife, in a variety of interesting ways. "June-bug?" he asked.

"Don't be silly," Rachel scolded, starting to look stern again.

"Olivia?" he persisted, in an innocent tone that caused her to narrow her gaze once more.

"Yes, Olivia," she retorted, but then her whole countenance brightened. "Oh, Trey, wouldn't it be wonderful if Olivia found a husband? She might join in once in a while then, become a real member of the community—"

Trey gave a deep and suitably long-suffering sigh. "I don't know why you women can't seem to accept the fact that she doesn't *want* to be a part of things. Seems to me, you'd be tired, the whole bunch of you, of having a door virtually slammed in your face every time you try to invite Miss Olivia Wilcott *Darling* over for tea."

Rachel looked troubled. "Anybody—well, any *woman*—could see that poor Olivia wants to be one of us, wants it with all her heart," she said. "It's just that she doesn't seem to know how to have a friend, or how to be one."

" 'Poor Olivia,' " Trey scoffed, but gently, because he loved his wife, loved the way she cared for everybody and everything around her. "That woman's been a thorn in my side since she got here. Yammering about her chickens, and how the noise from the Brimstone makes them so nervous, they won't lay. Landry figures she must have been weaned on pickle juice, and I'd say he's right."

Rachel stood, straightened her skirts. She looked particularly lovely that morning, with her skin glowing and her dark hair done up in a loose knot just above her nape. He wanted to take the pins out, one by one, and watch those gleaming ebony tresses fall around her shoulders, down her back. He wanted—

She shook a finger at him. "Don't you dare," she warned, as he started around the desk.

He held out his arms and did his best to look mischievously beseeching. His good friend Landry claimed that tactic always worked with his Miranda, no matter where they happened to be at the time.

Rachel backed up until she was pressed against the door. "Trey Hargreaves—" she murmured, as he advanced.

He braced his hands against the woodwork, one on either side of her, bent his head, and took her mouth with his own. She resisted at first, then, with a little moan, put her arms around his neck and kissed him back.

Trey reached down with one hand and turned the key in the lock.

There were ladies, he thought, and there were *ladies*.

Fortunately for him, Rachel was both.

Over at the general store, a buxom, smiling woman greeted him from behind the counter, and announced that her name was Cornucopia and he was mighty welcome in Springwater. And who was he, by the way?

Jack inclined his head slightly, in polite acknowledgment. He didn't reckon he'd ever encountered anybody as aptly named as Cornucopia. She was just the sort of woman he usually took to, in fact, ripe as peaches at the end of August, red-headed and friendly and generously made. Peculiar how his thoughts kept turning back to Miss Olivia, thin and prim and skittish as she was.

"I'm just a drifter," he answered, in his own good time. By then, he was inspecting work boots, fine, sturdy ones with thick soles and laces fit to withstand a few brisk pulls in the morning.

"You're the first boarder Miss Darling's had since she opened that place," Cornucopia volunteered, crossing the room to stand beside him. The mercantile smelled pleasantly of shoe leather and coffee beans, peppermint candy and pipe tobacco and a hundred other things.

The scent of Miss Cornucopia's lemon verbena perfume stood out, just the same.

He offered her a brief, sidelong grin. "I'll be needing a couple of pair of denim trousers and some other things, too." He raised one of the boots slightly. "You have these in a size eleven?"

She receded a little, but her eyes sparkled with good-natured determination. He decided he liked her.

"I suppose so," she answered. "I'll just go on back and see. Anybody comes in, you tell 'em I'll be right with them."

Jack nodded. "I'll do that," he said, struck by her willingness to trust him, a total stranger, alone with all that merchandise, a lot of which would have been easy to pocket, not to mention the big cash register with all its fancy chrome scroll work.

By the time she returned, he'd selected several pairs of woolen socks, some new long johns, and a couple of heavy plaid shirts. As an extravagance, he chose a book, too—a collection of adventure stories. Once he'd paid for his purchases, including the boots Miss Cornucopia brought from the storeroom, he'd pretty well spent all the cash he had on hand.

It didn't much matter, he decided. He'd found a place for his horse over at the Springwater Station, taking care to deal with a young stablehand and no one else, and paid for the animal's looking after in advance. He had the things he needed for his new job, and a clean, warm bed to sleep in, and he could plan on breakfast and supper at Miss Olivia's table, at least for the next couple of months. He'd have to do without the noonday meal, but he'd been hungry many a time in his life, and it had yet to kill him.

"You give Miss Olivia my best regards, now," Cornucopia called cheerfully, when Jack opened the door to step out onto the wooden sidewalk. "Tell her I've got some new sheet music in. Been saving it just for her."

Jack gave his hat brim a light tug in farewell. "I'll do that," he said. So Miss Olivia was musical. Now that was interesting; he would never have suspected. She seemed a mite too jittery to settle herself long enough to learn to play an instrument.

Back at the house, he tarried on the porch and knocked before entering, even though he had Miss Olivia's permission to walk right in, since he'd paid his rent in advance and all. He didn't want to startle her, since her nerves appeared to be delicate, so he rapped at the glass oval on the door with his knuckles, waited in vain for an answer, and finally went inside.

He peeked into the parlor and found there the piano he hadn't noticed when he arrived, even though it was in plain sight, and thought of Miss Cornucopia's new sheet music. He missed a quiet evening's entertainment—his mother had a singing voice fit to rival an angel's, and his father could make any fiddle dance in his big hands. He wished he'd spent another few pennies to buy a song for Miss Olivia to play; it would have been a friendly gesture, that's all. More for his own pleasure, he allowed, than hers.

Arms full of bundles, he mounted the front stairway and nudged open the door of his room with the toe of one worn-out boot. She'd made his bed, raised the window to let in the crisp autumn air.

He put the packages down carefully, on top of the bureau, and took off his coat. It gave him pause, to think of her smoothing his sheets, fluffing his pillows, straightening his blankets. It made him feel things he hadn't allowed himself to feel in a long, long time. Things were awakening inside him, sprouting like seed pushing up through warm soil, and all of them centered around Miss Olivia.

As much to distract himself as anything else, he opened the parcels and began, methodically, putting everything away. When he was through, he folded the wrapping paper neatly, tied the separate strings together, and wound them into a ball. It never occurred to him to stuff the items into the stove downstairs; he'd known his share of hard times and besides, a person never knew when they'd need a bit of twine or a scrap to write on.

When he'd done everything else he could think of, which wasn't much, he went down to the kitchen and was pleased to find a pot of coffee waiting on the range. He poured himself a mug full, added sugar, and went to the window over the sink, which overlooked the backyard.

That was when he saw Miss Olivia storming back from the chicken coop, all a-fury, with a basket over one arm, her face, indeed, her whole countenance, a fascinating study in consternation.

Jack grinned to himself and enjoyed the simple pleasure of watching her.

She entered the house with a clatter, and didn't seem surprised to see him standing there in her kitchen, a cup of her coffee in his hand. "Look," she said, thrusting the basket, now tilted, toward him. "Just look!"

He looked, and saw nothing at all.

"That's just the point," she burst out, for all the world as if he'd answered aloud, her high cheekbones pink with outrage, her sherry-brown eyes snapping, her thick rosewood hair wind-tossed, so that tendrils of it fell around her long, slender neck. "Not one egg. Not one! And do you know why, Mr. McLaughlin? Do you know why?"

He took a steadying sip of his coffee. "I can't say as I do," he replied carefully.

"Well," she huffed, "I'll *tell* you why."

"Okay," he said, affably enough, and waited.

"It's all that shooting and shouting and carrying on down there at the Brimstone Saloon, that's what it is. My chickens are so frightened, they can't even—they can't even be proper chickens!"

He wanted to laugh, wanted it so much that he

took a gulp of coffee to keep from doing so, and promptly scalded the whole inside of his mouth.

"I'm not going to stand still for this!" she ranted, hanging up the basket and her cloak and fetching up a wash basin. "I plan to attend that town council meeting tomorrow night, whether I'm welcome or not, and make my opinions known!" Jack set his coffee aside, wiped the back of one hand across his lips. His throat, tongue, and the roof of his mouth smarted so fiercely that his eyes watered. As for Miss Olivia's opinions, he figured everybody probably knew more than they wanted to about those as it was, but it would have been downright risky to say so, with her in high dudgeon and within grabbing distance of the cast-iron poker next to the stove.

Damn, though, he really wanted to grin.

"Maybe you ought to do just that," he said carefully, but he was thinking. *Can I watch?*

She opened the stove reservoir and began scooping water industriously into the basin. "It's not as though I'm asking so very much," she went on, stomping over to the sink with her vessel of warm water, where she proceeded to soap up her hands and scrub them with a vengeance. "I just want to live in peace. I want eggs for my boarders—"

He wanted something entirely different—to take this contrary, bustling woman into his arms and kiss her. Not just once, and not chastely, either, but a whole bunch of times. Employing his tongue.

"I reckon I can get by without eggs," he offered.

She glared at him over one slim shoulder. "That, Mr. McLaughlin, is not the point."

He reached for his coffee again, and saw that his hand was unsteady. Fortunately, Miss Olivia was too caught up in the henhouse drama to take notice. "I see," he said meekly, even though he didn't see at all and felt about as meek as a young ram in rutting season. It was enough to throw a man, that was for sure and certain.

"Are you all right?" Miss Olivia asked. She'd gone pale.

Her concern almost undid him. He lifted one hand and squeezed the bridge of his nose between a thumb and forefinger. "Fine," he lied. "I'm fine."

"Sit down," she commanded, pulling a chair over from the table.

He wasn't sick, nor was he about to swoon like some—well—some old maid. All the same, he sat. Lord knew, though, it wasn't going to cure what ailed him.

"You're ill."

"I'm not."

She ignored him, got out a clean strip of cloth, pumped cold water over it at the sink, wrung it out. Brought it over and pressed it against the back of his neck. It felt damnably good, useless gesture though it was.

He'd been in Olivia Darling's house for one day, and already he wanted to tell her things he'd never told anybody. About his nightmares, for example.

About that one hour, that one moment, that had changed everything. Everything.

If he had any sense, he'd leave. Now. Today.

She stroked his hair, and he knew instantly that the gesture had been unplanned, perhaps even unwilling, but her touch scalded through him like a flood of hot lamp oil all the same.

She stared at him, and he realized he must have stiffened like somebody waving a lightning rod in the rain. They were both quiet for a long, unsettled moment.

Then, being a female, she spoke.

"You might be quite handsome, with a haircut and a shave," she observed. It was clear, from the shaky note in her voice and the flush in her cheeks, that she'd taken herself by surprise, saying that.

He started to stand. Once he'd been barbered, they'd know him instantly, even from a distance.

Placing one hand on his shoulder, Miss Olivia pressed him easily back into the chair. "Just a trim, then," she said, very softly. It was that tenderness that spoiled his resolve.

He glanced up at her, attempted to lighten the moment with a grin. The way he figured it, he might just go crazy if she handled him too much, even if it was only to cut his hair a little, and tidy up his beard. "I guess it depends on how much you want to charge."

She hesitated, then smiled. "You're my first boarder. That should entitle you to some special consideration."

Their gazes locked for an instant, and then they both looked away.

He bore an uncomfortable resemblance to his old self, after Miss Olivia barbered him, he thought, much later, when he stood staring into the mirror over the bureau in his room, but as long as he was careful, it shouldn't matter too much. Given that he'd be spending most of his time underground for the next little while, it was unlikely that anyone would recognize him before he was ready to make his presence known.

He went to the window, raised the sash, and stood looking out over Miss Olivia's yard and chicken coop, toward the Springwater Station. Lamplight glowed from every window, and the sight filled him with a sweet and ancient ache. After a long time, he turned away, found the book he'd bought at the general store earlier in the day, and stretched out on his bed to read.

Olivia paused, there in the parlor, and lifted her gaze to the ceiling. Her fascination with Mr. McLaughlin was ill-advised, not to mention highly improper, and yet she couldn't seem to stop thinking about him. For all his rustic appearance and reserve, there was something fine about him, something dignified and very intriguing.

She'd be insane to let herself care for such a man, she knew—he was a saddle bum, after all, a mere vagabond. Perhaps even a rustler, or a bank robber. And he surely had a woman somewhere or, for that matter, a wife.

The idea of a Mrs. McLaughlin filled Olivia with such anguish that even her concern over the state of her frenzied hens was displaced. *Not a wife*, she thought, closing her eyes tightly. *Please, not a wife*.

Then, because she'd done the supper dishes and fed the chickens and there was nothing else to do, she raised the lid that covered the piano keys and ran her fingers over them in a flowing, sparkling trail of notes.

Aunt Eloise, despite her comfortable circumstances, had not been a generous woman. However, she had provided Olivia with music lessons from the very first, perhaps to keep the grief-stricken girl occupied and, thus, out from underfoot, perhaps because she enjoyed a rendering of Chopin or Mozart herself, once in a while, and had never learned to play. Whatever her reasons, Olivia was grateful, for she passed many otherwise lonely hours at her piano.

Slowly, softly, she began a rendition of her favorite, "Lorena," a ballad popular with all factions during the war. The tune was really more suited to a fiddle, but she loved it because it was so romantic. She closed her eyes and lost herself in the flood of notes.

When she finished and opened her eyes, Mr. McLaughlin was standing beside the piano, watching her.

"My goodness," she said, "you startled me." It

was a fib, and a coy one at that, and Olivia did not admire herself for such a deceit, however innocent. On some level, she had been aware of Mr. McLaughlin from the moment she'd opened the front door to him the night before.

"That was beautiful," he said. He sounded hoarse, and just then she glimpsed such misery in his eyes that she wanted to rise and take him into her arms, hold him tightly, and smooth his hair.

"I'm afraid I'm out of practice," she demurred, looking away to give him time to recover his composure. To give herself time to do the same.

"Please," he said, sitting down in the horsehair chair nearest the piano. "Play something else. A hymn, maybe."

She was about to launch into "The Battle Hymn of the Republic" when discretion overtook her—she'd noticed the soft, Southern meter to his speech right away—and chose "In the Garden" instead. When she'd finished that, she didn't dare look at him; the very air seemed to pulse with emotions of every sort, his, her own, those of the lonely and frightened men who'd sung the same songs around Union and Confederate campfires, 600,000 of whom never found their way home again, whether the road back led north or south.

She never knew how many songs she played that night, only that she kept making music until the small of her back ached and her fingers would no longer do her bidding. Then, at last, she stopped, stood, glanced over to find that Mr. McLaughlin was still seated, unmoving, his head back, and his eyes closed.

"Good night," he said, just when she'd begun to fear that he'd up and died, right there in her front parlor. "And thank you."

She resisted an urge to lay her hand on his shoulder again, the way she'd done in the kitchen. "Good night," she replied, in an oddly choked voice, and, after turning down the wicks in various lamps around the house, retired to her room.

CHAPTER

❦ 3 ❧

JACK WAS TOUCHED, that first morning, to see that Miss Olivia was out of bed, even though dawn had yet to break. She was wearing a simple dress, her hair trailing down her back in a single thick plait. The coffee was already perking, and she had a slab of salt pork sizzling in a skillet, along with some cut-up boiled potatoes left over from supper. There were eggs, too; evidently, the chickens had passed a restful night.

His throat tightened as he stood there, looking at her. She might have been sixteen, so softly did she wear the light of the lanterns, and she was more than pretty, she was beautiful. He felt an highly imprudent desire to move that braid gently aside and plant a soft kiss on her nape.

"Morning," he said instead.

"Good morning, Mr. McLaughlin," she replied, all business. She dished up a plate of food and carried it over to the table. "I'll get your coffee."

He nodded. "You're up early," he commented, and immediately felt foolish. It was obvious that she was up, wasn't it, and any idiot would have known it was early.

She glanced back at him over one shoulder. "Yes," she said, with a little frown. "I am."

"I know our bargain included breakfast," he said, sitting down, pulling his plate toward him, and taking up his fork, "but I could have fixed it for myself. No need your getting up with the"—he glanced down at the eggs—"chickens."

"Nonsense," she replied, fetching the coffeepot and coming back to stand beside him, filling his cup to the brim. "An agreement is an agreement." She nodded toward the drain board, next to the big metal sink, where a shiny tin lunch bucket awaited. "There's your dinner," she said.

"We didn't—"

She looked cheerfully exasperated. "It's only bits and pieces from supper," she pointed out. "No sense letting good food go to waste."

He laid down his fork. He'd done a lot of less-than-honorable things in his life, but he still had some pride, despite it all. "I don't take charity, Miss Olivia," he said. And he meant it as much as he'd ever meant anything before.

"And I don't give it," she replied. "If you're going to be pigheaded, I'll take that pail down to the Springwater Station and dump it in the McCaffreys' hog pen. Seems like a waste, though." She shrugged. "It's up to you. I'm not about to argue."

He began to eat again, because he had a long day ahead and he knew he'd be half sick with hunger by suppertime if he didn't. He gave the lunchpail a suspicious glance. "Just leftovers?" he asked. They'd had a good meal the night before—some kind of pie, with chunks of chicken in it. Shame to feed something that good to the pigs.

"Just leftovers," she confirmed.

"All right, then," he grumbled, and ducked his head, because all of the sudden, he couldn't meet her gaze. "You friendly with the McCaffreys?" he ventured, when several minutes had passed.

She sat down at last, with only a cup of coffee in front of her. Jack hoped he hadn't eaten all there was of the breakfast, leaving her to go hungry. "We're acquainted," she allowed. "Why do you ask?"

"I heard they were good folks, that's all."

"They are," she agreed immediately. "They were very kind to me after the accident—"

He felt a quivering sensation in the pit of his stomach, just to imagine her in any sort of danger. He wanted to protect this woman from everything that might hurt her, past, present, or future, crazy as it seemed. "What accident?"

She sighed, and a faraway look came into her eyes. "I was on my way to Choteau, traveling by rail, intending to take the Springwater coach here. Only something went wrong." She paused and bit her lower lip, and the distant expression was replaced by ghosts and shadows. He'd seen the same look in many a soldier's eyes, the reflection of too many battles, too much suffering and death. "The train went off its tracks out there, somewhere, in the wilderness. The weather was freezing and—and everybody was killed, except for myself and two little boys. Doc Parrish and Savannah adopted them, and I stayed at the Springwater Station until—until I felt a little less shaken. Jacob and June-bug looked after me, and wouldn't take a penny for their trouble."

He was silent.

She sighed again. "They're close knit, the people in this town," she said dreamily. "Almost like family. Jacob McCaffrey is the patriarch—he sort of oversees things, settles disagreements and such."

He knew somehow that she wasn't a part of that family, knew she kept herself apart from the others for some reason. "Maybe you ought to go to him about your quarrel with the Brimstone Saloon."

She shook her head. "I won't bring Jacob into this. He served his stint as mayor, and now the job belongs to"—she paused, for the merest fraction of a second, and tightened her mouth in distaste—"Gage Calloway."

"You don't care for this Calloway fellow, I take it?"

"He's as bad as Trey Hargreaves and Landry Kildare and all the rest of them. They all think I'm just a fussy spinster, complaining to get attention." All of the sudden, her eyes were awash in tears, and Jack wanted to go out and personally trounce every man on that council, starting with the ones she'd just named and working his way through the rest. She looked straight at him, blinking. "It's the *principle* of the thing, you see."

He figured if he didn't leave right then for the mine, he'd one, be late, and two, wind up taking Miss Olivia Wilcott Darling onto his lap and drying her tears with the edge of the tablecloth. No sound ideas in that bunch, he thought.

He set his plate, utensils, and cup in the sink, put on the coat he'd left hanging on the peg next to the back door the night before, and reached, with only the slightest hesitation, for the dinner pail. "That was a fine breakfast, Miss Olivia," he said gravely, "and I'm obliged for the rest, too."

She turned in her chair, pressing the back of her hand first to one eye, then to the other. "I'll have supper on when you get back, and water heated, too. You'll be wanting a bath."

This time he was the one to blush. A man had to be naked to take a proper bath, and thinking about that and Miss Olivia, in close sequence, was just plain unsettling.

"That'd be good," he said awkwardly, and then he left.

It was cold outside that morning; hard to leave a warm house. And a warm woman.

Down the road, lamps were burning in the windows of the Springwater Station and the barn beyond. It was still plenty dark, but Jack pulled the brim of his hat down a little, nonetheless. With any luck, the boy would be out there alone, doing chores, like he had been the night before, and he wouldn't encounter anybody else. Not yet, anyway; not until he was ready.

He entered the open doorway of the stables, instantly met by all the familiar, and oddly comforting smells of hay and horseflesh. The boy was seated on a bale of hay, milking an old cow, and he grinned as Jack entered. "Mornin'," he said.

Jack nodded. "Mornin'," he replied. It made him fitful, setting foot on the McCaffreys' property at all, but there was nowhere else to leave the roan. Miss Olivia's chickens probably wouldn't take kindly to sharing the coop with an ornery gelding.

What that town needed, he thought, somewhat irritably, was a good blacksmith and a livery stable.

"My pa was askin' about you," the boy said, looking proud and friendly. He'd finished the milking, and came to stand at the stall gate and watch while Jack saddled the roan. "Name's Toby. My Pa's Jacob McCaffrey. He said you ought to stop in one of these times and say howdy. He always likes to welcome a newcomer, my pa. My ma, too."

My pa is Jacob McCaffrey?

Jack ducked his head, even though the kid was a stranger and couldn't possibly recognize him. "I keep to myself mostly," he said, leading the roan out of the stall and mounting up just inside the barn's gaping doors. "You tell your pa thanks just the same, though."

The boy looked puzzled, and maybe a little stung. Then his blue eyes flashed in a way that put Jack in mind of somebody else, somebody he'd left behind, back in the long-ago. After all these years, the loss was still a hollow ache within him. "Well then mister, it's your loss, if you don't want to be sociable."

Jack tugged at his hat brim, ducked his head, and rode out of the barn.

Olivia was dressed for the town council meeting when Mr. McLaughlin returned from work that evening, looking about as cold and tired and as hungry as any man she'd ever seen. Immediately, her heart went out to him, and without thinking about it, she patted her carefully arranged hair, just as if she were fussy about such things.

"There's fried chicken in the warming oven," she said, in a businesslike tone, so he wouldn't think she'd been primping for him. "Mashed potatoes and gravy, too, and some kernel corn. The hot water reservoir is full, and the bathtub is in the pantry. It will probably be easier if you use the kitchen—I imagine you're too worn out to be carrying buckets up the stairs."

His clothes, hands, and face were black with dirt. He set the empty dinner pail on the drain board without taking his eyes off her. "You want me to bathe in your kitchen?" he asked, disbelieving.

She felt her face heat up yet again. She'd blushed more since meeting Jack McLaughlin, she decided, than in the whole of her life. "I'll be away from the house, at the town council meeting. You should have plenty of time to eat, wash, and make yourself decent."

A white, white grin flashed in his grubby face. "Suppose they throw you out on your ear? Those fellas on the town council, I mean," he said. "Far as I know, they don't let women vote in Montana Territory. That means they probably won't make you welcome."

Olivia straightened her spine and looked down her nose at him, which was not easy given that he was considerably taller than she was. "I'm not paying them a social call," she said. "I'm going to that meeting to give them a piece of my mind."

He sighed, carefully removed his coat, and hung it up beside his hat. "Maybe you'd better let me go along," he said. He wasn't grinning anymore.

"And let them think, for one moment, that they've cowed me into bringing a *man* to back me up, that I couldn't face them on my own? Not for anything in the world, Mr. McLaughlin." She filled a basin with water and handed it to him so he could scrub his face and hands before eating.

"You had supper?" he asked.

"I've drawn all the sustenance I need from righteous indignation," she said loftily.

"In my experience," he retorted, "that makes for sorry fare."

"Good night, Mr. McLaughlin," she said. "No doubt you will be asleep when I get home."

He sighed and began soaping and splashing at the drain board. "No doubt," he agreed.

She was reluctant to leave, and that annoyed her. She'd been full of conviction before he'd suggested accompanying her. Determinedly, she took her everyday cloak down from its peg, placed it around her shoulders, and reached for the doorknob. No sense in dillydallying. She had a mission to carry out.

Five minutes later, she was standing outside the back entrance to that despicable hellhole, the Brimstone Saloon. Lamps glowed in the windows, and she could hear tinny piano music coming from inside, along with raucous masculine laughter and the click and clatter of pool balls.

It seemed especially cold, out there in that street, and for a brief moment, Olivia considered going back to the house and asking Mr. McLaughlin to accompany her after all. The only thing that stopped her was the distinct possibility that he had decided to bathe before having his supper, in which case he might be stark naked by now, right there in her kitchen.

Besides, she decided, the chickens were depending upon her.

Lifting her chin, not to mention her hems, Olivia marched boldly toward the rear door and, when she got there, knocked smartly.

"Come in," called a masculine voice, without enthusiasm.

Olivia drew a deep breath, pushed open the door, and stepped inside.

They were all there—Trey Hargreaves, Landry Kildare, Gage Calloway, Doc Parrish, even Scully Wainwright, who would have ridden a considerable distance to attend, given that his ranch was some ten miles from town. All of them looked at her in surprise, except for the doctor, who bit back a grin and settled comfortably in his chair as though expecting a show.

The others' expressions ranged from openmouthed shock—Mr. Kildare and Mr. Wainwright—to polite but profound irritation—Mr. Hargreaves and Mr. Calloway.

"I've come to talk about my chickens," Olivia said.

Doc Parrish curved the side of one hand loosely against his mouth, cleared his throat, and ducked his head for a moment.

"Your chickens?" Mr. Hargreaves demanded. He kept his voice at a low pitch, but he was intimidating all the same.

Olivia took a step forward, mostly because she wanted more than anything to turn tail and run, and she'd never hear the end of it if she did. "I am a citizen of this town, gentlemen," she said, putting only the slightest emphasis on the last word. "I have the right to live in peace. And this place"— she waved both arms, taking in the whole of the

Brimstone Saloon—"this *place* is a menace. My rooster will not even crow in the mornings, and my hens are at their wits' end."

Doc Parrish cleared his throat again.

Landry Kildare remembered his manners—at last—and rose from his chair. "I'll see you home, Miss Olivia. You oughtn't to be in a place like this."

She wasn't going anywhere, unless they dragged her, and she'd have them all arrested if they so much as touched her. "Sit down, Mr. Kildare," she said. "It is a bit late for courtesy, don't you think?"

Mr. Kildare went red and sank back into his chair. Doc Parrish's eyes were sparkling—dare she think it—*encouraging*. Might she have one ally in this, the enemy camp, after all?

Trey got up, disappeared into a room that was probably his office, and returned with a chair. Setting it before the table like a witness's seat in front of some grand tribunal, he gestured elaborately for Olivia to sit.

She did, with a sniff. Inwardly, she was most grateful for the offer, since her knees had become dangerously unsteady.

"What," Mr. Hargreaves began, in a patronizing tone, as he took his own seat again, "would you have us do?"

"I would have you close this place," she said.

He sighed and squeezed the bridge of his nose between a thumb and forefinger. "I'm sure you can understand," he replied, after a long silence, "that that is impossible."

She leaned forward in her creaky chair. "Why?"

"Because," he answered wearily, looking her in the eye, "it is a thriving business. A part of the community."

She blinked. She would not disgrace herself by weeping in front of these men, no matter how impossible they were to reason with. "My rooming house is also a part of the community," she pointed out. "And my chickens provide sustenance for my boarders. *When* they are not too frightened by gunshots and whooping trail hands to lay."

Gage Calloway, who had replaced a retiring Jacob McCaffrey as mayor, bit down hard on his upper lip and then laughed anyway.

Olivia glared at him. "You are all prosperous men," she said. "Perhaps it is funny to you. To me, it is a very grave situation indeed—my very livelihood is at stake."

Mr. Kildare looked pained. He was not a bad man, she knew. None of them were, really. They were simply hardheaded, obdurate, and, well, *male.* "Nobody here wants to put you out of business, Miss Olivia," the rancher said quietly.

"No," Trey added, gazing at her in bewilderment, "Miss Darling is the one who wants to put someone out of business. Me, to be specific."

"You're a rich man," she accused, growing angry now that her initial timidity was subsiding a little. "You own the lion's share of a silver mine. You live in the finest house in town. *Surely* you do not need the income from a saloon!"

Mr. Hargreaves made a tent of his fingers, beneath his chin. "You're right," he said. "I don't need the Brimstone. But Springwater does. Out here, a town without a saloon hasn't a chance of surviving."

Olivia was very nearly moved to violence, although she managed to contain herself in the end. "That," she said, rising to her feet with all the fury of a queen about to order the chopping off of heads, "is patently ridiculous."

Mr. Hargreaves stood, too, with a suppressed sigh, and so did the rest of them. Including Doc Parrish, who hadn't said a word during the entire confrontation. Neither, for that matter, had Scully Wainwright, though it was plain from looking at his face that he would stand by the other members of the council.

"Nevertheless," Trey said regretfully—the charlatan—"I have no intention of closing the Brimstone, now or ever." He reached into his inside coat pocket, took out a sleek leather wallet. "However, I am willing to compensate you for any inconvenience to your—chickens."

There were snickers around the room; Olivia kept her head high and her shoulders straight and did not look to see who was laughing at her. When Mr. Hargreaves held out a sizable bill, an amount equal to several months rent from a regular boarder, it was all she could do not to reach out and snatch it from his hand.

"I neither need nor want your money," she lied.

She'd been on the verge of asking for credit at the general store, so dire were her circumstances, when Mr. McLaughlin appeared and had taken a room. Her pride just wouldn't allow her to reach out and accept funds that might have come from the sale of liquor and the flesh trade, that was all. Not while she had that precious twenty-dollar gold piece hidden in her stationery box.

She swept up the members of Springwater's town council in a single, furious gaze. "You have not heard the last of me, gentlemen," she said. Then she turned on one heel and walked out.

She was standing in the alleyway, drawing in deep, restorative breaths, when she realized someone was beside her. It was no real surprise when she turned and saw Doc Parrish.

"I'll see you home," he said.

She pulled a handkerchief from the pocket of her cloak, wadded it, and blotted at both eyes. "I can't go there," she replied.

"Why not?" he asked reasonably.

"Because there might be a naked man in my kitchen," she answered.

He laughed then, took her arm. "All right, then," he said, "I guess I'll just have to accept that remark at face value. Meanwhile, you can come to our house and have a late cup of tea with Savannah."

She turned, searched his face to see if he was mocking her. The moon was nothing more than a sliver of light, so it was hard to tell, there in the shadows.

"Come on," he urged, somewhat gruffly, and the next thing Olivia knew, she was being escorted toward the Parrishes' front gate.

"Do you agree with them?" she asked, when she thought she could trust herself to speak without giving way to a torrent of tears and thus humiliating herself completely. "About the saloon, I mean?"

He considered the question as he opened the gate and waited for her to step through. "I can see both sides of the argument. That saloon does bring a lot of business into this town."

Olivia stopped, there in the middle of the stone walkway leading to the Parrishes' large front porch. "It doesn't bother you? The noise—the shooting? What about your children, Doctor?"

He sighed. "My children don't frequent the Brimstone Saloon," he answered, with a tired smile in his voice. "And neither do your chickens."

While she was still trying to come up with a reply to that amazing—and, of course, entirely irrefutable—statement, Savannah stepped out onto the veranda, hugging herself against the evening chill. October was waning rapidly, and the first silent notes of winter chimed in the air.

Her smile looked warm in the lamplight coming from the nearest window. "Olivia!" she said, pleased. Then a worried expression crossed her face. "You're not sick, are you?"

"She just needs some female company and a cup of tea," Doc said.

Savannah came down the steps and linked her arm with Olivia's, tugging her toward the door, lest she bolt, no doubt, but her words were addressed to her husband.

"You'd best go down to the station and look in on June-bug. Toby came by a little while ago and said her arthritis was paining her something fierce."

"I'll get my bag," he told his wife, with a nod, and followed the two women inside.

The Parrish house was a pleasant place, clean and simply furnished, though there were toys of various kinds scattered from one end of the parlor to the other. Olivia felt a pang of envy, looking at that cheerful clutter. Her own place was neat as the proverbial pin; nothing ever out of place, and quiet. So quiet.

"Let me take your cloak," Savannah said gently, and Olivia was too weary, too defeated to object to her neighbor's hospitality. She nodded and complied, and sat staring into the fire while her hostess went to the kitchen for tea.

When she returned, she had to zigzag between the dolls and the miniature fire wagon, the top and the storybooks, balancing a silver tray carefully in both hands. Upon it was a china pot, two cups and saucers, and containers of sugar and cream, and the scent of rich Ceylon tea mingled with the smells of newly bathed children, wood fires, dried flowers from last summer's garden, and beeswax.

"Now, then," Savannah said, when she'd served the tea and seated herself in the chair next to Olivia's, "tell me." Her eyes twinkled above the rim of her cup. "Did you *really* go to the town council meeting?"

CHAPTER

4

FOR A FRACTION of a second, Olivia was taken aback by her neighbor's powers of discernment. Then she realized that the Doc must have told Savannah about the town council meeting before leaving the house. Perhaps in the kitchen, while the tea was brewing.

Briefly, the way a person will sometimes worry a sore tooth with the tip of their tongue, she allowed herself to envy that ordinary husband-and-wife intimacy. Then she sat up very straight, cup and saucer held carefully but properly in both hands, and answered, "Yes. I did attend tonight's meeting—for all the good it did."

Savannah looked delighted; she leaned over the arm of her chair, her cheeks flushed, her blue eyes full of laughter. "Oh, what I would have given to see their faces when you stepped over the threshold!"

Olivia sighed. "Surely I'm not the first woman to brave the stronghold," she remarked.

"Springwater women are made of stubborn stuff," Savannah avowed, "but that's one bastion June-bug and the others have never been able to breach. Even my Pres says men need somewhere to go that's absolutely their own."

"As if women didn't," Olivia said mildly.

Savannah laughed. "That's exactly what I'm going to tell him the very next time we have that particular conversation."

Olivia felt unaccountably weary, in those ensuing moments, and so alone. Until she thought of Mr. McLaughlin, bathing in her kitchen, that is. Perhaps, by now, he was in bed, resting on the clean, crisp sheets she herself had laundered and pressed . . .

She turned her mind forcefully back to the matter at hand. "In any case," she said, "I might as well have addressed my chickens as those men. I can't help thinking I would surely have gotten a more intelligent response."

Again, Savannah laughed. She seemed to genuinely like Olivia, to enjoy her company. She reached across the space between their chairs and patted Olivia's arm. "You ought to speak with June-bug McCaffrey. She holds the Brimstone in the same low esteem you do."

Olivia shifted slightly in her chair. "And you? How do you feel about the place, Mrs. Parrish?" She knew, of course, that before marrying the doctor, Savannah had been Trey Hargreaves's partner, half owner of the saloon. One couldn't even pass through Springwater without hearing about that.

"Savannah," the other woman corrected firmly. Then she sighed. "I guess I don't mind it so much as I should," she confessed, after some thought. "I lived another life before I came here, and I know from experience that there are lots of worse places. Compared to some of the beer halls I've seen, the Brimstone is practically a cathedral."

Olivia set her teacup aside, and it rattled slightly in its delicate saucer. For a little while, she'd almost dared to hope that a friendship was blossoming between herself and Savannah, but alas, the Brimstone Saloon would always be a bone of contention between them. She stood. "I'd—I'd best be going. It's getting late."

Savannah stood, her face a study in troubled surprise. "Did I say something wrong?"

"Well," Olivia began sadly, "it does seem that we'll never have the same outlook, at least in regard to that—that place."

"I see," Savannah said quietly. "You think we have to agree on everything to be friends. Is that it?"

"Friends are people with a great deal in common," Olivia said. In her mind, she heard the echo of Aunt Eloise's voice, railing because Olivia, at seventeen, had shyly brought one of the other students home for tea, one day after a piano lesson. *You mark my words, missy,* the old woman had harped. *A girl like that won't look to a great clumsy house mouse like you for friendship. What on earth could the two of you have in common? No, it's not your friendship she's interested in, it's my money, and you may rest assured that all the rest of them are just the same.*

It was not reasonable, her nursing an old and seemingly irrelevant hurt the way she ofttimes did, Olivia knew that, but there had been many other such remarks, and over the years her aunt's words had intertwined and woven themselves into a sturdy, perhaps unbreakable mesh. A web that, to that very day, remained tightly wrapped around her heart and her soul.

"Friends," Savannah retorted gently, "are people who like each other, Olivia. That's all. And I like you, whether you're comfortable with the prospect or not. There it is. I like you very much, June-bug likes you, and so do Rachel and Evangeline, Miranda and Jessica. All you have to do is let us show it."

Completely at a loss, Olivia glanced around the room, perhaps a bit anxiously, for her cloak. Surely by now, Mr. McLaughlin had finished his ablutions, and she could go home. She felt a sudden, powerful drive to play her piano, to hammer out the most thunderous of Beethoven's chords, to play and play until she'd smothered and stilled Aunt Eloise's relentlessly critical voice once and for all.

Savannah took a light hold on Olivia's shoulders. "We're not going to give up on you, Olivia. We're just not the sort to do that."

Olivia could only nod. Her heart was wedged into her throat and it had been a trying day and the first dark clouds of a sick headache were gathering at the base of her skull. Aunt Eloise might as well have been standing at her elbow, raving away.

Savannah released her, but not before Olivia saw the sympathy and the sadness in her eyes. She went to fetch the cloak, extended it almost reluctantly. "It feels like we might get snow tonight, don't you think?"

Olivia well knew the remark was meant as a sort of conversational lifeline. She shivered and managed a faltering smile. In truth, she had been so intent on reaching the town council meeting without losing her resolve that she hadn't even noticed the falling temperature. Now, in retrospect, she felt the echo of it biting into her very bones. "It is cold out," she said.

With a smile, Savannah nodded.

Well, Olivia thought, if they could agree on nothing else, there was always the weather.

The first flakes of snow were already beginning to fall as she hurried across the road, doing her best to turn a deaf ear to the customary carryings-on down at the Brimstone Saloon. It wasn't even Saturday night, but the clientele was yahooing all the same.

She rounded the house and went in by the back door, half expecting to find her boarder lounging in her large copper bathtub, a legacy from Mr. Calloway, the house's former owner, but the kitchen was empty, and dark except for the light of one lantern burning low in the middle of the table.

At once glad and disappointed, Olivia removed her cloak and hung it on its peg next to the door. Then she checked the stove reservoir, expecting that it would need filling, but Mr. McLaughlin had apparently attended to that chore. His supper dishes were washed and dried and neatly stacked on the drain board, and when she peered into the storeroom just off the kitchen, lantern in hand, she caught the coppery glimmer of the tub, hanging tidily from its nail in the wall.

She raised her eyes to the ceiling, wondering if he'd gone to bed. No doubt he'd been exhausted, after a day of slaving in the bowels of the earth, and he probably would not welcome a serenade of thunder. On the other hand, the music was rising in Olivia like lava in a volcano; she did not know if she could contain it without going mad.

She was still tossing between one sharp horn of her dilemma and the other when she heard Mr. McLaughlin's footsteps on the rear stairway. She could not think why his appearance caught her so unprepared, but it did. He was quietly handsome, hair and beard groomed, clothes clean and new. He carried a book in one hand, using an index finger to mark his place, and though Olivia suddenly yearned to know the title, she couldn't make it out without squinting and craning her neck.

"I thought I'd like to play the piano for a while," she said, testing the waters. Indeed, the house was her own, and she could do what she pleased, but if Mr. McLaughlin packed up his few belongings and left, she would be in dire financial straits.

"I would enjoy that," he replied, very quietly. His eyes seemed to caress her—but that was probably just a trick of the lamplight, or of her foolish emotions. She was tired, after all, and confused, and not a little discouraged.

She simply nodded; as with Savannah, she felt tongue-tied all of the sudden. Perhaps, she thought miserably, she was incapable of accepting a kindly gesture from anyone, however innocent. It was, she supposed, one more flaw in her character.

She left the kitchen in a hurry, leaving the lantern behind on the table, and made her way to the parlor. There, her best globe lamp was burning, the light shining through its ornately painted china globe in a variety of soft colors.

She sat down on the piano bench, lifted the lid that covered the keys, and flexed her fingers. Then, forgetting all about Jack McLaughlin, all about the men and women of Springwater, and even Aunt Eloise, she began to play. She played until her spirit had wept the tears she could not allow herself to shed, played until she was physically and emotionally spent, until her hands were aching and she could be certain of a sound and dreamless sleep.

Upstairs, relaxing on his bed, the book of adventure stories bought at the general store lying forgotten on his chest, Jack listened to the tempest of music rising up through the floorboards, at once heartrendingly beautiful and swelling with fury, and knew precisely what he was hearing.

He smiled to himself. Whatever she wanted the rest of the world to believe, Miss Olivia Darling was a passionate woman. While all that sweet rage flowed over him, a wild and churning river of notes, he couldn't resist imagining what it would be like to be the recipient of all that intensity, to match it with his own.

He closed his eyes. He'd been with a lot of whores in his life, and a few lonely widows, too, but for the most part he'd avoided decent women. To his way of thinking, a man didn't have a right to enjoy a lady's favors unless he intended to put a gold band on her finger. And in that case, he could damn well wait until after the ceremony.

Olivia was most definitely a good woman, that was plain. She deserved a far better man than a mere saddle bum, like him, a drifter with more cause for shame, given his past, than pride. All the same, it was easy enough to picture her stripped to the skin, arching under his hands and his mouth and finally his hips, plunging her fingers into his hair and, in the end, calling his name, over and over.

He opened his eyes abruptly and sat bolt upright on the side of the bed, letting out a long breath. Then, bracing his elbows on his knees, he thrust both hands into his hair. The book had long since fallen to the floor.

He'd worked like an ox all day, and he was numb with fatigue. He needed to put out the lamp, undress, and go to sleep, but Miss Olivia and her music had gotten inside him in a way nothing and no one had ever done before.

Coming to Springwater at all had not been an easy decision; following a long stretch in a Yankee prison, he'd turned raider out of pure, cussed spite, and led nuisance attacks on federal occupation troops and their supply trains for eighteen months or so. He'd kept that up until a man—a kid, really—was killed, fighting back. When that happened, he'd come to his senses and taken to the straight and narrow path. Chances were good, though, that he was still wanted, east of the Mississippi. And that young blue-belly was sure as hell still dead.

He'd drifted for years after that, riding from town to town, ranch to ranch, mulling things over in his mind while he herded cattle or shod horses in some livery stable, working it all through. It was hard enough, just being there, so close to Jacob and June-bug, and yet with a chasm of regret to separate him from them, and now there was Olivia.

He hadn't figured on meeting a woman—especially a skinny, contentious spinster—and feeling so many new and turbulent responses, all of them rooted in her. He'd known Olivia for just two days, and already she was at the center of his thoughts, whether he wanted her there or not.

Gradually, the music softened, then ebbed away.

He listened as she moved about the lower floor, probably locking windows and doors, heard her climb the back stairs. He saw the light of her lantern, a golden line beneath his door, lingering there for the better part of a minute before moving on.

Then she was gone; her own door closed in the distance.

He kicked off his boots, unfastened his suspenders, pulled his shirt out of his pants and began to unbutton it. All the while, he wondered what she'd wanted to say to him, pausing out there in the corridor the way she had. It couldn't be a coincidence that she'd hesitated in just that place.

"Leave it alone," he said to himself, and finished undressing. "Just leave it alone." Then he turned down the lamp and got into bed. It seemed wider that night, his bed, colder and emptier, too, and blind-tired as he was, a long time passed before he slept.

The shout awakened Olivia from a deep slumber, and she sat up, gasping, certain that she herself, entangled in some horrid dream, had made the sound. When she heard it again, she realized it had come from Mr. McLaughlin's room.

She snatched up her wrapper, pulled it on over her nightdress, hurried down the hall, knocked upon his door, and admitted herself before she so much as questioned the propriety of doing such a bold thing.

He yelled a name, raw-throated, though she couldn't rightly make out what it was. Surely he'd been calling to a wife or a sweetheart, Olivia thought; there had been such raw, desolate emotion in his voice. There *was* a woman somewhere, she was sure of it, or had been once.

"Mr. McLaughlin!" She lit the lamp on his bedside table, saw that he was still tossing and turning. The sheets were twisted about his middle and his thighs, and his chest, heaving with the effort to breathe, was bare. She dared to press a hand to his shoulder, but gingerly. "Mr. McLaughlin!"

He opened his eyes, blinked in the unexpected light, and let out a groan.

"You were dreaming," Olivia said. She had to give the man some reason, after all, for barging into his room in the middle of the night.

He sat up, his breathing still ragged and shallow, and Olivia automatically retreated a step. She couldn't help staring at his chest; she'd never seen a man in a state of even partial undress before, and she found the sight fascinating. His muscles were hard, and beautifully defined, and she wanted to trace their length, one by one, with the tips of her fingers.

"I'm sorry," he said. "For waking you, I mean."

She forced herself to look away, to occupy her trembling hands and her eyes, oh especially her eyes, by pouring a glass of water from the small pitcher she had brought in earlier and holding it out to him. "Don't apologize," she said, with a calmness she most certainly did not feel. "These things happen."

He took the glass with a hoarse thank you and swallowed its contents in a few lusty gulps. He still looked haunted, even distracted; he might well have forgotten Olivia's existence, never mind her presence in his room. He gazed up at the ceiling as though some terrible scene were being played out there, and him unable to look away.

Leaving the lamp burning, making a definite point of *not* looking at any part of his anatomy other than his face, Olivia backed toward the door, very conscious, all of the sudden, of her plaited hair, her wrapper and nightdress, her bare feet. "Well—if you're all right—I'll say good night," she faltered.

" 'Night," he answered. He was reaching out for the water pitcher when she closed the door.

It was pitch dark in the corridor, and cold, now that all the fires were out.

Back in her own bed, Olivia pulled her top sheet, blanket, and quilt up to her chin, one by one. All the while, she was thinking of Mr. McLaughlin and his bare chest. She closed her eyes and heard his voice again, in her memory. Heard the desperation, the fear, the fathomless sorrow.

Olivia was filled with envy for the unknown woman, whatever tragedy had befallen her, envied the love Jack McLaughlin bore her, a love so strong that it was with him even in sleep.

* * *

The night crew had dug until they hit a wall of rock, and left the problem to the day men. It was Jack's job to crawl into the hole on his belly and elbows, set a charge of dynamite in place, and back out again. He'd been grateful for this job when he got it, and he was grateful still, but that didn't mean he had to enjoy himself.

It was cold and dark down in that mine, and after only a couple of days, he was beginning to forget what sunlight looked and felt like. When he got back up into the fresh air again, at the end of a long day, it would be well past sundown.

Reaching the main shaft, where the rest of the day men waited, he nodded to the man with his hands on the plunger. The next few seconds seemed to drag by, and the silence was deafening. Then the blast came, shaking the ground above and below and all around the small band of miners. The usual shower of pebbles and dirt rained down.

Everyone stood still, covering their heads and maybe holding their breath, like Jack was doing, until they knew whether the walls of the mine would give way and bury them alive. It could happen at any time, of course, but it was especially likely after a blast.

Jack was the first to take up his shovel and head into the rubble. The others followed, and they dug, all of them, until their legs and arms were numb with exhaustion and cold, and then they dug some more.

"You reckon we got to it this time?" Ben Williams asked, working beside him, referring to the fresh vein of silver they had reason to believe snaked off from the now-spent mother lode. A young man with a family, Ben had been on his way to California to seek his fortune, but some bad luck had found them, so he and his wife and their two little daughters were wintering over with the McCaffreys. They had little money, Jack knew, Ben being the sort who was content to do all the talking, and both he and the missus helped out around the stagecoach station to defray some of their room and board.

Jack didn't pause in his digging; if he did, he wasn't sure he'd be able to get himself going again. He would get through his shift by listening, grateful for his partner's garrulous nature, which allowed him to keep his own counsel. He concentrated on advancing himself, hand over hand, from one thought of Olivia to the next, through the day's work. By anticipating the hot, fragrant supper that was sure to await him when he got to the place he was already starting to think of as home, the bath he'd take in the kitchen, in front of the glowing stove, the clean bed where he would sleep, if he was lucky, without dreaming.

"It's there," he answered belatedly. He could feel that silver, cold and pure in the dark depths of the earth, just waiting to make its way from the ground to the assay office to Trey Hargreaves's burgeoning bank account.

"You ever think what it would be like, owning an outfit like this?" Williams asked.

"No," Jack answered honestly. He didn't care much for money, having found the stuff to be of small comfort when comfort really mattered, and his needs were simple. He'd saved most of his wages for as long as he could remember.

Lord, but he did long to light someplace, once and for all. He'd begun to dwell, at least part of the time, in a world of the mind, a world where he went by his own name, and proudly, without a beard to disguise his face and a pack of lies to hide his past. "You?"

"I wouldn't steal or nothin' like that," Ben said, shoveling away, "but it sure would be a fine thing to be able to buy my Sally those gewgaws and trinkets women value so highly. I'd get dolls for my little girls, too, and let them each have a kitten. Build a real house."

Jack smiled to himself, knowing Ben couldn't see his face in the gloom. "I reckon you could do all of that, in due time anyway, on the wages you earn here at the Jupiter and Zeus."

Ben sighed. "Sally won't hear of it, my workin' in a hole in the ground for the rest of my days. Her pa was a coal miner, back home in Kentucky, and he died of the black lung. No, sir, I wouldn't be here at all if our grub hadn't run out before time and our wagon hadn't broken down."

"It's not so bad a place," Jack allowed. "Spring-water, I mean."

"That's true," Ben said, "and the McCaffreys are as fine o' folks as you could ever hope to meet, anywhere you went, but there ain't much work around here outside this mine."

"You know anything about blacksmithing?" Jack asked, and then wished he'd held his tongue. He wasn't going to stay on in Springwater, wasn't going to get himself a forge and a livery and the tools to shoe horses, no matter how appealing he might find the prospect now.

" 'Bout as much as I do about parting the Red Sea," Ben answered, and they both laughed.

Five endless hours later, they reached the fringe of the new vein, Ben and Jack and the others, and a boy was sent aboveground to carry word to Trey Hargreaves. His response, an order to take the rest of the day off with full pay, was greeted with a cheer that all but set the walls of the pit to rumbling.

Jack was glad as hell to rattle up in the metal cage, operated by a pulley system, and set his feet on the snowy ground. The daylight was muted, nearly blotted out by storm clouds, but it was there nonetheless, and Jack reveled in it.

Everyone except for Williams and Jack himself made straight for the Brimstone Saloon. Ben wanted to go back to his family, maybe get in some extra chores, and Jack—well—he didn't really belong anywhere, but he was grateful just to look at the sky and to breathe fresh air.

He took Miss Olivia by surprise, that was obvious, showing up in her kitchen without warning the way he did. She had just stepped out of that big copper tub of hers, and her freshly washed hair fell in glorious tangles and ringlets well past her waist. Fortunately—or unfortunately, depending on how you assessed the situation—she had managed to get into her pink and white flannel wrapper, but she was not only naked beneath it, she was wet.

Jack's mouth went dry, and he couldn't speak, couldn't move, either to retreat or advance, for the life of him.

"What are you doing here?" Olivia demanded, her cheeks flaring with color and her wonderful eyes flashing with indignation and something else, too. Something that lifted his heart a notch or two above its usual plane.

He cleared his throat. "I believe I live here," he said.

She stared at him, clasped the front of her wrapper closer to her bosom, which only served to emphasize the lithe but womanly figure beneath. "You know very well what I'm talking about. You're not due back from the mine for hours yet." A worried expression came into her eyes, took some of the shine off. "You didn't lose your job, did you?"

He finally remembered his manners and turned his back. "No, ma'am. We struck a fresh vein of silver today, and Mr. Hargreaves was so happy about it that he turned us all loose. I guess I should have gone over to the Brimstone, with the others, and bided there a while."

"Trust Mr. Hargreaves to get his wages right back from those misguided men by filling them with his whiskey and beer." She sounded huffy, and he knew she was preparing to flee. He wondered why she hadn't already done so, in fact, but the workings of a woman's mind, like the ways of God, were past finding out. In his experience, better than half the things females said and did were beyond the comprehension of a mere man, and whenever he'd dared to venture a guess, he'd been wrong.

"I'll just wash up," he said diplomatically.

She made no reply, but for a barely audible *harumph* sort of sound, and then he heard her hurrying up the rear stairs.

He took the coffeepot from its shelf, carried it to the sink, and pumped water into it, smiling to himself the whole while. While the coffee was brewing, he lugged the bathtub out into the yard and emptied it onto the half-frozen ground.

Snow was beginning to fall again, the flakes big as chicken feathers, and for the first time in a long while, he felt a stirring of the joy he'd taken in such days, back when he was a boy. The sledding would be good, if that weather kept up, though the nearest hill was a long way off.

Whistling, he carried the tub back inside, set it in the middle of the floor, and began pumping more water.

* * *

Seated at her vanity table, her silver-backed comb in one hand, Olivia listened to the noises from the kitchen. She was almost completely certain that Mr. McLaughlin was taking a *bath*, in the middle of the afternoon, when anyone, anyone at all, might come knocking at the back door and catch him in the altogether.

It was scandalous.

She dared to meet her own eyes in the looking glass. She herself had very nearly been caught, but that was different. This was her house, and it wasn't as if she were at liberty to bathe in the evening, with Mr. McLaughlin always somewhere about. Oh, she might have found the proper privacy in her room, of course, but carrying the water upstairs, not to mention the tub itself, was simply too much work. Emptying it again afterward would have been pure drudgery.

Downstairs, Mr. McLaughlin was singing. It wasn't a tune she recognized, but that didn't matter. The sound of his voice touched something inside her, something she'd managed to keep hidden from everyone she'd ever met. Until he came along, that is. He'd upset everything, turned her thoughts upside down, brought her senses to life. Worst of all, he'd made her poignantly aware of her own loneliness.

She brought herself up short. There was no sense in indulging in silly fancies. The fact was, she was thirty-two. Much as she loved children, it was most unlikely that she'd ever have any of her own. She'd been passed by, where marriage was concerned, left on the shelf. Indeed, her storybook prince had clearly been detained, and Mr. McLaughlin, as attractive and intriguing as he was, was surely just a frog.

Jacob McCaffrey and Trey Hargreaves stood on the back veranda of the house Trey and Rachel shared with their children, blowing blue cigar smoke into the crisp air of a snowy, end-of-October evening.

"This time of year always makes me think of the boys," Jacob confided, gazing off into the distance. Trey knew his friend was referring to the twin sons he and June-bug had lost in the battle of Lookout Mountain, near Chattanooga. "We used to go huntin', long about this time." He paused and came as close to smiling as he ever did, but his mind was still far away. "Will, he didn't care much for it, though he was never a coward, mind you. Wes, now, he was a fine shot."

Trey waited. Jacob didn't want or expect an answer. A long time passed.

"What sort of man is he?" Jacob asked. "That new feller, I mean." He was referring to the stranger who lived at Miss Olivia's, the one Trey had hired on to set dynamite charges in the mine. If Springwater was like a growing and rambunctious family, which it was, then Jacob was its head, and he took a genuine interest in everybody who came and went.

Trey sighed. "Quiet. Calls himself Jack McLaughlin, but I'd bet my next shipment of whiskey that he's lying about that and a lot more."

Jacob regarded him thoughtfully. "What makes you think that?"

Trey shrugged. "Just a hunch," he admitted. "But it's a strong one."

"You take him to be bad news, this McLaughlin?"

"Maybe," Trey allowed, after some thought. "Maybe not. He's no greenhorn, and he sure as hell doesn't lack for guts. Many a brave man would rather go hungry than shimmy into holes and light fuses all day." He sighed again, shook his head. "No, the truth is, I like him. If he wants to keep his true name to himself, I guess that's his business. He wouldn't be the first."

Jacob chuckled in agreement. "My June-bug's fit to perish from curiosity. Only thing that's kept her from going over there to the rooming house to take a gander at him is the fear that Miss Olivia will think she's come to see whether or not there's a scandal brewin'."

Trey smiled and drew deeply on his cigar. He was going to have to give this habit up, he thought, though he didn't relish the prospect. Rachel said it was bound to kill him, and she was seldom wrong about anything.

"They've all been trying to get Miss Olivia to join in their hen parties ever since Pres and I hauled her out of that overturned railroad car," he said, meaning the female contingent. "With him under that particular roof, they're likely to redouble their efforts."

"You know what that means," Jacob said.

Trey nodded. "By Christmas, the ladies of Springwater are going to know more about that poor man than he knows about himself."

CHAPTER

❧ 5 ❧

THE VERY NEXT Sunday afternoon, immediately after church, the ladies of Springwater met to sip tea and plan their campaign to win Miss Olivia Wilcott Darling around to their way of thinking once and for all. They chose June-bug McCaffrey's spacious home for the purpose, being as their number was steadily growing and she had all those tables in the public room of the stagecoach station. Everybody, with the possible exception of Olivia herself, knew the town was run not by the council, meeting every other week in the back room at the Brimstone Saloon, but from right there within their midst. The men only *thought* they were in charge, and the female sector was more than willing to allow their husbands to live out the rest of their lives—hopefully long ones—in blissful ignorance.

From the beginning, the gathering was a-bustle with talk of Miss Darling's bold intrusion at the town council meeting only a few days before.

Miranda Kildare giggled, one of June-bug's prized china cups in hand, recounting her Landry's stunned consternation over the whole matter. "If you could have seen his face when he came home and told me about it," she said, eyes shining. "I declare he wouldn't have been any more surprised if Lady Godiva had ridden right into that meeting."

Rachel Hargreaves, carrying a platter of currant scones fresh from the McCaffrey oven, laughed in response. "Trey was fit to be tied. He thinks the woman is out to ruin him, single-handed." She shook her head at the idea.

Jessica Calloway took a sip of tea, keeping an eye on her twin nieces, fetching blond toddlers, who were playing on a nearby blanket, far enough from the fire for safety, and near enough for warmth. "Gage says he knew he'd live to regret selling his house to a total stranger," she said, with a soft smile of agreement. Jessica, herself a relative newcomer to Springwater, published the *Gazette*. Although they still lived in the cramped quarters above the office and the tiny pressroom, she and Gage had purchased land at the edge of town and were planning to build a large house.

June-bug, never happier than when she was square in the middle of some commotion, was flushed with the joy of having a houseful of company and things to wonder about. "Who would have thought she'd let a strange man live under her roof thattaway?" she speculated, almost under her breath.

"She does run a rooming house," Savannah Parrish put in. Like the others, she'd brought her children, and the two oldest, her adopted boys, were overseeing little Beatrice as carefully as if she were made of translucent china.

June-bug put both hands on her hips and chuckled. "You know, I've been so all-fired bent on makin' a friend of that woman that I plum forgot all about her bein' in business and all."

"It surprises me," Evangeline Wainwright declared. Pretty and fair-haired, Evangeline had been among the first women to live at Springwater. "That Miss Olivia Wilcott Darling would risk ruination by stooping to commerce, I mean. Especially when it involves letting strangers sleep under her roof."

"You don't like her, do you?" asked young Sally Williams, a pretty, brown-haired creature, small and fragile looking as a wren. Being shy, she usually kept to the outer edges of their gatherings. "I think she's just afraid."

Evangeline reached out and squeezed Sally's hand. "I don't know Miss Darling well enough to dislike her," she said gently. "It's just that she's so prim and remote, and here we're all falling over ourselves trying to get her to come to a tea party or a quilting bee once in a while."

"Stuck up, that's what she is," Sue Bellweather insisted. Sue tended to take the dark view of everybody, until they'd proven themselves over and over again. "Did you see her at church this morning? Why, butter wouldn't have melted in her mouth!"

"She's afraid," Sally Williams said again. Her voice was no more forceful than before, but just the fact that she'd spoken up a second time indicated strong opinions on her part.

"Afraid?" Dorothy Mathers, the new schoolmarm, wanted to know. Dorothy was a plain girl, tall as a man and broad in the shoulders, but like as not, she'd be married off before long, and they'd be trying to lure yet another teacher to Springwater. "Good heavens. It isn't as if we've been *shooting* at her, or calling her names."

Sally's eyes, brown like her hair, were bright with quiet conviction. "Maybe she figures you wouldn't take to her, if you really knew her."

Sue Bellweather drew in a breath. "You mean, she might have a *past*?"

Evangeline dismissed the question with an impatient wave of one hand. "For goodness' sake, Sue, we *all* have pasts."

"Amen," said Savannah, with a raise of her teacup. Although she wasn't smiling, her eyes twinkled with laughter.

"That wasn't what I meant," Sally said. For her, this was an oration; she probably hadn't talked so much in the whole two and a half months she'd been in Springwater. Her cheeks were flushed, and her voice trembled a little. "It isn't easy for some folks, comin' to a new place, meetin' people, fittin' in. Specially if they've been scorned a time or two.

Miss Olivia, she's just tryin' to keep from bein' hurt."

A thoughtful silence descended, following this insightful comment, but the lull didn't last long. Silences never did, when the women of Springwater got together.

Rachel went over and put one arm around Sally's small shoulders. "We'd never be unkind," she said gently. Everyone knew that, while Rachel had been referring to Olivia, her words were meant as a reassurance to Sally as well.

Sally's eyes were fever bright, and she nodded, swallowed. "You've been good to me and mine. I ain't sayin' you haven't. But when we first came here, down on our luck, out of money and food, I was about as scared of you folks as I ever been of anybody. I don't know what we would have done if you'd turned us away."

Again, the women were quiet, though the children made up for that well enough.

"What we need to do," June-bug said, brightening, "is plan ourselves a Christmas pageant, over to the church. Time we had one anyhow. We could ask Miss Olivia to head up the whole doin's."

"She's musical?" Evangeline asked.

It was Savannah who nodded. "I've heard her at that piano at all hours of the day and night, playing like her heart would break. I think that's how she sorts through her feelings."

Just about everybody in the room understood why Olivia would need such an outlet. Even with friends and husbands and babies, the Western frontier could be a bleak and lonely place, especially for women. They pined on rare occasions, all of them, for the places they'd left behind, for the dear friends, the mothers and fathers, sisters and brothers they might never see again. How must it be for a spinster, with no husband to turn to for solace, no children to warm her heart?

"Poor thing," murmured June-bug.

"June-bug's right," Jessica said. "We ought to have a pageant. Here we have that nice church and our own organ." She paused, looked around at the others with one fair eyebrow raised. "Christmas Eve would be a good time. Then the children would have all of November and most of December to practice."

Dorothy, the schoolmarm, gave a heartfelt sigh, no doubt concerned that Olivia would refuse their request, thus leaving the entire burden of the exhibition to fall on her shoulders. After all, none of them had any reason to believe that Olivia would agree to the plan. So far, she'd turned down every single invitation, except for tea at Savannah's the night of the town council meeting, and she hadn't been precisely herself then, had she?

"Well," Miranda said, frowning prettily, "she *does* come to church every Sunday."

"Who's going to ask her?" Evangeline wanted to know, and everybody in the room looked straight at June-bug. Of all of them, she'd come the closest to reaching Olivia, since the latter had spent some time with the McCaffreys, following her dramatic arrival the year before.

"I'll do it," June-bug said, with resolve.

The announcement met with enthusiastic applause.

Olivia stood at her parlor window, backbone rigid, watching as June-bug McCaffrey picked her way up the snowy walk. November had arrived in the night, wearing a white and glittering cloak, but the sky had cleared and the sun was shining fit to dazzle the eye.

Looking up from her effort to traverse the treacherous flagstones without injury, June-bug smiled cheerily and waved. So much for the possibility that she hadn't seen Olivia there, behind a lace curtain, watching her approach. If it hadn't been for that, Olivia might have pretended to be away from home.

Instead, she opened the door and greeted the other woman with a wobbly but sincere smile. June-bug McCaffrey was not an easy person to hold at arm's length.

"Whee," June-bug cried, with a little laugh, as she mounted the porch steps. "It's cold out here!"

"Do come in," Olivia said, and was surprised to realize that she was glad to have company. Mr. McLaughlin had gone to work, as usual, and that great, empty house felt about as cozy as a tomb. Once she'd taken June-bug's cloak and gloves and settled her in a chair close by the fire, she hurried into the kitchen to brew up a pot of her best Ceylon tea.

While she was attending to the task, who should come through the back door but Mr. McLaughlin, and him not due back for hours. He was black with mine dirt, like always, but for all that, the sight of him gave Olivia a quivery feeling deep down, in a twilight place lost somewhere between flesh and spirit.

He grinned and hung up his hat. "Hargreaves closed the mine early again today," he explained. The question must have been clear in her eyes.

She tried to seem unconcerned. "I see," she said, and went on with her tasks, perhaps with a little more clatter than was necessary. "Well, you'll just have to wait to bathe, because I've got company in the house. It just wouldn't be right, your being naked in the kitchen with June-bug McCaffrey right there in the parlor."

He seemed to go uncommonly still, teetering on the edge of another smile, as though some passing magician had turned him into a granite headstone. "That so?" he asked, after a very long time. His voice was gravelly, and Olivia could have sworn he was on the verge of turning right around and leaving.

"You're much too dirty to set foot in my parlor," Olivia said, stating the obvious. It was just that he seemed to need for her to say something ordinary. Not, she reflected, that she'd said anything *extra*ordinary. "You'll just have to meet Mrs. McCaffrey another time."

He might have met the McCaffreys and numerous other people the day before, but he'd refused to go to church with her, saying he needed his rest, and she hadn't pressed him. All the same, she'd been more than moderately disappointed.

"I guess I will," he agreed, and he seemed torn between bolting out the door and racing for the rear stairs.

Olivia was unaccountably relieved when he chose the stairs.

"So, you see," June-bug chimed happily, "we really need your help with this pageant. We mean to have angels and shepherds and, Mary and Joseph, of course. Maybe even a real baby in the manger—heaven knows, we got a passel of 'em around here. Why, this is just about the *dernedest* thing we've ever thought up."

Olivia was no fool; she knew a gambit to draw her into the social circle when she encountered one, and perhaps June-bug and the others hoped to wrangle a little gossip about her boarder into the bargain, but the truth was, she was getting tired of saying no. Tired of spending all her time alone in that big house, with nothing to do most days, once the chickens had been fed, the sweeping and dusting finished, and the beds made up.

She took a sip from her teacup, pretending to consider the matter. "It does seem like a very ambitious undertaking," she said, at some length.

"Well," June-bug replied, with her customary

honesty, "it will be that. No question about it. But you're the only one of us that can play the piano—" Here, she paused to cast an admiring glance at the grand instrument Gage Calloway had left behind when he sold Olivia the house. " 'Cept for Mamie Riley, o' course." Mrs. Riley, nearsighted and tone deaf, pounded out an exuberant accompaniment to the hymns every Sunday morning, invariably giving Olivia a headache. "Mamie's gettin' on, you know, and her nerves most likely couldn't take it."

Olivia knew she would be working mostly with children, and the idea heartened her in a way she hadn't expected. She adored the little creatures, though she had had no real experience in dealing with them. Surely they would be easier to manage, though, than adults. "All right," she said, speaking hastily, before her courage failed. "I'll do it."

June-bug looked both startled and delighted, and she nearly spilled her tea, getting to her feet. Was she that anxious to leave?

"That's the best news I've had since Trey Hargreaves struck silver!" she cried, beaming, and when Olivia rose from her chair, more from reflex than intention, the other woman embraced her warmly.

Olivia stood somewhat stiffly in June-bug's arms, but she did not pull away. She could not, in fact, recall the last time anyone had exhibited open affection for her. Certainly Aunt Eloise had never done that sort of thing, and her father, Eloise's only brother, had been a distant man, thirty years older than his flighty wife. Olivia's mother, whom she remembered as a nervous creature, forever fainting or bursting into tears, had been most concerned with herself.

June-bug was still exuberant, gripping Olivia's shoulders and giving her a gleeful little shake. "Thank you," she said. "*Thank you* for saying yes!"

Olivia laughed, in spite of herself. She felt a swell of joy surge up inside her—normally that would have frightened her, being so foreign a feeling—but the tears that came to her eyes were not born of fear. "I hope I can live up to your expectations," she said, and though she gave the words the tone of a jest, she meant them. At that moment, disappointing June-bug McCaffrey seemed like the worst thing that could befall her.

The older woman placed warm hands on either side of Olivia's face. "You'll make us all proud," she said. "I just *know* you will. Now, I'd best be getting back to the station. Jacob and Toby and the others will be wantin' their supper." She paused. "Maybe you and your boarder would like to join us," she said.

Crafty old thing, Olivia thought, amused. "I'm afraid I've got supper all planned," she said. In truth, they were having leftovers from yesterday's Sunday dinner of ham, grits, and gravy, but she knew Mr. McLaughlin wouldn't accompany her to the station any more than he'd gone to church, and besides that, she wasn't ready to be quite so sociable herself. Just agreeing to plan and orchestrate the Christmas play had left her feeling a little enervated.

"Another time, then," June-bug said. A few minutes later, bundled in her cloak once again, she was trundling back down the walk toward the gate. A new snow was falling, and a wintry twilight lay like folds of purple silk on the plains and the slopes of the distant hills.

When Olivia carried the tea things back to the kitchen, she was only partly taken aback to find Mr. McLaughlin there. He'd scrubbed himself clean, and his hair was still wet and ridged from combing. He was even wearing clean clothes.

And he looked so fine that Olivia nearly dropped the loaded tray.

"I took a spit bath," he said, eyes dancing.

A picture came unbidden to Olivia's mind, and she felt her cheeks burn. She set the tray on the drain board with an eloquent clatter, just to let him know she didn't approve of such dashing remarks.

He laughed. "Sorry," he said.

He did not look the least bit remorseful to Olivia. "You aren't anything of the sort," she countered, with a sniff. "Do go and read a book or something. I won't have you underfoot when I'm trying to make supper."

He pulled a chair away from the table, turned it the wrong way around, and sat astraddle of it, his arms resting loosely across the back. "I'd rather watch," he said.

Olivia cast a sidelong look at this boarder of hers, wondering at the change in his manners. Although it was not a commendable alteration, she wasn't sure she precisely disliked it. To hide this unsettling fact, she shrugged and went about her business.

"That woman," he began, and there was a serious note in his voice now, even though she could tell he was making an effort to sound casual. "Was that June-bug McCaffrey?"

Olivia glanced at him, nodded. "She wanted a peep at you, you know. That's one of the reasons she came by."

He grinned, but the expression didn't quite catch in his eyes. "Oh?" he said. "I'm sorry I disappointed her."

Another lie, Olivia thought, and wondered. "Some other time," she replied.

"You're going to play piano for the Christmas play," he commented mildly, resting his chin on his forearm as he watched her.

Olivia turned on him, narrowed her eyes. "You were eavesdropping!"

He thrust a hand through his hair. Yet again, Olivia itched to shave off his beard and trim back those unruly tresses. She had a feeling it would be like unveiling a magnificent statue. "Not exactly. I was just hanging around at the top of the stairs, that's all." He neither looked nor sounded apologetic. Just interested and sort of, well, *sad*. "That kid—Toby. He's the McCaffreys' son?"

Olivia frowned, puzzled, but relaxed a little. "June-bug told me she and Jacob took him in a few years ago, when his father abandoned him. Later on, they adopted him."

"I thought they were a bit long in the tooth to have a boy that age," he said.

She went into the pantry to fetch the ham from the newfangled icebox Mr. Calloway had put in when he built the house. "Stranger things have happened," she said, returning. "My father was well into his fifties when I was born."

He watched her with an appreciation frank enough to fluster her, even if she didn't entirely want him to stop. He seemed oddly perplexed, even a little shaken. "Was he, now? And your mother?"

"She was twenty or so. He had money when she married him."

He arched an eyebrow. "*That's* a cynical thing to say," he observed dryly.

"They were unhappy," she said, and felt sad to remember it. Her father had stayed away most of the time, preferring his Boston club, or maybe the home of a mistress, to the family home. He'd been a spendthrift, as it turned out, and died penniless, despite the appearance of wealth. Turnabout was fair play, so she fixed her gaze on her boarder. "And your family, Mr. McLaughlin? What are they like?"

He was quiet, and she thought he paled a little, there in the glow of the lamps, but she couldn't be certain. The light simply wasn't that good. "Jack," he said, and his voice was throaty. It gave Olivia that peculiar quavering sensation again.

" 'Mr. McLaughlin' will do perfectly well."

"It won't," he argued quietly. "My name is Jack."

She was pleased by his insistence, though she would not have admitted as much to him. Indeed, she could barely admit it to herself. "All right, then—Jack. Where do you come from? Who are your people?"

"I grew up in Nebraska," he said.

Another lie. Nebraska didn't account for the soft Southern inflection to his voice. "I could have sworn you were from Dixie," she said, just to let him know he wasn't fooling her in the least. Well, maybe he was, a little, but not so much that he ought to be congratulating himself or anything.

He sighed and smiled, and he looked very tired all of the sudden. "I might have passed through there once or twice. Picked up a word or two of the lingo."

"And your family?"

"Farmers. Nebraska farmers. They're gone now."

"Any brothers or sisters?" She was slicing off thick chunks of ham by then, laying them in the skillet she'd set on the stove.

He hesitated, or at least she thought he did. "No," he said finally. "Just me. What about you? Do you have sisters and brothers someplace?"

She shook her head. "I was an only child. My parents died when I was a young girl, and I went to live with my aunt." She busied herself salting the ham, even though it didn't need salting, just so she could hide her face for a few moments.

"Was she good to you, this aunt of yours?"

She didn't look at him. "You *are* curious tonight, Mr. McLaughlin."

"Jack."

She sighed. "Jack. No, she wasn't particularly kind; she kept account of my numerous shortcomings, which she was ready to list in detail on a moment's notice, and she never let me forget that I was dependent on her for every bite of food that went into my mouth." Now what in the name of heaven had made her say something so personal?

She heard the chair scrape, and then he was behind her, his hands resting on her shoulders. He turned her gently to face him. "Olivia," he said. That was all. Just "Olivia." Then he bent his head and touched his lips lightly, ever so lightly, to hers. There was no more to the kiss than that, but it made her heart lurch and sent heat pulsing up her neck and into her face all the same.

She should have told him to pack his things and leave, immediately, that very night. She should have slapped him across the face, or reported him to the law. But instead of doing any of those things, she just stood there, staring up at him, so near that she could feel the warmth of his breath on her face, the heat and power of his body tugging at her, bidding her to come closer, and closer still.

He stepped back, let his hands fall to his sides,

and his shoulders slumped a little. "I shouldn't have done that," he said. "I'm sorry."

Don't be, she thought, in a flood of sweet despair. *Don't be sorry.*

He turned away then, put the chair back in its place at the table, and went to stand at the sink, staring out at the snowy night. The evening shadows accentuated his imposing back and shoulders, his lean waist and hips, his long, powerful legs. "I don't want you to be afraid of me, Olivia," he told her, without turning around to face her. "Not ever."

It was all she could do not to go to him, to slip her arms around his middle and lay her cheek to the space between his shoulder blades. She could imagine how his skin would smell, through the fabric of that fresh shirt. "I'm not afraid," she said. It was not, she knew, a sensible way to feel, given that he was almost a complete stranger, and without question a prevaricator. Nonetheless, there it was, sensible or not.

At last, he turned. His eyes were haunted by a host of ghostly regrets and ancient sorrows. "Why?" he rasped. "Why do you trust me, when you know—?"

"When I know you're probably lying about your name and being from Nebraska and maybe a dozen other things, too?" she finished for him, without rancor.

He looked away, then made himself look back. She knew the exasperation she saw in his face was directed at himself, not her. "Yes," he ground out, after a long, difficult silence. "Why, Olivia?"

She turned to attend to the ham, which was beginning to sizzle in the pan. It was much easier to answer when he wasn't looking at her with those eyes that seemed capable of searching the innermost reaches of her soul. "I don't know," she said, and gave a rueful little laugh. All of the sudden, her throat was aching with tears she dared not shed. Once begun, she feared, the torrent might never cease. "Maybe I'm turning foolish in my old age."

"Your what?" he asked, sounding honestly bewildered.

Olivia was profoundly grateful that the conversation had taken a new turn. She sniffled. "I'm thirty-two, after all," she said. "A spinster."

"Ah," he responded, as though considering some profound and mystical quandary. "A spinster."

She sniffled again. "If I wanted to hear the word echoing back at me, Mr. McLaughlin—or whoever you are—I would scramble out onto the roof and shout it out to the whole of Springwater."

The gentleness in his voice was almost her undoing; she could have endured outright mockery far more easily. "Maybe you just haven't met the right man yet," he suggested quietly.

She stabbed at the slabs of ham with a vengeance and turned them hard, causing the grease to spit and snap. She was terribly afraid she *had* met "the right man," and that he was, at one and

the same time, entirely the wrong man. "It's a
way of saying that nobody chose me. Nobody—
wanted me."

She gave up on the ham then. Just flat gave up
on it. What in the name of heaven was causing her
to talk this way, like a blathering, self-pitying fool?

Jack crossed the room and shoved the skillet
back off the heat, and even though it seemed for
the length of a heartbeat that he was about to
take Olivia into his arms, he kept his distance. "Is
that what you think?" he asked, and he sounded
amazed. Even angry.

She went to the table, dragged back a chair, and
sank into it, breathing deeply and rapidly, covering
her face with both hands. "Stop," she whispered.

He laid a hand on her shoulder, and sent fire
spilling through her system by that simple and otherwise innocent gesture. "Olivia," he said. "Another time, another place—I would have been proud
to court you."

Would have been.

She lowered her hands, raised her chin and
made her backbone straight as a broom handle. "I
do not need your pity, Mr. McLaughlin."

He did not step away, did not lift the weight of
his palm from that place where her neck and
shoulder met. "Believe me, Olivia. What I feel
toward you is something else entirely. What I
meant was—I can't offer you anything. Once,
maybe I could have, but not now. And you deserve
a far better man anyhow."

She resisted a ridiculous urge to press the fabric of her skirts to her face and wail disconsolately. "I don't recall asking for your affection—Jack."

"You didn't. But I would have asked for yours, if things were different. Oh, yes, indeed, I would have asked and asked, until you said yes. Until you were my wife, sharing my bed, carrying my babies."

"Stop," she said again. It was too painful to imagine such things, when she knew, when they both knew, nothing was going to come of it. Nothing was going to change, not at this late date.

But that was wrong, she thought, all her joy over June-bug's visit evaporating like steam from a bucket of fresh cow's milk. Something *was* going to change. Jack McLaughlin would get on his horse, one day soon, and ride away from Springwater forever, never once looking back. And she would remain behind, scrabbling for the scattered pieces of her heart.

CHAPTER

❦ 6 ❦

"WHAT DID OLIVIA say about the pageant?"
Rachel demanded, the moment June-bug entered
the stagecoach station, directly following the visit.
"Did you see *him*—close up, I mean?"

June-bug untied the laces of her cloak and surrendered it to her friend to hang for her, all the
while shaking her head. It had left her with the
strangest feeling, being in that house, a dizzying,
instinctive sort of quickening, as though she were
on the verge of some shattering discovery. "Miss
Olivia's goin' to plan the play," she said, almost
musing. "As for the boarder—he was there, all
right. I heard him come in the back way. But he
never did set foot in the parlor." She gave a small
chuckle, combined with a shrug, all the while don-
ning her apron and tying it behind her. "Not that
you'd expect him to, him just back from the mine
and everything. Still, it was—well, it was—odd."

Just then, Jacob came out of the pantry, carrying

a kettle in those big, work-worn hands of his. "You two still at it?" he asked, with a glint of amusement in his dark eyes. "Leave the poor man be. He'll show his cards when and if he's ready."

June-bug took the kettle from him with a little wrench, but she was smiling, and the same fierce and reckless love she'd borne him on their wedding day, more than forty years before, burned within her still. Through it all, the hard early days, when they'd worked from sunup to sundown, just to stay even, the joyous times, the war and the losses, the terrible losses, that flame had never so much as flickered. "If I wanted your opinion, Mr. McCaffrey," she said sweetly, "I'd have asked for it."

He leaned down—way down, being over six feet tall, while June-bug stood barely above five—and planted a light kiss on the top of her head, where her hair was parted. If she had a penny for every time he'd kissed her in exactly that way, she reflected, why she'd be richer than Trey Hargreaves and Scully Wainwright put together. "My sweet bride," he teased, and she laughed and swatted at him.

At the same time, though, in a secret part of herself, she wanted to weep—an unaccountable fact that had nothing to do with Jacob and everything to do with the man hiding out over there in Miss Olivia's house.

Rachel, meanwhile, was putting on her own cloak and smiling. "I'd better get home," she said. "Emma's been watching the little ones ever since school let out for the day."

Jacob, the most chivalrous man June-bug had ever come across, looked up from his wife's face to meet Rachel's eyes. "I'll walk you over," he said. The Hargreaves house was just across the road, and the day wasn't quite gone, but that was Jacob. He'd been born mannerly, June-bug reckoned, and fetched up right.

Rachel dismissed the idea with a smile and a wave. "Good heavens, Jacob," she said, "I can certainly see myself to the other side of the street." She shifted her gaze to June-bug, one hand resting on the door latch. "You'll let me know, if you find out anything?"

In a sidelong glance, June-bug saw Jacob roll his eyes. "Maybe we ought to set the Pinkerton people on this feller," he speculated.

June-bug gave him an affectionate shove with one hand, the empty kettle held against her side in the curve of her other arm, but she was looking at Rachel all the while. "O' course I will. And expect the same from you."

Rachel nodded, opened the door to a brisk November wind that made the fire dance on the hearth, and took her leave.

"You seen Toby in the last little while?" June-bug inquired, turning around and heading for the kitchen area. "He better not be late for supper again. I declare, ever since he took a shine to Emma Hargreaves, he's gone more than he's home."

Jacob wasn't to be put off. "The boy'll be here,

right enough, once he smells food cookin'," he replied, going to the mantel and taking down his pipe which, being a prudent man, he did not make use of inside the house. "Meantime, Miss June-bug, I'd like to know just what it is about that McLaughlin feller that has all you females in such a high dither."

June-bug was quiet for a long while. It wasn't that she didn't want to answer—she shared virtually everything with Jacob, him being as much a part of her as her hands or her heart—but that she didn't exactly understand the thing herself. She turned, searched her husband's craggy, beloved face, and shook her head once to show she was confounded.

"I can't speak for the others," she said softly, after a long time, avoiding Jacob's searching gaze the whole while. When she went on, though, she made herself look at him directly. "Everytime somebody new comes to town, I start wonderin'—I start thinkin' of the boys." Her eyes began to smart. "I guess I'm still lookin' for them to come ridin' in one fine day, even now." She paused, sniffled. "They've been so much on my mind lately, Will and Wesley have. More than what's usual—and I don't rightly know why."

Jacob nodded, fiddling with the pipe in his hand, but he held June-bug's gaze. He was a steady man, Jacob was; he never flinched from much of anything. Still, losing their sons had just about broken him, same way it had her. "There ain't a day—an hour—goes by that they don't cross my mind."

June-bug let her forehead rest against Jacob's strong shoulder for a long moment, and when she looked up at him again, it was through a haze of fresh tears, even though she was smiling. "You remember the time Wesley got himself stuck way up there in that pine tree? Poor little devil was a whole day gettin' down, with you and Will workin' out in the fields and me at the missionary aid meeting in town."

Jacob chuckled, a low, rumbling sound that June-bug loved, the way she loved thunder on a hot summer day, and birds singing on a cool, bright morning. "I should have taken him to task for that, more than I did," he said. "Problem was, I was so glad he hadn't broken his neck that I couldn't bring myself to get after him."

"You never was the kind to raise your voice to anybody," June-bug said, laying her palms flat against her husband's powerful chest, feeling his heart beating strong under her hand. It wasn't something she took for granted, Jacob's heartbeat; a few years back, she'd nearly lost him. Would have done, if it hadn't been for the Doc.

He sobered, a change that would have been all but imperceptible to anybody but June-bug, for Jacob was a man of solemn countenance. A body would never guess, to look at him, that he'd been hallelujah-happy for much of his life, as had she. "Don't think I don't have my regrets where Will and Wes are concerned," he said. "That last day, Wes and I parted on poor terms. I said some harsh words to him, June-bug, and I can still taste them on my tongue, bitter as gall. I reckon I'd give twenty years of my life for a chance to take them back."

"Don't you go tormentin' yourself, Jacob McCaffrey," June-bug scolded gently. "They knew you loved them, Wes as much as Will. No, sir, it was bound to happen, all of it, like it was written in the stars or somethin'. I guess we got to trust that the Lord understands why, even if we don't."

Jacob arched an eyebrow. "I mean to discuss that very thing with the Lord, soon as I set foot in heaven," he said. "As it is, I fail to see His reasonin' in the whole matter."

June-bug stood on tiptoe to kiss the cleft in Jacob's chin. "Just don't go traipsin' off to the Promised Land anytime soon. You'll wait for me, if you know what's good for you."

He laughed out loud. Then he lifted June-bug plum off the floor, his hands at her waist—time was, he could make a circle that way, with his thumbs and fingers meeting round her middle easy-like, but she'd spread out a little over the years—and swung her around once, just like he'd done way back, when they were sparking. "I do indeed know what's good for me, Mrs. McCaffrey," he said, and gave her a sound kiss before setting her back on her feet, where she wavered a bit, dizzy. "Best thing in the world for me is you. And you can bet

I'll wait; even heaven would be a sorrowful place without you there to keep me in line."

June-bug was still light-headed from the kiss. Such interludes always left her that way; with her husband, she always felt like a new bride. "Jacob McCaffrey, for shame. It is the middle of the *day*." It wasn't, though, with suppertime coming on.

He laughed again. "You, woman, are my lawful wedded wife, night, day, and noontime," he reminded her, as if she needed reminding, long as they'd been married. Then he swatted her on the bottom and took himself outside to smoke that pipe of his while she started supper, letting her mind wander while she worked.

Oh, Lord, she prayed silently, *I don't reckon I understand Your reasons for taking our boys away any better than my Jacob does. They were such fine lads, both of them, hardworking, with strong minds and hearts and souls, quick to laugh and always ready to help when help was needed. They'd have made good husbands and fathers, Lord, just like they made good sons, and it seems a waste that they never got the chance to really live, either one of them.*

I don't mean to be complaining, but You know, sometimes, I can't recall their faces. My own babies! Why, whenever I think of them now, it's as if they've come together somehow, to make up one man, instead of two.

She smiled, a little sadly perhaps. *I do thank you most sincerely, though, for that husband of mine. He's as fine a work as You ever done, and I'd admire to keep him for a long, long while, if it's all the same to You.*

Olivia's chickens were in a state, squawking and flapping their wings fit to raise a stiff wind. Jack, standing in the back doorway smoking and watching the first purple shadows of night sneak across the snow, was confused. There was no undue noise coming from the direction of the Brimstone Saloon—at least, no more than usual, which eliminated the most likely possibility.

Hoping to stem the disturbance before Miss Olivia got her back up and went marching off on another of her hopeless crusades, he headed for the chicken coop.

The door squeaked on its hinges when he pulled it open—he'd have to oil the hardware right away—and the stink of all that manure struck him first thing. He squinted into the darkness, expecting to find a fox or a weasel or maybe a stray cat.

Instead, a child darted toward him, striking his middle like a cannonball, but the doorway was narrow and he had a good hold on the back of a ragged coat before the culprit could slip past.

At first, he couldn't tell if the kid was male or female, what with all that matted hair and ground-in filth. The wiry little critter was strong, whichever gender it was, and Jack had some trouble holding on. He almost smiled when he realized that this small, enterprising thief had not come merely to steal eggs; he—or she—was clutching a very disgruntled hen under one arm.

"Now, who would you be?" Jack asked, holding on tight. It was always his way to be kindly with little folks, but thieving was thieving, and it wouldn't be right to make light of the matter.

Fierce blue eyes scalded him from the center of the small, smudged, hunger-pinched face. "You got plenty of chickens," the kid answered. "You ain't gonna miss just one."

"That isn't the point," Jack said. "For one thing, those aren't my chickens to miss or not miss. For another, somebody else having plenty doesn't give you the right to steal." *Hunger could have a real peculiar effect on a person's morals, though*, he thought grimly. He'd seen that sort of desperation many a time, during the war, in the faces of enemies and fellow Rebs alike. He'd swiped a weathered apple from a tree or a potato forgotten in somebody's field on more than one occasion himself. He remembered the gnawing pain of starvation all too well, and it was plain that this little imp was no stranger to the experience, either. "Now, I believe I asked for your name."

"Jamie," the kid replied.

Well, that didn't help much, where gender was concerned. He'd heard of girls bearing that name, though it was more often given to a boy. He sighed. "Where are your folks?"

"Don't have any."

"I see. None at all."

"Nope," said Jamie.

"How'd you get here, then?"

That was when Olivia appeared, drawn, no doubt, by the incessant complaints of the purloined hen. Clutching up her skirts, she came briskly toward them, over the snow-crusted dirt path.

"Good heavens, Mr. McLaughlin," she said. "Unhand that child."

"It'll run away if I do," he reasoned.

"*It?*" she echoed, evidently incensed by his choice of words. The child, meanwhile, looked from one adult to the other, as though they were tossing a hot coal back and forth between them.

He raised his eyebrows in an unspoken challenge, defying her to tell precisely which sort of chicken thief they had here.

"Here's your old chicken," Jamie said, thrusting the bird toward Olivia. "It's skinny anyhow. Meat's probably tough."

"Why don't we find out?" Olivia asked reasonably. There was no condescension in her voice at all; she might have been carrying on a pleasant chat with another grown-up. "Mr. McLaughlin, if you would be so kind as to put that poor fowl out of its misery? In the meantime—" She looked at the child again. "What am I to call you?"

"Jamie," came the enigmatic reply.

A look passed between Olivia and Jack, his a little smug, hers conveying a warning. "Well— Jamie—" she said, making a valiant effort, "let's just go inside, out of the cold. I'll peel some potatoes for supper, and you can wash up. We'll have a nice long talk while Mr. McLaughlin here is attending to that chicken."

"You gonna fry it?" Jamie asked, almost breathless at the prospect.

Jack couldn't fault the kid for being eager. He'd had Miss Olivia's fried chicken himself, and it was worth the grim preliminaries. It paid not to think too much, that was all.

"Certainly," Olivia said, and held out one hand.

The child hesitated, then put out a grubby mitt and allowed himself—or herself—to be led into the house.

"Girl," Olivia mouthed when, fifteen minutes later, Jack came in with the cleaned and plucked chicken. The sound of splashing, along with Olivia's pronouncement, indicated that the little raider was in the pantry, having a bath.

He handed her the chicken, and she washed it carefully before cutting it up into pieces to be floured and fried in snapping-hot bacon grease. "She tell you where she came from?" he asked, scrubbing his hands at the basin Miss Olivia set out for the purpose.

"She's been traveling with a distant relative," she answered, in hardly more than a whisper. "Sounds like he was a peddler of some sort."

"Was?"

Olivia sighed. In the pantry, the kid began to

sing in a voice so clear and sweet that Jack would have thought there was an angel in Miss Olivia's bathtub, if he hadn't known better. "Either he's dead, or he left her behind. She's been on her own for a while—like Toby McCaffrey was—living by what she could scrounge or steal. Now that the weather's turned cold—well, I guess that forced her to come closer in to town."

At one time, Jack would have been amazed to know that such a thing could happen, that a mere child could be left to fend for itself but, like hunger, he'd seen the phenomenon many times since the war. Most folks, no matter what their age, had had a close acquaintance with hard times, at one point or another.

"How old do you reckon she is?"

"I don't have to reckon," Olivia said matter-of-factly, stirring and making things sizzle and smell good over there at the stove. "I know. She told me she was nine on her last birthday." She paused, smiled, this woman who so intrigued him. "Of course, she's really only eight."

Jack frowned. "How do you know that?"

"I just do." She seemed happy, Olivia did. Happier than he'd seen her, and while that pleased him, it also roused a degree of envy in him, made him wish he'd been the one to bring that light to her eyes, that note to her voice. "I'm a woman."

No refuting that, he reflected. The knowledge was keeping him awake nights. One of these days, for pure lack of sleep, he was going to miscalculate the length of a fuse or something, down there in the mine, and blow himself and ten or twelve other men right into the Kingdom. No doubt the good Lord would be surprised to see them.

"What are you going to do with her?" Jack asked, when the splashing went on, indicating that the kid wasn't eavesdropping.

Miss Olivia frowned in a way that made him want to kiss the little crease appearing between her fine eyebrows. "Well, I don't know, Mr. McLaughlin. I hadn't thought that far ahead."

"I imagine the Parrishes would take her in. Like they did those two little boys after the train wreck." Instantly, he regretted mentioning that calamity, for Olivia's eyes darkened at the memory, and some of the soft-apricot tint faded from her cheeks. No doubt it haunted her, that experience, the way certain recollections of the war did him.

She appeared to consider the idea, however, then shook her head decisively. "No, I'll attend to Jamie myself, I think. Someone's sure to claim her. But I would like for Dr. Parrish to examine her, make certain she's all right. You could step across the road and fetch him, after supper, if you wouldn't mind."

It was the first favor she'd asked of him, so he couldn't refuse, though the idea made him feel uneasy. Springwater was a small town, after all, and the less contact he had with the locals before he was ready, the better. "I'll do that," he said.

Jamie, clad in one of Miss Olivia's shirtwaists,

with a silk scarf for a belt, her scraggly blond hair wet-combed and her face scrubbed clean, sat warily at the table as supper was served. She was sure to bolt like a deer if anyone made a sudden move, but her eyes followed that platter of fried chicken as though it might lead her to some holy place. She ate four pieces before she even slowed down, and two servings of mashed potatoes and gravy after that. She was preparing to tuck into a dried apple pie when Jack excused himself from the table, carried his plate and utensils to the sink, and took his coat down from the peg by the back door.

"I'll save you the Doc's fee," he said, with a half-grin. "That kid is healthier than anybody this side of the Missouri River."

"I don't need no doctor," Jamie protested, but she was too intent on the pie to make a strong case. "I ain't sick." Jack hoped there'd be a slice or two left by the time he got back, for he did favor sweets.

"Atrocious grammar," Miss Olivia commented, unmoved. She'd long since finished eating, but she seemed to be in no hurry to wash up the dishes and either play the piano or vanish into her room to read, the way she usually did.

"Huh?" Jamie asked, forehead crumpled.

Smiling to himself, Jack went out, and smelled snow in the air.

Dr. Parrish tugged the stethoscope from around his neck and tossed it into his bag. "Just malnourished," he said to Miss Olivia, who was standing on the other side of the bed where the child lay watching them both with eyes the size of bear tracks. "She'll be fine."

His mind, he had to admit, was not on the child. He was thinking, instead, of the man who had appeared on his front porch an hour or so before, hat brim drawn low over his face, the collar of his coat raised. So this was the mysterious boarder, whom no one had met in broad daylight, apparently, other than Miss Olivia herself and Trey Hargreaves, who'd hired him to set charges in the mine.

Pres was a great believer in minding his own business, a knack his wife and her friends couldn't seem to master, but there *was* something about Jack McLaughlin that stirred his memory. He'd seen that walk before, heard that voice—but where?

"Doctor?" Olivia said, and he realized she must have been speaking to him while he was letting his mind roam. Bad habit, in a doctor, he reminded himself.

"I'm sorry," he said. "I was a little distracted just now."

She smiled, and for the first time—he was virtually blind to every woman but Savannah—it struck him that she was pretty, in a rather prim sort of way. "Actually," she said, "I was asking Jamie if she was afraid of you."

Pres squeezed the bridge of his nose between a thumb and forefinger. His rounds had been particularly grueling that day, and he longed to eat the meal Savannah was keeping warm for him, to read to his children, and talk quietly with his wife. Sometimes, Savannah was all that kept him sane, he thought. The demons he'd acquired during the war would be with him until he died, he knew that, but when he lay down with Savannah, and she took him in her arms, he could forget. For a little while, he could put what he knew of the world out of his mind, out of his heart, out of his spirit, and if he hadn't loved his bride for a thousand other reasons, he would surely have adored her for that one alone.

He bid Olivia and the little girl a quiet good night, said he'd let himself out, and headed for the rear stairway, not wanting to track through Miss Olivia's fine house with God-only-knew-what on his boots.

In the middle of the stairs, he met McLaughlin, who was carrying a lantern in one hand and a plate of apple pie in the other. The two of them stopped, face-to-face, and Pres's legendary memory, which was both blessing and curse, pulled hard at a far corner of his mind.

He'd seen this man before, he was almost sure of that, but where? Lying on an operating table, during the war, awash in blood? Probably. McLaughlin would have been just one of hundreds of wounded, terrified boys to cross paths with Pres. He'd never known any of their names, they came and went too fast for such niceties as that, but their faces often returned to him in his nightmares. He frowned.

From the expression in the eyes of Miss Olivia Wilcott Darling's star boarder, he didn't want to be remembered. His jawline tightened. "The little girl's all right?" he asked.

"Just hungry and in need of some mothering."

The boarder nodded. He was trying to look pleasant, but Pres knew he hadn't expected to encounter anybody other than Miss Olivia or the child on that stairway, and he would have gone to almost any lengths to avoid the confrontation.

Pres thrust a hand through his hair and sighed. He was hungry, he was weary through and through, and he needed to be with Savannah, if only to sit across a table from her, or in the chair next to hers, before the fire in the front room. "I'll say good night," he said. "It's been a long day."

McLaughlin gave another brisk nod, and they let each other pass without speaking again.

They were lying on their bellies in deep grass, their rifles beside them. Overhead, cannon fire boomed, fit to rend the sky into jagged pieces, and Will could literally smell the fear in the air. He would have readily admitted—had he been asked, that is—that a good share of that apprehension was his own. Nobody inquired, though, least of all Wes.

He scowled at his feckless brother; they might have been playing soldier in one of the fields at home, for all the concern Wes showed. God in heaven, didn't he understand that this was *real*?

That those people over there on the other side of that nameless creek wanted to kill every last Reb between there, wherever the hell they were— somewhere in North Carolina, Will figured—and Florida?

"Daddy'd be real proud if he could see us now," Wes breathed, and sighted in his squirrel gun on nothing.

"Thank God he can't," Will answered, and pushed the barrel of his brother's peashooter down into the grass. "Be careful with that thing. We're in enough trouble, with all those Yankees buzzing over yonder like a swarm of scalded bees. You shoot one of our own and that'll be the end of your military career."

The irony of the words "military career" was plainly lost on Wes. He was still grinning. "You ain't scared, are you, Will?"

"Hell, yes, I'm scared," Will said, with spirit. "You would be too if you had the sense God gave a rotted tree stump."

"We can take them Yankees. Why, the two of us could face 'em all down on our own if it came to that." He started to get up. "I'm tired of waiting."

A bullet twanged overhead just as Will grabbed Wes by the fabric of his shirt and slammed him back to the ground. "You move from that spot before Cap'n McLaughlin says," he warned, through his teeth, "and I might just shoot you myself."

Wes was irrepressible, even in the face of a cou-

ple of hundred well-armed, well-fed, pissed-off
Yankees. He looked downright cocky, in fact. "I'm
gonna win me a medal 'fore this is over," he said.
"Take it home for Mama to show off to her
friends."

"She'd rather have you than every medal in the
Confederacy," Will answered, but he spoke in a
low voice. He knew Wes wasn't listening to him
anyhow.

That was when Cap'n Jack McLaughlin ordered
a charge. Wes sprang up, eager to protect the Confederacy. Will followed suit, bound and determined
to protect Wes. After all, he'd promised.

The world split apart in the next few moments—all those Rebs were running through the
fields, splashing through the creek, Wes right there
in the thick of it all. The Yankees, as expected,
opened fire with a line of cannon and rushed forward with bayonets.

Will fought with a savagery he hadn't known
was in him; so much was at stake: not slavery, not
federal gold, but his mama and daddy and only
brother. The whole South, damn it, and the only
way of life he'd ever known.

Wes gave the Rebel yell a hundred times, if he
gave it once, and he wielded the squirrel gun as a
club when there was no time to reload. He'd have
died that day, all the same, if Will hadn't stayed
close by, and shot one particular Yankee with murder in his eyes.

Long as he lived, though, he'd never forget the

look on that northerner's face when the bullet
exploded in his gut. It came to Will then, if it
hadn't before—at least, not in the daylight—that
the blue-coat had had a family, too. A home and a
history and private hopes that would never come
to pass.

The sudden appearance of a battalion of Confederate cavalry saved all their asses that day; Will
could admit that, if Wes couldn't. The horsemen
scattered the Yankee infantry in all directions, sent
them racing back across that blood-red creek, trip-
ping over fallen men from both sides as they went.

That night, hunched over a scrap of paper, close
by the campfire, Wes recounted the glories of the
day in a letter home. His brother was hearing the
cavalry bugles, Will supposed, and the welcome
thunder of Confederate artillery. Will was hearing
the screams.

"I'm gonna get me a horse and sign on with the
cavalry," Wes said, his eyes bright in the firelight as
he fixed that dreamer's gaze of his on Will.

"How do you figure on doing that, on twelve
dollars a month?" He didn't point out that they
hadn't been paid since they'd joined up; none of
them had, except maybe the officers. Some of the
boys didn't have boots, let alone horses, and most
of them might just as well have carried sticks, like
kids playing in the schoolyard, useless as their
small-caliber, brought-from-home rifles were. Guns
made for hunting rabbits and squirrels weren't
much use against federal-issue carbines.

"You know, Will," Wes speculated, with his usual good-natured persistence, "the trouble with you is, you think little puny thoughts." He looked even younger than he was, face smeared with dirt and streaked with sweat, hair rumpled and in need of trimming, clothes torn and stained from crawling in the grass half the time and mud the other half.

Keep him safe, Will prayed silently, even though he didn't place much store by such things as prayer anymore. Not since the first time he'd seen a boy he knew from home, lying on his back in another creek, in another field, arms flung wide, chest a mass of gore, staring up at the sky with startled eyes.

Somebody, somewhere in the darkness that lay just beyond the short reach of the fire, brought out a mouth harp, and the strains of an old, sweet tune filled the air like tears. The boys, talking before, forks clattering against metal plates, fell silent, listening with a sort of sad reverence.

Will blinked and averted his gaze.

Home seemed further away than ever.

CHAPTER

7

IT WAS SNOWING a little, the next morning, when Olivia and Jamie set out for the schoolhouse, side by side. Jamie was clad in an ill-fitting dress borrowed from little Beatrice Parrish, across the street, and rather than the shyness one might have expected, the child exhibited a touching eagerness to attend class. As best she could recall, Jamie told Olivia, during the short walk, holding her napkin-wrapped lunch carefully in both hands, she'd never been to school before.

"Do you think I'll know how to read, time I get home?" she asked, looking up at Olivia with wide, hopeful eyes, eyes the same pale, delicate blue as a spring sky.

The word "home" pinched Olivia's heart, and for a moment, she dared to hope that no one would come to claim this adventurous little urchin, that she might stay, become Olivia's ward, or even her adopted daughter, and grow up right there in

Springwater. At the same time, she knew it was unlikely—yes, the Parrishes had taken the two small brothers from the train wreck into their hearts and homes, but Doc and Savannah were married. Pillars of the community. She, on the other hand, was a newcomer, a relative outsider, and a spinster.

She swallowed. "I—I suppose that depends," she began, recalling Jamie's question at last, "on whether or not you know your letters and such. It does take time to learn to read. Everything worthwhile takes time and effort."

Jamie frowned. Beneath their feet, the ground was hard and rutted, furred with a coat of hoary frost, and there were frozen puddles everywhere. "Oh," she said, at last, sounding disappointed. "You have all them books. I was hopin' I could read some of them 'fore I have to go away."

The schoolhouse was just ahead, on the other side of the road. It faced the despised Brimstone Saloon, an example of poor planning if Olivia had ever seen one. "Where would you go?" she asked softly, and not for the first time. "Do you have family somewhere?"

Jamie dragged her lower lip beneath her front teeth and pondered the matter at some length before answering. "I have a ma someplace, I think. But maybe not. Axel used to say she was dead. Then he'd say she just left us, because I was bad."

Tenderly, Olivia touched the child's shoulder. Together, they proceeded across the road, toward the schoolhouse gate. The Brimstone, meanwhile, was already open for business, and discordant piano music tumbled out into the crisp, dry air like a hundred tiny, rusted cowbells, shaken up and poured out of a bucket. "Was Axel your father?"

Jamie shook her head. "Don't think so," she said. "If I ain't gonna learn to read, how about countin'? Will they teach me *that* in this place, at least?"

A smile touched Olivia's mouth and was gone again, before the child caught sight of it. Obviously, Jamie was beginning to take a dim view of a school that could impart so little knowledge, even when given a whole day to accomplish the task. "You'll learn arithmetic," she said. "If you work hard and pay attention in class." *If. If this dreadful Axel person doesn't come back to claim you. If the town fathers, in their infinite wisdom, don't decide to send you away to some girls' home, far from Springwater. Far from me.*

The child emitted a heavy sigh. "Well, that beats all. Sounds like I'm gonna come out of that place with nothin' in my head but what I already know."

Olivia wanted to laugh. At the same time, she wanted to cry. In any event, she had time to do neither, for they had reached the schoolhouse gate, and Miss Dorothy Mathers opened the door and stepped out, beaming.

"And who do we have here?" the teacher asked, her breath making fog in the air.

Whom, Olivia thought automatically, but at least she didn't correct the woman aloud. For her, that was progress. "This is Jamie," she answered. "Jamie, Miss Mathers. Your teacher."

Jamie assessed the brawny young woman with unflinching thoroughness. "Can you teach me to read and count?" she demanded.

Dorothy laughed. "In time," she replied, and held out one hand. "You come on in here, Miss Jamie, and get yourself settled." All the while she was speaking, she kept her gaze, curious and friendly, fixed on Olivia's face. Jamie scampered inside. "Now where did she come from?" Dorothy asked, in a low voice.

Briefly, Olivia explained Jamie's arrival, taking care to leave out the fact that she'd been in the process of stealing a chicken at the time.

The teacher seemed inclined to chat that morning. "I hear you're going to plan the Christmas pageant," she remarked. "The children will enjoy that, all the singing and dressing up and reciting their pieces and such."

The words warmed Olivia, despite the biting breeze sweeping down from the distant, snowy mountains, despite the ever-thickening fall of fat white flakes, made her feel a part of the community in a way she hadn't before. "Thank you," she said, somewhat shyly.

The other woman nodded. "We get through around three o'clock," she said, and Olivia turned away.

She didn't go directly home—the prospect was a lonely one, with Jamie at school, Mr. McLaughlin gone to the mine, and only her chickens for company—but made for the general store instead.

A small bell sounded above the door as Olivia stepped inside, shivering a little, grateful for the welcoming aromas of sawdust, coffee beans, leather goods, and smoke from the woodstove in the center of the store. Cornucopia greeted her with a warm smile and rounded the counter. Her bridegroom, whose name Olivia could not recall from the brief announcement printed weeks before in the *Gazette*, had gone to Texas, right after the wedding, to bring back another herd of cattle.

"Look at you," she said. "Chilled right through. Come sit by the stove and have a cup of coffee."

Olivia might have sidestepped the invitation on another day—she was not unaware that Cornucopia was curious about Mr. McLaughlin, like everybody else in town, and probably hoping to pry out some tidbit of information in the course of conversation—but she was feeling purposeful that morning, even cheerful. "I'd like that," she said. With a polite nod, she began the process of shedding her cloak—pushing the hood back, untying the laces at her throat, laying the heavy garment aside, over the back of one of the chairs encircling the stove.

Cornucopia fetched a cup and poured coffee from the large community pot warming on top of the potbellied stove. "You want sugar? Cream?"

Olivia shook her head and took a chair. "Thank you, no. Just coffee." The cup was deliciously warm in her chilled hands, the scent of the strong, fresh brew restorative, all by itself.

Since there were no other customers in the store at the moment, Cornucopia apparently felt at liberty to languish a while. After serving Olivia's coffee, she sat down in a nearby chair, sighed cheerily, and rested her feet, crossed at the ankles, on the chrome rail surrounding the stove. Then she simply sat there, gazing at Olivia and beaming, chin propped in one hand.

Olivia took a nervous sip from the cup; the coffee was stout and delicious, well worth the sleepless night she would probably pass because of it. After that first taste, she sighed and relaxed a little. "I've come for yard goods," she said, feeling a need to break the silence.

"You're fixing to make up some duds for the little girl."

Olivia blinked, surprised, yet again, at how fast word traveled in and around Springwater. They might as well have had an old-fashioned town crier, strolling the streets clanging a bell and shouting out the latest news, so efficient was the grapevine. "Well," she said. "Yes."

Cornucopia smiled. "I've got some nice scraps from things I've made for myself," she said. "No sense in your paying good money for new cloth when mine's just been setting there, going to waste."

Olivia found the store mistress's offer not only heartwarming, but a great relief. Once Mr. McLaughlin's rent money ran out, she'd be flat broke, and there was no telling when she'd get another boarder. "Thank you. That's—that's wonderful." She braced herself to be quizzed about the strange man living under her roof—nobody ever gave anything away without expecting something in return, after all, Aunt Eloise had drummed that into her—but Cornucopia took up an entirely different topic.

"We're all looking forward to the Christmas pageant," she said. "It's been a long time since most of us have seen something like that."

Olivia relaxed again, took slow, delicate sips from her coffee, not because she was inclined toward daintiness, but because she didn't want the occasion to end too soon. She had not realized how lonely she was until she had begun to let other people into her life—first, Mr. McLaughlin, then June-bug McCaffrey, and then little Jamie, who claimed she'd never had a last name. And now here was Cornucopia, seemingly determined to become her friend.

Cornucopia's eyes took on a dreamy, reflective glint. "We used to put on a play every year, back home in Virginia, even during the war." She smiled, softly and perhaps a little sadly, and returned to the here-and-now with a blink of her eyes. "I was Mary once. Another time, I got to be an angel. Mama made wings for me, out of wire and cheesecloth. I had them for years, those wings, but they got lost somewhere along the way betwixt there and here."

Olivia was touched by the brief story, and it occurred to her that this was a chance to offer a special gift to the whole community of Springwater—memories of theatrical glory for the participating children, and the delight of an old and dearly familiar ritual for the parents and other adults. All of the sudden, the resignation she'd felt toward the project was replaced by resolve: the first Springwater Christmas pageant would be as spectacular as she could make it. In one area of her mind, she was already planning the music. They would sing all the old favorites, inviting the whole assembly to join in, and the script would of course be based on the second chapter of Luke, though she intended to take some license. Surely God would not mind the addition of a few lines for each of the shepherds and the Wise Men, and perhaps a handful of the angels . . .

"You want any help with the sewing," Cornucopia was saying, "you just let me know."

Olivia laughed. Every member of the cast would need at least the indication of a costume, and she was going to have her hands full directing the music and the recitations. "All right. I need help."

"Good," Cornucopia said, with obvious satisfaction.

Just about then, the door opened, and Miranda Kildare came in, followed by her husband, Landry.

They were both bundled up against the cold, and while Miranda smiled an obviously genuine greeting as soon as she stepped over the threshold, Landry averted his gaze every time it crept in Olivia's direction.

"What can I do for you today?" Cornucopia asked, getting up. The Kildares might have been making a social call, Olivia thought, the way they were welcomed.

Miranda shivered happily and hugged herself. She was young and beautiful and hugely pregnant, and Olivia felt a pinch of envy as she looked at the other woman. All the same, she decided then and there that she liked Miranda; she was simply too friendly and engaging *not* to like. "We've come to send off for some Christmas presents for the boys," she said. "You don't think it's too late, do you?"

Cornucopia had risen from her chair and taken up her place behind the counter. "Plenty of time," she said. "I'll fetch the catalog. Landry, help yourself to some of that coffee. You know where the cups are."

Mr. Kildare was still self-conscious; no doubt, Olivia's visit to the town council was fresh in his mind. It certainly was in hers, and she was, truth to tell, enjoying his discomfiture enormously.

"Miss Olivia," he said gruffly, with a nod, taking Miranda's heavy cloak and bonnet before removing his hat and lined leather coat.

"Hello, Mr. Kildare," she replied.

He fetched a mug from the shelf on a nearby

wall, carried it to the stove, and filled it from the big pot. Cornucopia and Miranda were already chatting in the background, discussing catalogs and snowstorms and the forthcoming Christmas pageant, all in a bright tangle of words.

Mr. Kildare took the chair Cornucopia had just abandoned and set one booted foot on the stove railing. Only then, when he was finally settled, did he meet Olivia's gaze.

He cleared his throat. "I don't reckon our older boys will be much interested, but our next to youngest, Isaiah, is looking forward to that play you're putting on," he said. "Little Joshua's just barely talking, so he doesn't go to school yet."

Olivia smiled to herself and cast a sidelong glance in Miranda's direction. "Looks as though the new baby will be arriving soon," she said, and blushed, wondering, the moment the words were out of her mouth, what had gotten into her, causing her to make such a personal remark.

Landry, on the other hand, relaxed visibly, and finally smiled. His eyes shone with delight, and she saw that he had a certain mischievous charm, like a well-meaning, overgrown boy. "I sure hope we get a girl," he said.

Whatever her differences with this man and his fellow members of the town council, Olivia could not help liking him for the joy she saw in his face, the love he so obviously bore his wife and his children, born and unborn. The Kildares had everything anybody could ask for, to her way of thinking—a home, each other, healthy children, and a whole town full of loyal friends.

Miranda, having overheard his comment, made one of her own. "I *am* having a girl this time," she said. "And that's all there is to it."

Everyone laughed, including Olivia. A certain festive sweetness swelled in the center of her heart, and outside, the snowfall thickened until the buildings across the street were barely visible.

While Miranda and Landry were examining the catalog, Cornucopia went into her living quarters at the back of the store and brought out the "scraps" she'd mentioned earlier. Olivia was overjoyed by the selection—there were brightly colored woolens, calicos, even silks and velvets. She ran a reverent hand over a length of lush forest green, and her eyes must have been shining when she met Cornucopia's gaze.

"These are so beautiful. Surely you have need—"

Cornucopia dismissed the idea with a wave of one hand. "I can't use them—there isn't a full bolt in the lot. They're just right for your girl's dresses, though. I think this woolen here"—she indicated a rich blue cloth—"would make a real nice little coat."

Olivia's throat was constricted, and her eyes stung. She had to look away for a moment, for the sake of her dignity.

Cornucopia reached across the counter and touched her hand lightly. "Here, now," she said softly, "don't you go getting sentimental over a pile of sewing scraps. I'd have given them to the ladies for their quilts, but they like to cut their squares from shirts and dresses—things that have a story behind them."

"You are very generous," Olivia managed. Then, as the snow came down thicker and faster, she was reminded of the passing of time. She bought a length of lawn to make drawers and petticoats for Jamie, white flannel for nightgowns and, after saying good-bye to the Kildares, braved the weather to make her way home.

She had half hoped that Mr. McLaughlin would be there when she arrived, released from the mine early because of the worsening storm, but the house was empty, and it was cold. She busied herself building up the fire in the kitchen stove, then fetched her sewing box and assessed the stock of lovely cloth Cornucopia had given her. She would put some aside for a quilt, and use a portion for the pageant costumes, too.

She started with the flannel first, cutting the pieces for two small nightgowns; because of the generous fit, she didn't need to measure Jamie before undertaking the task.

The day passed rapidly, though Olivia barely noticed, so intent was she on her sewing. While she snipped and stitched, she hummed every Advent hymn she could remember, and still the snow came down. She had already lighted several lamps when she glanced up at the wall clock above the table and saw that it was nearly three o'clock.

Jamie would be getting out of school at any minute.

Her heart soared on a swell of excitement; in a hurry, she extinguished the lamps, put on her cloak, and dashed out. The air was cold enough to sting her fingers and toes, even through gloves and sturdy shoes, but she barely noticed.

Just a week before, she had been a lonely woman, with an empty life. Now, she felt as though she had been made new. Suddenly, her life was full of activity and purpose; the people of Springwater deemed her trustworthy to put on their first Christmas pageant. She had Jamie to look after, and Mr. McLaughlin—Jack—to talk with of a night. They shared interests, such as music and books, she and her boarder. Maybe she would even ask him to teach her to play checkers.

Why, it was almost as if she had a family of her very own . . .

The recklessness, the sheer danger of that thought halted her in midstep.

Have a care, warned a familiar voice, forever lurking somewhere in the back of her heart, amid the shadows.

As quickly as that, her joy evaporated. Mr. McLaughlin had never planned to stay in Springwater—he'd said so, right off—and it was certainly possible that Jamie would either run away or be taken from her. Best not to let them get too close.

But wasn't it already too late? Despair swept

over her, but she turned her back on it resolutely. She was very good at that.

The doors of the schoolhouse parted with a crash just as she reached the gate, and shouting children raced out, chasing each other, reveling in the storm, making snowballs and flinging them in all directions.

Olivia sidestepped one such missile herself, and chose to believe it had been thrown in her direction accidentally.

Jamie hurried toward her, waving a slate. "I'm all the way up to *H*," she boasted with a smile so wide she could have tucked the ends into her ears. Ignoring the snowballs and the gleeful shouts of the other children, she held the small chalkboard up for Olivia to see. Very carefully, Jamie had written the first eight letters of the alphabet.

Olivia was genuinely impressed. "You must be very intelligent," she said, opening the gate. She'd finished one of the flannel nightgowns, except for the hem, and she was eager to present it.

"What's 'extulligant'?" Jamie asked, looking up at her as they started for home.

Olivia repeated the word correctly. "It means you're smart," she said.

Jamie beamed. "Oh. Well, I *told* you that, first thing." She looked back over one painfully thin shoulder. "That red-haired boy there—his name is Johnny. He says anybody who don't know their alphabet by the time they're nine has to be stupid."

"Hmmph," Olivia responded. "Pay no attention

to him. It is *what* we learn that matters, and how much, not when we learn it."

When they arrived at the house, stomping snow off their feet at the back door, they found that Mr. McLaughlin had returned. He was surprisingly clean, considering that he'd spent the day crawling about in the tunnels of a silver mine, and he'd brewed a pot of coffee and helped himself to a slice of leftover pie.

"I can write every letter up to H," Jamie told him, while Olivia was still helping the child out of one of her own wool jackets, designed to wear with a skirt and shirtwaist, but doubling, for the present, as a coat.

Mr. McLaughlin looked suitably impressed. "That's real progress," he said.

Olivia felt unaccountably flustered; glad of his presence, and at the same time, thrown off balance. What a peculiar effect he had on her, she thought, disgruntled and full of an odd, cautious, raging bliss.

"I'll get supper started, since we're all here," she said, hurrying over to clear away the debris of the afternoon's sewing frenzy.

Jamie had caught sight of the small nightgown, hanging over the back of a chair. Her eyes went wide, and Olivia saw her throat work as she swallowed. She approached the garment as though it were a religious relic, and reached out a tentative hand to touch it.

"You needed something of your own to sleep in," Olivia said, very softly.

Jamie looked at her in bewilderment. "This is mine?" she asked, and the note of wonder in her voice made Olivia want to pick the child up and embrace her.

Out of the corner of her eye, Olivia saw that Mr. McLaughlin was watching the scene with interest.

"Sure it is," she said. "I've got yard goods for dresses, too," she added.

"I ain't never had anything like this," Jamie whispered. "Do I have to leave it here when I go away?"

Olivia bit her lip. She was, of course, moved by the little girl's pleasure in an ordinary flannel nightgown, but it was the reference to the inevitable departure that nearly undid her. She tried to speak, and found she couldn't.

Mr. McLaughlin, meanwhile, had crossed the room to rest one large hand on top of Jamie's blond head. "I reckon Miss Olivia means for you to keep that," he said quietly. "Since she went to the trouble of stitching it up to fit and all."

Jamie bit her lower lip so hard Olivia feared she would break the skin. "I'm obliged," she said, sounding more like an adult than a child.

Olivia smiled. "After supper," she said, making her tone brisk in an effort to disguise her emotions, "you can stand on a chair and I'll pin up the hem."

"Will it be ready for me to sleep in? Tonight?"

Olivia nodded. "Tonight," she said, and turned away to mix a batch of cornbread batter to go with the pinto beans and salt pork she'd kept simmering on the stove since her return from the general store that morning.

After supper—Jamie ate with the same voracious appetite she'd exhibited the night before—Mr. McLaughlin insisted on washing the dishes. Olivia was deeply appreciative, though she hoped he didn't expect a corresponding reduction in his rent, and she set about hemming Jamie's nightgown.

When the task was finished, the child insisted on going straight to bed in her new nightgown, even though it wasn't yet five o'clock. Olivia finally conceded the point, and was surprised when she looked in on Jamie a little after six and found her sound asleep.

She crept down the rear stairs, planning to start on a dress, using one of the woolens. The blue, she thought—that would match Jamie's eyes, and it could certainly be counted upon to keep her warm.

For some reason, she was not expecting to encounter Mr. McLaughlin again before morning, but there he was, chair drawn up close to the stove, head bent, reading from a book. Olivia recognized a rather dry history of the Roman Empire, taken from her own small collection. Like most of the other volumes, that one had belonged to Aunt Eloise, and still bore her starchy signature on the title page. Marking her possessions had been very important to Aunt Eloise.

"Hope you don't mind," Mr. McLaughlin said,

holding the book up. He was keeping his place with one index finger, as she'd seen him do before.

"Of course not," she replied briskly. "Heaven knows, I won't be reading it any time soon."

He smiled, and it seemed, that smile, in the cozy, lamplit kitchen, on this snowy night, to shine from within him, like some internal flame, rather than simply resting lightly on his lips before flying away. "It was a fine thing, what you did for that little girl," he said.

Olivia had to turn away, lest he see too much in her face, see that she was a fool, dreaming foolish, futile dreams. Taking the length of blue woolen from the stack of folded cloth, she held it up in both hands, assessing its size and suitability. While Jamie was standing still—at least, *relatively* still— she'd taken proper measurements. "Thank you," she said, when she trusted herself to speak.

"Take care, Olivia," he said quietly.

She stopped, turned to face him. "What do you mean?"

"I think you know," he said. "That child is half wild, and whatever she's told you, she most likely belongs to somebody, somewhere. Don't get too attached to her. You're liable to wake up one morning and find her long gone, and that might just break your heart."

He was a fine one to talk, when it came to being long gone and breaking hearts, though of course she couldn't say that out loud.

Olivia felt angry color surge into her face, though she knew he was right, but somehow, just since his arrival, she'd lost her ability to close off her feelings, to choose whether or not she wanted to care for someone. "Merciful heavens, Mr. McLaughlin," she said, a little snappishly, "you make it sound as though she's a stray dog."

"You know I didn't mean it that way," he scolded, but gently. Quietly. "I don't want to see you hurt, that's all. And I thought we agreed that you wouldn't call me 'Mr. McLaughlin' anymore. My name is Jack."

"No," Olivia said, spreading the fabric on the well-scrubbed table, "it isn't."

"It will do for the time being," he said, and went back to reading his book.

She was glad he was there, even though they'd had words, for his mere presence was a secret joy to her. For the thousandth time, she wondered how she would bear it when he finally went away, once and for all.

The evening was companionable, a pleasant change from the lonely nights Olivia had endured for so long. Jack read, and she sewed, and they said very little to each other, while beyond the steamy windows the snow continued to fall.

Eventually, they said good night, and went to their separate beds, and Olivia lay stiffly, even rigidly, upon her cool, starched sheets, staring up at the ceiling. During the day, she could hold her worries at a distance, but when she lay down to sleep at night, they always caught up with her, like a pack of patient, slavering wolves.

They encircled her now, nipping and yowling, tearing at the flesh of her spirit. She thought about losing Jamie, so soon after finding her. She thought of Jack McLaughlin, mounting his horse and riding out, leaving Springwater behind forever.

The tears she was too proud to shed in daylight pushed their way to the surface and trickled over her temples into her hair.

It wasn't until Sunday morning that Jamie rebelled. The moment Olivia mentioned going to church—it was an opportunity to wear one of several new dresses, after all—the child scrambled under her bed and hid there, dug in like a stubborn house cat clutching a rug.

"Come out of there this instant," Olivia said firmly. Her arms were folded and she was tapping one foot.

Jamie shook her head. "You go on ahead," she said, with stout determination. "I ain't goin' in that place. No, ma'am."

Some instinct alerted Olivia to Jack's presence; she glanced back and saw him leaning in the doorway, one shoulder braced against the jamb. He looked amused, but he had the good sense not to offer his opinion, whatever it might have been.

Olivia dropped awkwardly to her haunches, the skirts of her Sunday dress pooling around her on the bare wood floor. "Going to church," she said, as reasonably as she could, "is part of growing up to be a lady."

"I don't want to be no lady."

Olivia closed her eyes and offered a brief, silent prayer for patience. "This is unsuitable behavior," she said. "Now, stop dillydallying. We'll be late."

"I done told you already, Miss Olivia," Jamie replied. "I ain't going."

Olivia heaved an exasperated sigh. "Why ever not?"

"Because the roof'll fall in on my head," Jamie replied, with conviction. "Axel always said so."

Against her better judgment, Olivia looked at Jack again, and saw him raise his eyebrows. "Nonsense," she told the child.

It was then that Jack finally ambled over, crouched down, and held out one hand to the little girl. "Come on out, kid," he said gently. "You and I will play some cutthroat checkers while we wait for Miss Olivia to come back and fry us up another chicken."

Jamie considered the proposition, tossed a wary glance in Olivia's direction, and wriggled out of her burrow. "All right," she said, utterly serious, "but I ought to warn you, mister: I'm real good at checkers, and I'll most likely beat you."

Jack grinned. "I'll take my chances," he replied.

Olivia sighed, rose to her feet as gracefully as she could, and took herself off to church.

CHAPTER

8

"I WAS HOPING your boarder would join us for this morning's church service," said Sue Bellweather, stepping into Olivia's path when she stood up at the end of the closing prayer to make for the door. She never stayed for the social hour, though she supposed she would have to amend that habit, now that she had charge of the Christmas pageant.

Olivia drew a deep, measured breath and released it slowly. The fingers of her right hand, resting on the back of the pew in front of hers, clenched. She relaxed them only by a conscious effort. "I'm afraid Mr. McLaughlin is not a religious man," she said, and attempted a pleasant smile.

"He sure does keep to himself," Sue said, frowning. "Like he's got something to hide. You don't suppose he's an outlaw, do you?"

The possibility had certainly occurred to Olivia before, especially in the darkest hours of the night, when she sometimes lay awake, recalling perfectly dreadful stories she'd heard about the fate of women who allowed strangers into their homes. Now, though, in the bright light of an early winter day, she felt honor bound to defend Mr. McLaughlin. "Jack is no outlaw," she said, trying—and failing—to smile again.

" 'Jack,' is it?" Sue asked, in a self-satisfied tone of voice.

Other members of the congregation were beginning to jam the aisle behind Sue, like too many logs trying to pass through a flume at the same time. "Oh, for Pete's sake," Rachel Hargreaves said, tugging the woman out of the line of traffic to stand between the pews. "Leave Olivia alone."

"Amen," said Savannah.

"And hallelujah," added June-bug McCaffrey.

Sue made a huffing sound. "It's not as if the rest of you don't wonder about him yourselves," she pointed out.

Olivia would never really know where her response came from; the invitation was out of her mouth before she had time to analyze it—or its many ramifications. "Perhaps all of you would like to stop by my house for tea," she said.

"Right now?" Miranda Kildare asked, obviously surprised.

The faces of the other women reflected their friend's reaction.

There was no going back, Olivia decided. Besides, it served Jack McLaughlin right, this unexpected visit from the women of Springwater;

bad enough that he refused to attend church himself, but he'd led little Jamie down the same path of irreverence. Even now, the two of them were probably embroiled in a rousing game of checkers, and never mind that it was the Sabbath.

"Yes," she said, squaring her shoulders. "Now. Unless you have other plans?"

The men generally passed Sunday afternoons over at the McCaffreys' place, drinking coffee and swapping tales, Olivia knew, while their wives stitched and chatted across the street, in Rachel Hargreaves's parlor.

June-bug, Rachel, Savannah, Miranda, Jessica, and Evangeline all hastily denied having plans, while Sue Bellweather just stood there, looking smug. And so it was that the ladies of Springwater followed Olivia home through the diamond-bright snow that day, every one of them amazed. Some of their children followed along as well, planning to spirit Jamie outside to play.

Olivia had hoped Mr. McLaughlin and Jamie would have set up their checkerboard in the front room but, not surprisingly, they had chosen the kitchen. It was, after all, the most comfortable room in the house.

"We might as well go into the dining room," Olivia said cheerfully. "There's more room there, and it's warmer." The parlor fireplace had not been lighted, and there was a distinct nip in the air, even inside. Furthermore, the dining room opened onto the kitchen, where she'd last seen Jack.

When Olivia had settled her company around the long and seldom-used table, taken their cloaks and coats and bonnets, and stirred the dying fire on the hearth, she proceeded to the next room. She half expected Mr. McLaughlin to have disappeared, for he couldn't possibly have missed hearing the entrance of Springwater's female aristocracy, but there he was, seated across from Jamie, embroiled in a game. It looked as though Jamie's warning that morning was well-taken: she was obviously winning.

Jack looked at Olivia with full knowledge of her purpose in his eyes. There was a hint of challenge in his smile. "You have company," he said.

"Yes," Olivia replied, still a little nettled by the easy way he'd dealt with the child that morning before church, showing her up. "They'd all like to meet you." She turned her attention to Jamie for a moment. "There are some children out front, waiting for you. Bundle up, though—it's very cold."

Jamie looked from one adult to the other, weighing the situation, then dashed off to put on warm clothes and join in the fun outside.

Jack stood, in the meantime, and Olivia figured he'd make for the stairs, or even the back door, but instead he executed a courtly half bow, one arm resting gracefully across his middle, and said, "Far be it from me to disappoint the ladies of Springwater."

Jamie appeared again, briefly, in the doorway.

"You better come back and finish this game," she warned, her gaze fixed on Jack.

"Shark," Jack replied, and headed straight for the dining room.

Confounded, but secretly pleased, Olivia followed, watched as he faced the women sitting on either side of the long formal table, quelling their chatter just by arriving. "Ladies," he said, "it is indeed an honor. My name is Jack McLaughlin." Only then did he glance back at Olivia. She saw fire in his blue eyes, and noticed that he didn't look directly at any of the guests. "And how should I address these charming creatures?" he inquired.

Still taken aback, Olivia stumbled over her answer. "Well—they're—they're the founders of the Springwater Quilting Society."

"And," said Jessica Calloway mischievously, "we have names." She stated hers, and all the others followed suit, one by one. It was plain that they were enchanted, every last one of them, with the possible exception of June-bug McCaffrey.

She was peering at Jack, her eyes narrowed in concentration.

It seemed to Olivia, who had stepped to his side sometime during the exchange, without realizing she was doing so, that jovial though his manner might be, he was being especially careful not to look directly at Mrs. McCaffrey. He finally took his leave, very graciously, and returned to the kitchen.

When Olivia entered to make tea, busying herself at the stove, she found him sitting alone at the table, glowering at the pieces on the checkerboard. Upon noticing Olivia, which seemed to take a moment or so, he shoved back his chair and crossed the room to stand next to her.

"That," he accused, in a terse whisper, "was a dirty trick."

Olivia did feel a certain degree of chagrin, but she wasn't about to let him know it. "If you really have nothing to hide," she said, keeping her voice at the same level as his, "it seems to me that you shouldn't care."

"I never said I didn't have anything to hide," he pointed out, and she could see by his eyes that he wasn't joking. "Believe me, I do. I have my reasons for wanting to keep to myself, Olivia, just like you do."

She stared at him. "You *are* an outlaw," she breathed.

"No," he said. "I am not an outlaw—not in the way you're probably thinking, anyway. I'm just an ordinary man, trying to attend to my own affairs. I would suggest that you do the same."

Jack McLaughlin was anything but ordinary, but it wouldn't pay to say so. Not just then, at least, when he was all but in a temper.

For a long interval, nothing was said. They just stared at each other. Finally, Jack's jaw worked visibly, and he started to speak, then muttered something under his breath and left the room by way of the rear stairway.

Olivia stood very still, gazing at the place where

he'd been standing, and nearly burned herself on the tea kettle.

June-bug McCaffrey sat on the side of the bed she'd shared with Jacob for so many years, clad in her nightgown, her hair flowing loose. Her tarnished silver-backed brush lay forgotten in one hand as she stared off into the distance. Into the past.

She couldn't stop thinking about that stranger. Why, when he'd stepped through the doorway that afternoon, into Miss Olivia's dining room, her heart had skittered over several beats and then hammered so hard that, for a moment, she'd honestly thought she might swoon.

It could not be. It simply couldn't.

And yet—

She hadn't mentioned the encounter to Jacob, because she knew what he'd say. He'd remind her that she'd been struck by such resemblances before; she'd encountered several men, in her travels, who looked so like one or the other of her lost sons that the mere sight of them had stopped her breath and turned her tongue and throat dry as sand. All in an instant. And each time, she'd been wrong. Each time, she'd been bitterly disappointed.

Jacob came in just then, gave her that slight, tilted smile that always cheered her, no matter how bad she was feeling. He'd been out to the barn, he and Toby, settling the animals down for the night, and the scents of snow and pipe smoke clung to his clothes.

"You gonna tell me what's botherin' you, woman, or am I supposed to guess?"

June-bug managed a smile. There was no sense in trying to hide anything from her husband; he knew her too well. "It happened again," she said. "That young feller boarding over at Miss Olivia's. I finally got a look at him. And he's the spitting image—"

"Of one of our boys," Jacob finished gently, when her voice broke on a hoarse note of misery and fell away. He sighed and began unbuttoning his black shirt. "Which one was it this time—Will or Wes?"

Tears sprang to June-bug's eyes, and she pressed her lips together for a moment, in an effort to stem the tide of an old, old sorrow. "That's what hurts so much, Jacob," she confided, touching the back of one index finger delicately to her nose and sniffling. "I couldn't have said which one he looked like. After all this time—why, it just seems like they've melted into one person, in my mind, at least. My own children!"

Jacob came to stand before her, drew her to her feet, and held her close against his powerful chest. "It's been a long time, darlin'," he said, and kissed the top of her head.

She clung to him. "I do love you so, Jacob McCaffrey."

His answering chuckle rumbled up through his

chest, and she took pleasure in the dearly familiar sound. "And I love you, Miss June-bug. Now, let's put Miss Olivia's boarder out of our minds and get us some sleep. The mornin' stage will roll in early tomorrow, and the passengers will be lookin' for breakfast."

She knew it was true, and she was grateful. It was the hard work that had kept her from brooding too much over the years, the work and Jacob, her dear, dear Jacob. "Hold me just a moment longer," she said, and buried her face in his shoulder.

He tightened his embrace, kissed her once again, on top of her head.

In time, she was calmer, and they put out the bedside lamp and lay down to sleep. Jacob was soon snoring, like he always did, but June-bug was wide awake. She'd accepted that that McLaughlin feller wasn't Will or Wesley, either one, but that didn't stop her from thinking about them. From remembering.

They'd been mischievous boys, the pair of them, though Wesley had a particular genius for getting himself *and* his brother into trouble. When they were eight or nine, for instance, cavorting at the swimming hole with some of their friends, Wes had sneaked out of the water, gotten dressed, stolen Will's clothes and gone right on home, whistling to himself.

Will had always loved to swim, so he was the last one to leave the pond. June-bug smiled in the darkness, recalling how he'd walked all the way home, through the fields, like Adam leaving the Garden, with nothing to cover him but a pair of leafy twigs torn off a bush. He'd been mad enough to spit, and Wes had hidden out in one of the sheds half the night, just to keep out of his way.

The tears returned, and June-bug sniffled again. How was it that she could recollect things like that, how they'd looked then, how the Tennessee sunlight had shone in their fair hair, how they'd felt so solid when she embraced them, and smelled of fresh air and green grass, but was unable to separate their faces in her otherwise vivid memories of the morning they went away?

Even now, after so many years, she ached whenever she recalled that morning, recalled how Wes had sneaked off, well before sunrise, taking nothing but his squirrel gun and a bedroll, but she didn't flinch from the images. Will had gone after his brother, determined to drag him home by the scruff if it came to that, and he'd brought Wes back with him, it was true. He'd stayed only long enough to say a fare-thee-well and fetch his own gear, though, and then they'd left together, the pair of them. She could still see them walking away, shoulder to shoulder on that fateful spring morning, framed in an aura of light.

Wes had been talking about going to war for so long that neither she nor Jacob had truly been surprised. Heartbroken, yes. Frustrated, certainly. But not surprised.

Will, on the other hand, would never have left

the land, given a choice. No, Will had gone—dear God, the truth was burned into June-bug's soul just as surely as if somebody had branded it there—Will had gone because she'd left him no choice. She'd raised him up to look after Wes, knowing right away that he was the stronger of the two. She'd made him promise that he would take care of his impetuous brother, no matter what. Will hadn't wanted to go to war, not deep down; had believed, as Jacob had, that it was a foolish fight, one the South couldn't possibly win, but he'd gone. Because of Wes.

Because of her.

The pain of her regret was still ferocious enough to make her cry out; she clasped a hand over her mouth to hold in a sob. *Forgive me*, she pleaded, in silence, but for once, she wasn't talking to God. No, she meant the words for her sons, the babies she'd waited for so long, and kept for too short a time. *Wesley. Will. Forgive me.*

Jacob rolled over. "June-bug," he said, taking her into his arms again. "Let them rest, darlin'. Let them rest. Our boys are gone."

With that, June-bug's composure was broken. The loss seemed as fresh, as final, and every bit as shattering, as the day word of it reached them from Chattanooga. She wept now, as she had wept then, and many times since, without restraint.

He ought to leave, Jack thought to himself, that night, while little Jamie slept and Miss Olivia went over piles of sheet music at the kitchen table. She had a Bible open to the second chapter of Luke, and every once in a while, she paused to scribble notes on a sheet of paper. Her lower lip was caught lightly between her teeth, and the vulnerability of her nape made him want to kiss her there.

He sat next to her, trying to concentrate on the ancient Romans, but they weren't a very appealing bunch, for the most part. Some married their own sisters, and none of them seemed to have a stitch of loyalty toward their friends. If they weren't stabbing or poisoning each other, they were putting their fingers down their throats so they could move on to the next feast and gorge themselves all over again. He was losing patience with the whole outfit.

Besides, Miss Olivia presented a more-than-minor distraction, to say the least.

He should have been angrier with her, he guessed, but the truth was, she had a right to invite guests to her own house whenever she chose to do so. He was a boarder, and nothing more. If he didn't want to be seen—not up close, anyhow—he should ride out of Springwater. Anybody with a lick of sense would do just that. The trouble was, when it came to Miss Olivia Darling, he had about as much judgment as one of those chickens out there in that ramshackle coop.

She raised her eyes from the work at hand. "Is there something you want?" she asked, having sensed, no doubt, that he was watching her.

He didn't dare answer that particular question honestly, though he'd have had no trouble making up a list. "Why did you do it?"

For a moment, he thought she was going to make some flippant reply, like, "Do what?" She didn't, though. She blushed a little, and it took an effort, he could see, for her to meet his eyes.

"I'm sorry," she said, very softly.

He'd reached across the table and taken her hand before he thought about it, and she didn't pull away. It was a small thing, yet it filled him with a desire he'd thought himself incapable of feeling. "I wasn't looking for an apology. Just an explanation."

She looked away, looked back. And left her hand in his, even though he felt her tense, poised to withdraw, maybe even to flee. "I don't know why I did it," she answered, and as inadequate as the answer was, he knew she was telling the truth.

He smiled at her and gently released his fingers. He thought he saw the briefest flicker of disappointment in her eyes, but that was probably wishful thinking. For a few moments, they just looked at each other, neither one speaking.

Then Jack broke the silence. "I've been thinking—maybe I ought to move on right away, instead of waiting."

She bit her lower lip. "Oh," she said, staring hard at the tabletop.

"When I came here, I figured I knew what I was doing. What I'd say to make things all right. Now,

I'm not so sure there's any way to do that." He was talking to himself when he uttered those words, as well as Olivia. He laced his fingers together, fearing that his hands would shake visibly if he didn't. "Seems like I'd do more harm than good by staying."

"Why?" she asked softly. His words had wounded her a little, he could see that. "Why would it be so wrong to stay?"

He sighed. "There's a lot I can't talk about, Olivia. Not without speaking to some other people first." He thrust a hand through his hair and tried his damnedest to give her some part of a reason. "A long time ago, I was somebody else. A while back, you asked if I was an outlaw—and I—I said I wasn't. In some ways, that was a lie—"

God, how he wanted to tell her everything. He longed to settle down, do ordinary things, like having a shave and getting his hair cut to a decent length. Like calling himself by his right name again—assuming he could ever get back into the habit of answering to it. He'd been going by "Jack McLaughlin" for so long, he sometimes forgot who he really was.

Again, she looked as though he'd punched her. She sat up very straight; it broke his heart to know she was bracing herself. "Just what sort of an outlaw were you?"

He wanted to flee from the dread he saw in her eyes, but he'd done more than enough running as it was. "I was involved in some raids, after the war. Somebody was killed."

She went white. "Did you do the killing? Or condone it?"

"I was there," he said. "I didn't pull the trigger, and I would have stepped in, but the fact is, the thing was over with before I knew what happened."

"Dear God," Olivia whispered, closing her eyes.

He wanted to die, seeing the horror in her face. "I left after that, took up honest work," he said, and it was the God's truth. He'd turned his back on the gang he'd been riding with, but the law had been after him for a long, long time.

"You're wanted?"

"Maybe," he said. "I don't know. A lot of years have gone by."

"There's more, isn't there?"

He held her gaze. Nodded. "I'll tell you everything," he said, "but, like I said, there's somebody else I have to talk to first."

"You mean Jacob and June-bug McCaffrey, don't you?"

He was startled at first, but he figured he'd probably given himself away. "Yes," he ground out.

"Who are you, Jack?"

"Don't ask me that, Olivia. I can't tell you. Not yet."

"But you will?"

"Yes."

"I guess that will have to be good enough," she said. Then she got up from her chair, turned away from him, and busied herself at the stove.

He rose, awkwardly, and stood there, just watching her, for a long while, knowing full well that she wouldn't want him around anymore, once she'd heard everything he had to say. Chances were, the McCaffreys wouldn't, either, though they'd be glad enough to see him at first, he imagined.

Desolate, he finally strode across the room, intending to grab his coat and hat and head for the Brimstone Saloon, a place he'd avoided so far, but a single thought stopped him in his tracks.

He spoke hoarsely. "If you don't want me to come back here tonight, I'll understand."

She did not look at him, made, it seemed to him, an unnecessary amount of noise, raising and lowering the stove lids and sliding pots and pans around on the cast iron surface of the range. "If you were going to murder me in my bed," she said, "I suppose you would have done so by now."

He grinned, without amusement. Her words were small comfort but, then, he couldn't rightly expect anything more. He went out, closing the door quietly behind him.

Olivia stared at the door for a long time, as though by doing that she could make Jack turn around, come back, listen to reason. At the same time, she knew she wouldn't see him that night. Maybe not tomorrow, either, or ever again. The thought was almost intolerable, even though she had every reason to believe that she and everybody else in Springwater would be better off without him.

She'd always regarded herself as an intelligent woman, and a fairly good judge of character, and her instincts told her that Jack was a fine man, whatever secrets lay in his past. Yet he'd admitted to taking part in a killing, however indirectly, and he'd warned her that there was worse news to come.

Could she have misjudged him? She certainly wouldn't be the first woman who'd ever made such a mistake.

Exhausted emotionally, she folded her arms on the table and laid her head down in an effort to collect herself. After some time, she began to feel a little less shaken, and returned with deliberation to the task of planning the Springwater Christmas pageant. She had not wanted to accept the project at first, but now she was glad she had—glad she had music to think about, angels and shepherds, Wise Men and all the rest. She didn't know what she would have done, without something to keep her busy.

It was exceedingly late when she decided to retire for the night; even the lights across the street, in Dr. Parrish's study, had been extinguished. The usual raucous music flowed from the Brimstone Saloon, but she'd become enured to that, she supposed, for it seemed the least of her problems, in light of recent events.

She could no longer deny, to herself at least, that she did indeed love Mr. McLaughlin—or whoever he was. He hadn't so much as kissed her, really—just touched his mouth to hers that once—certainly hadn't behaved in any fashion that could possibly be called untoward. All the same, whenever he was near, Olivia was overtaken with all sorts of peculiar and undeniably wanton passions.

She walked slowly through the house, banking fires, putting out forgotten lamps, pausing at the parlor window to peer through yet another snow-fall toward the center of sin and depravity that was the Brimstone Saloon.

She waited there for an interval, hoping to catch a glimpse of a familiar figure coming down the road toward her front gate, but the vigil proved a futile one. Finally, she turned away and, carrying a single candle in one hand, mounted the stairs.

It wasn't until she'd gotten undressed, donned a nightdress, and climbed into bed that she realized Jamie was there. As her eyes adjusted, Olivia could make out the child's hair, her white gown, and, finally, her small, pale face.

"Is he gonna come back, Miss Olivia?" The question was heartrendingly urgent. "Jack, I mean? I heard the door shut, and when I went to the win-dow, I saw him headin' up the road."

Olivia sighed and settled into her pillows. "I don't know, Jamie," she answered sadly.

"Did I do somethin' wrong? Maybe I shouldn't have beat him at checkers all them times—"

Olivia wanted to weep, but she knew that would

merely upset the child even more than Jack's departure had done. So she slipped an arm around Jamie's shoulders and squeezed gently. "No, darling. It has nothing to do with you."

"Honest?"

"Honest."

Jamie snuggled a little closer to Olivia's side, like a kitten curling up next to its mother. Her voice was very small. "I want him to come back."

Another sigh escaped Olivia. She felt as though her heart had cracked down the middle, like soil hardened by a long drought, and silently she mocked herself for not knowing when she'd had it good. She'd spent a great deal of time over the years, chafing under the weight of the word "spinster" and all its connotations, and now she'd give anything to go back to those safe days. Back to the time when she hadn't cared, hadn't listened for the sound of one man's voice, one man's footsteps. "So do I," she replied at last. "Oh, yes, Jamie—I want Mr. McLaughlin to come back, too. But I don't know if he'll be able to stay here with us."

"I was hopin' we might make a family," Jamie confided. "Him and you and me. The McLaughlins."

Olivia blinked hard. "Maybe you and I can be a family, just the two of us."

Jamie sounded willing, if not confident. "It won't be the same, though," she said. "Will it?"

"No," Olivia admitted. "It won't be the same.

But that doesn't mean we couldn't be happy, just you and I."

"Can I stay in here with you? 'Til morning?"

"Yes," Olivia answered, after due consideration. "Just for tonight."

After that, Jamie drifted off to sleep, while Olivia lay wide awake, listening to the cold winter wind blowing in off the flatlands around Springwater, rattling the windows and howling beneath the eaves. When she heard the back door open and close, she told herself to stay in bed, but she could not do it. She simply could not resist getting up, pulling on her wrapper, and hurrying down the kitchen stairway.

He was there, at the stove, holding the pot of cold, stale coffee.

"You came back," she said. She hoped she didn't sound too happy, but if she did, there was nothing for it.

He favored her with a sheepish, crooked smile. "Seems I've lost my knack for drinking whiskey," he confessed. "Running, too, maybe."

She wanted to ask more questions, a million of them, but she wasn't about to risk upsetting the delicate peace between them and sending him out into the world again, perhaps never to return. She drew a chair away from the table, set it near the stove.

"I've never shaved a man before," she said, "but I used to trim Aunt Eloise's hair all the time."

He gazed at her, plainly as surprised by the statement as she was herself. "You want to cut my hair? In the middle of the night?"

She smiled. "You're wavering. If I wait until tomorrow, you might change your mind."

He grinned. "All right, then," he said. "I've got to admit, I'm tired of feeling like I'm hiding in a haystack."

Olivia laughed softly, not wishing to awaken Jamie. "Sit down," she said, and when he complied, she fetched her sewing shears.

He had a great deal of hair, enough for two or three men by Olivia's estimate, and as she trimmed it to a tidy length, it seemed to lighten, going from the color of aged golden oak to a shade more like corn silk. She snipped away as much of his beard as she could, while he sat patiently in that kitchen chair, but she had no razor. Presently, when she had done all she could, he stood and went up the stairs without a word.

Olivia did not expect him to return, but return he did, with a shaving cup and razor apparently garnered from the small store of belongings he'd brought with him.

"Might as well go the whole way, now that we've started," he said.

Olivia had just finished sweeping up the heavy locks of light brown hair, and she risked a glance in his direction when he helped himself to a basin of water, went to the small mirror affixed to the far wall, next to the door, and began to shave.

She found busywork, so that she could stay and watch his progress out of the corner of her eye, but nothing could have prepared her for the face he turned to her when he'd finished.

He was so handsome that, for a timeless interval, she completely forgot to breathe.

CHAPTER

❧ 9 ❧

W<small>HAT HAD SEEMED</small> like a good idea in the night, Jack reflected ruefully, studying his reflection in the mirror over the bureau in his room the morning following the shearing, had lost much of its appeal roughly five seconds after he'd opened his eyes. He looked—well, like himself. The self he'd been trying to leave behind for the better part of his life.

He rubbed his chin, now bare except for the daily stubble. June-bug had nearly recognized him the day before; if she or Jacob got a close look at him now, without the beard and mane of hair, the game would be up. It didn't seem to matter that facing them was the right thing to do, plain and simple; he was afraid—afraid of their grief, afraid of their justifiable anger, afraid of being overwhelmed by his own sorrow and guilt. Anybody would have said he was a coward. But "anybody" hadn't walked in his shoes, hadn't been there, on that battleground, awash in somebody else's blood, and no one who heard the tale secondhand could truly be expected to understand what had taken place that day.

He was due in the bottom of the mine in less than an hour, and he still needed to fetch his horse from the Springwater Station, a job he dreaded more that morning than ever, given his new appearance. He wasn't ready to face Jacob yet, though he knew it had to happen one day soon.

Leaning against the bureau, hands braced against the edges, he lowered his head. It would be no kindness to the McCaffreys, what he had to say to them. On the other hand, he didn't figure he'd have a chance of ever calling his soul his own, if he didn't. And then there was Olivia. Until he'd met her, he hadn't known it was possible to want a woman that much, and leaving her would be like having a part of himself torn away.

"Make the choice, you bastard," he muttered. "Go or stay. Tell the whole bitter, ugly story, or ride out and never look back. But decide, damn you. *Decide*."

He straightened, rubbed his chin. He'd been raised to believe that the truth was always better than a lie, even when it was hurtful to tell and to hear, and the conviction went bone deep. Still, he'd rather have saved Jacob and June-bug the gruesome details of their son's death, and all that had come later. In many ways, that was the worst part.

What he had to say to them could only add to their anguish, not assuage it. The vivid images, the sounds and smells, would haunt them after that encounter, instead of being his alone, they would impress themselves on the backs of their eyelids, inside their nostrils and ears. Honorable people, decent and good, they would bear the weight of his shame for the rest of their lives.

Forcibly, he turned his thoughts back to Olivia. She'd wound things into a tangle, bringing June-bug to the house while he was there, and there was no getting past that. No, sir. Best to deal with it all, at long last, and get on with things, one way or the other.

Olivia. She'd changed him in so many ways, almost certainly without even knowing she was doing it. He couldn't say for sure if what he felt for her was love—he'd never loved a woman, not the way Jacob loved June-bug, which was the way he knew it ought to be between a man and a woman—but he sure as the devil felt *something*. And it was something strong.

Whatever fool notion it was, it made him want to stay, stand his ground, carve out a place for himself—and for her—right there in Springwater.

He thrust a hand through his hair, now close-cropped and half a dozen shades lighter than he remembered it being, and heaved a heavy sigh. It wasn't just June-bug and Jacob, or Olivia, either, pressing on his mind. It was that little kid, whupping him at checkers right and left, and looking at him like he could set a crooked world back on its axis.

A light rap at his door interrupted his revery.

"Mr. McLaughlin?" It was, of course, Olivia's voice. He'd never heard her sing, but he reckoned she'd be good at it, just from the way she spoke. "I've got breakfast started."

He ground out some acknowledgment, forgot a moment later what it was, and turned to leave his room. He'd half-hoped Olivia might have lingered in the corridor, but there was nothing left of her but the soft, violet scent of her perfume.

Down in the kitchen, she poured him coffee and served up a plate brimming with corned beef hash. His lunchpail sat on the drain board, gleaming and no doubt full, and the window above the sink was trimmed with fresh snow, glowing like gold in the lamplight.

She stopped, after setting his food in front of him, and stared at him, as though he were some stranger, and not the same boarder she'd taken in just a few days back. Her cheeks turned a fetching shade of apricot, and she averted her eyes.

"It's just that you look so—so *different*," she murmured.

He grinned at her, not because he felt cheerful, or even particularly optimistic, but because being around her made him want to let out a yip and a holler, just for the hell of it. "If I didn't know better, Miss Darling, I'd figure you found me comely."

She blushed all the harder, looked away and

then back again. When she met his gaze once more, her eyes were flashing. "Please do not be arrogant, Mr. McLaughlin. Or should I address you by some other name?"

"You should call me Jack," he said evenly, no longer amused, "like we agreed."

"You won't be able to avoid them forever, you know."

He picked up his coffee and took a great gulp, mostly so he wouldn't have to answer, and scalded his tongue and the roof of his mouth good and proper. Left with a choice between spitting or swallowing, he did the latter, though he would have spat if he'd been anywhere besides Miss Olivia Darling's house.

"I didn't come here to avoid anybody," he said, choking a little, after biting back a couple of curses even less suited to polite company than spitting.

"Really?" She arched an eyebrow, set the coffee-pot down, and fetched him a glass of cold water. "Well, you seem to be doing a fine job of staying out of their way, it seems to me."

He downed the water gratefully, hardly taking a breath before it was gone. "This is my problem, Olivia. I'll handle it in my own time and my own way."

She sighed. "When I first met you, it struck me that there was something very familiar about you. Why is that?"

She was close—too close. He wanted to tell her, and yet he wasn't ready. He pushed his plate away, even knowing he'd be half-starved by the time the midday meal rolled around. His appetite was just a fine memory, like Tennessee before the war, like innocence and sweet dreams when he slept. "Good day to you."

"Hmmph," she said, subsiding a little and eyeing his food. It was the damnedest thing; the sky could be falling, but if there was a meal on the table, a woman would invariably insist that a man clean his plate. "Aren't you going to finish your breakfast?"

"No, ma'am," he said, pushing back his chair. He wasn't angry with Olivia, just frustrated, but it served his purpose—escaping that kitchen and her too-shrewd scrutiny—to stalk off. So he got his hat and coat and lunchpail and stormed out into a blustery wind, edged with the promise of more snow.

It was not his morning, evidently, for when Jack reached the stables behind the Springwater Station, there was no sign of young Toby. He raised his coat collar, pulled down his hat brim, and led his horse out of its stall, making quick work of saddle and bridle.

He wasn't quite quick enough, though; before he could mount up and make for the mine outside of town, Jacob appeared, at a little distance, carrying a steaming milk bucket in each hand.

"Mornin'," he said, either not looking directly at Jack or pretending not to—he was a crafty old codger, nobody knew that better than Jack

McLaughlin. "You must be that feller the ladies are all yammerin' about."

The barn was lit by only one lantern, God be thanked, and Jack was pretty certain he was standing in shadow, but Jacob had always had keen eyesight. "Mornin'," Jack replied. He'd been a kid when he last saw Jacob McCaffrey, not even shaving regularly; it was safe to assume his voice had changed since then, so he made no effort to disguise it. "Guess I'll be goin'."

If Jacob knew him, nothing in his tone gave a hint of it. Again, though, with Jacob, that meant damn little. Most of the time, the good Lord Himself was probably hard put to make out what was going on in that unfathomable mind. "Ya'll come on back for one of my June-bug's good Southern suppers," he said. "Tonight would do. She's makin' cornbread and beans boiled up with salt pork."

Jack, halfway into his saddle by that time, froze for a split second before settling himself to ride. It was probably just a coincidence, he told himself, Jacob mentioning the two foods Jack loved best in all the world—when cooked by June-bug McCaffrey, anyhow.

"Yes, sir," he said hoarsely, wondering, even then, if he'd be able to keep his word. "Maybe I'll do that, one of these nights."

"We'll look for you," Jacob replied affably.

Jack felt those Indian-dark eyes fastened on his back as he rode off, and the sensation didn't entirely let up until the town was well behind him.

He'd never been more tempted, since he'd first entered Springwater, to keep right on riding.

Olivia addressed the children of Springwater School that very afternoon. While the roles of Mary, Joseph, and the Three Wise Men would be awarded to those best suited for them, she said, anyone wanting a speaking part could be accommodated.

Little Isaiah Kildare raised his hand.

"Yes?" Olivia asked, affording him the same courtesy she would have shown any adult. By her lights, children were not, as some people seemed to think, a separate species, and they deserved to be treated with respect until they proved otherwise.

"What's 'accommodated'?"

A ripple of good-natured giggles flowed over the flock of little heads, and Olivia smiled.

"In this case, it simply means that everyone who wishes to be in the play can be. Again, with the exceptions of Mary, Joseph, and the first of the Three Wise Men, no one need speak if they'd rather not." She paused. "Everyone, however, will be expected to sing."

This roused a flurry of groans from the boys. They were finished with their lessons for the day, and the new snow was bright and deep and surely inviting. They obviously wanted to get outside and fling the stuff at each other.

Jamie stood up beside her desk and quelled the whole crowd with one sweeping look. Then she turned back to Olivia, smiled sweetly, and inquired, "If you don't sing, do you still get a costume?"

Olivia bit back a responding smile. Before this was over, some people would undoubtedly accuse her of playing favorites, but the fact of the matter was, Jamie did have a fine singing voice and the face of an angel. She might even be given a solo. "No," she answered.

This brought on a thoughtful silence, and Jamie sat down, having accomplished her purpose. Clearly, even the boys wanted to dress up as shepherds and kings and archangels. Again, Olivia stifled a smile.

"This is Friday, as you know," she continued. She might have liked being a teacher, she thought, for she enjoyed holding forth in front of a group. "On Tuesday afternoon, after school closes, those who are interested in joining the cast of the pageant should present themselves at the church. Parts will be assigned then."

Two little girls in the front row, wedged into the same desk seat, looked up at Olivia with thin, wonder-struck faces. She recognized them as the children of Ben and Sally Williams.

"Does it cost money to be in this pageant?" the bigger of the pair asked.

Olivia's heart melted in her chest, but for their sake, she did not reveal what she felt. "Absolutely not," she said. "Cloth for costumes will be provided—your mothers can do the sewing, I'm sure—

and I'll write out each of your pieces on a sheet of paper, so that you may practice on your own."

The sisters exchanged hopeful looks, and Olivia made a mental note to make them both angels—neither was old enough to play Mary—with lines to say, a Bible verse, perhaps, or a morsel of poetry.

One of the older Kildare boys raised a hand, and when Olivia called upon him, he spoke up loud and clear, smirking a little. "My ma said there'd be cookies and punch at this party. Maybe even a tree with baubles and the like. If we ain't in the program, do we still get cookies?"

Olivia tried to look stern, but she couldn't manage it. Her heart had already warmed to the project, taken refuge in it, and all the children of Springwater, in a peculiar way, were her concern. "I'm sure the refreshments will be offered to everyone," she said.

With that, her talk ended, and Miss Mathers dismissed her pupils, who were delighted, most of them, to have Saturday and Sunday spread before them; it must have seemed, to their young minds, a vast expanse of time. They fled, stomping and shouting, barely pausing to put on their coats and scarves and mittens, paying no attention whatever to their teacher's admonitions to take their leave in an orderly fashion.

Emma Hargreaves, beautiful young daughter of Trey, stepdaughter of Rachel, lingered. And because she tarried, so did Toby McCaffrey, who might otherwise have been among the first to depart. He watched Emma with calf eyes, as though determined to memorize every word she said, every graceful move she might make.

"If you wouldn't mind, Miss Darling," the girl ventured shyly, "I'd like very much to be your helper."

"I can certainly attest to Emma's helpfulness," Dorothy Mathers put in. She was gathering up discarded slates and reading primers from the tops of the desks, which stood in three short rows, linked one to another by ornate cast-iron rails. Springwater was proud of its new schoolhouse and fine desks. "She's already learned everything I could teach her. Now she merely comes to school to help me with the little ones, I think."

Emma blushed a little, under that lovely pale-cinnamon skin. Olivia divined, in a flash of insight, that Miss Hargreaves attended school for another reason, as well. As long as she kept going to class, so would Toby.

"You can ask Mrs. Calloway, too—over at the newspaper. I work hard." The child seemed so eager, almost stumbling over her words in the effort to convince Olivia of her competence.

Olivia took Emma's hand briefly, squeezed it. "I don't need anybody's word but yours. I'd be happy to have you for a helper, Emma," she said, and though the girl looked very pleased, it was Toby who let out his breath. Plainly a case of young love, Olivia thought, and felt the faintest twinge of envy. Oh, to be starting out in life, with all those choices yet to be made.

"Oh, thank you!" Emma cried, and embraced her impulsively.

Olivia hesitated, then laughed and returned the hug. "We'll see how grateful you are, missy, by the time pageant night comes around," she teased. "This is going to be a monumental task."

Emma's dark eyes were shining. "It will be wonderful," she said. "The best Christmas imaginable!"

If, Olivia thought, *Jack McLaughlin doesn't take to the road. If he doesn't break the McCaffreys' hearts—and mine—then yes, it will be a grand Christmas.*

Jamie was standing close to Olivia, already bundled up in her newly sewn coat. The blue, as Olivia had expected, suited the child perfectly. "Can we go home now?" the little girl asked. "I want to go home now."

Olivia resisted an urge to touch the child's forehead, checking for fever, so plaintive was her request. Instead, she nodded and got her wrap from the peg in the cloakroom. After a brief farewell to Miss Mathers, and a few more words with Emma, she and Jamie set off for the house.

While Olivia paused to scatter feed for the chickens, Jamie stood nearby, searching the already darkening sky.

"Come along," Olivia prompted, when she'd finished the small chore. Inside, she would start supper, in the hope that Jack would be home soon. In spite of everything, it raised her spirits, just to think of seeing him, hearing his voice, finding an excuse to touch his hand or his arm . . .

In a brief spurt of recalcitrance, Olivia considered marching right over to the marshal's office and asking to see the latest crop of wanted posters, just to see if she'd find a drawing of Jack's face on one of them, but soon dismissed the idea. The marshal, a Mr. John Henry Spencer, would think she was behaving like a hysterical spinster and probably tell everyone in town that Miss Darling thought she might be harboring a criminal.

"You reckon I'll still be around here come Christmas?" Jamie asked, trying to lend the question a casual note. She'd taken a place at the kitchen table and opened her reading primer, which she would probably pore over for hours, perhaps expecting to solve the mystery of the written word by willpower alone.

Olivia, busy until then, building up the fire and inspecting the contents of the larder, stopped. "Why, I hope so," she said, very softly. "Were you planning to leave us, Jamie?"

The child looked very small, and although her eyes, huge now, were indisputably blue, it seemed to Olivia that they'd taken on a gray cast, rather like a summer sky when a storm is moving in. "Something bad happened," she said.

Feminine intuition surging to the fore, Olivia abandoned everything, drew back a chair at the table, and sat down, taking Jamie's hands in hers. "What do you mean, sweetheart? Tell me."

Jamie blinked, and a single tear slipped, glistening, down her cheek. She dashed it away with the back of one wrist. "Axel's dead. He's out there, under the snow. I don't think I could find him again, afore spring."

"Tell me how he died," Olivia pressed gently.

Another tear fell. "I don't rightly know. He was drinkin' corn liquor by the campfire. He did that most every night. When I woke up, the fire was gone out and I figured he must be half froze, lyin' there the way he was. So I tried to wake him up. He just laid there."

Olivia smoothed Jamie's hair gently back from her face, with the backs of her fingers. "Oh, sweetheart, I'm sorry. You must have been very frightened."

Jamie nodded. "I was scairt all right." She paused and sniffled. "But that ain't the worst part. I was glad, too, Miss Olivia. I was *real* glad."

"Why didn't you tell someone? Before this, I mean?"

The little girl gave a sigh that was bigger than she was. "I'm an orphan now. Axel always said, when you ain't got no folks to look out for you, they'll put you in a home. He said they beat you when you're bad, and won't let you learn to read, and make you go hungry, too."

What a perfectly horrible man he must have been, Olivia thought, though she was not one to speak ill of the dead. Lord knew, there were plenty of uncharitable things she could have said about Aunt Eloise, aloud and to herself, but she'd always tried to honor the old woman's memory. She'd tried to be grateful; without her aunt, she would have been destitute after her father's death.

"What else have you neglected to mention?" Olivia asked, firmly but with kindness.

Jamie hesitated. "Lots of stuff," she said, in her own good time. "You ain't gonna like some of it."

"Go on."

A look of anguish filled the child's eyes. "I don't want you to hate me."

Olivia cupped the small face in both hands. "Listen to me," she said. "I will *never* hate you, no matter what. In fact, I'll do everything I can to keep you right here with me, provided you want to stay, that is."

Jamie nodded immediately, then crumpled her brow in thought. "Is there a lawyer in this town? We could go and talk to him, if there is. Get me adopted."

Olivia did not relish the prospect of approaching Gage Calloway, Springwater's only attorney— she was, after all, still smarting from the failure of her pilgrimage to the town council meeting—but he was allegedly very good at his job. She knew that consulting him was the only prudent thing to do.

"I'll pay a call on him first chance I get," Olivia promised. "In the meantime, I think we need to tell Marshal Spencer about your—about Axel's dying."

The color drained from Jamie's face. "He'll arrest me, the marshal will. He'll put me in jail and never let me out!"

"No," Olivia said, almost in a whisper. "No, sweetheart." Then, when Jamie began to sob, body racked with the force of emotions too big to contain in such a small body, she pulled the child onto her lap and held her there, rocking her gently and murmuring mother-things. "Shhh. No one is going to put you in jail."

"Axel—said—"

"Axel lied. Decent people do not lock up little children, sweetheart."

Jamie looked up at her. "But—but Axel said—I'd be the death of him—"

"Well," Olivia said, wishing Axel were still alive, so that she might have the pleasure of killing him personally, "you weren't. He died of the drink, Jamie, and probably exposure."

"Exposure?"

"Lying out in the cold the way he did."

"I covered him up with a blanket," Jamie confided. "He was snorin' when I did that. He always snored."

Again, Olivia stroked the little girl's fair, corn-silk hair. "Then you did everything you could have," she said. "Darling—did he ever hurt you in any way?"

Jamie shook her head emphatically, and some of

the spark returned to her eyes. "He'd've liked to whup me more'n once, all right, but he never could catch me," she whispered, with a wavery smile. Then she laid her head against Olivia's shoulder. "You can hang on to me a while if you want," she added.

Olivia kissed the top of the little girl's head and held her close. It was as comforting to her, she suspected, as to Jamie, that interlude. She felt strong, competent, more than able to see to the needs of this child and any other she might be fortunate enough to have. For once, Aunt Eloise's strident tones and harsh looks did not spring to her mind and cause her to doubt herself. In fact, it seemed that her guardian's face and countenance were fading from her mind, and she couldn't quite recall the sound of the old woman's voice.

Good riddance, she thought. You've haunted me long enough.

They were still sitting there together, no closer to having supper on the table, when Jack came in. He was black with dirt and clearly chilled to the marrow of his bones, but he was *there*. For Olivia, for today and for the moment, that was enough.

"We've just had a rather emotional discussion, Jamie and I," she said gently.

Jamie, dozing until then, opened her eyes and blinked. "Jack!" she cried, as joyously as if the archangel Gabriel himself had appeared in the kitchen.

"Hello, Smidgeon," he said quietly, but he was still looking at Olivia.

She set Jamie on her feet and stood, patting her hair with both hands before she could catch herself. "You'll be wanting some supper," she said.

He sighed. "I do believe I'm too tired to eat. I can manage a bath, but that's about all I've got the energy for."

She didn't argue with him—she could settle the matter of supper later—for the time being, she was just pleased to have him—well—home. Every day, she was afraid he would leave, even though he'd said he wouldn't, until he'd completed his business, anyway, and every night when he came through the door, she felt like celebrating. "I'll set the tub out in the pantry and fill it for you. It'll be a little cold, but—"

"I don't care about that," he interrupted. "I just want to be clean. And then I'd like to sleep until the middle of next week."

She smiled. "That," she said, "would *really* stir up the gossip."

He laughed; it was, for all its weariness, a richly masculine, pipe-smoke, and worn-leather sound, better than music, or birdsong, or the fragrant snap of an apple wood fire on a winter hearth. "We wouldn't want to do that. Besides, I've got to work again tomorrow."

Olivia made relatively quick work of heating water and filling the tub, and when she was finished, Jack came into the pantry and immediately started unbuttoning his shirt. She fled, precisely because she felt an untoward desire to stay.

What a beautiful man he was, she thought. Whoever he was, whatever his past, he was without question the finest specimen of manhood she had ever seen. Not, of course, that she was any authority on the subject.

For a while, there was splashing. Then a silence descended.

"He's sleepin'," Jamie said, with conviction.

"Dear heaven," Olivia muttered, "he'll either drown or catch his death. You can see your breath in there."

"I can hear him snorin'," Jamie insisted.

Olivia went to the pantry door and laid her ear against it. Sure enough, Jack had fallen asleep in the bathtub, and he was indeed snoring.

She tapped at the door. "Mr. McLaughlin!" she said.

No answer.

She raised her voice. "Jack!"

Nothing.

"You'd better go in there and get him," Jamie said seriously.

Olivia's heart lurched. "I can't do that!" Oh, but she wanted to. That was the disturbing thing; she wanted to see him—well, *unclothed*—in the worst way.

"Then I will."

"You absolutely *will not*," Olivia replied. She raised her chin. "I'll take care of this." She shaded her eyes, as if from a too-bright sun, and turned the latch. "Jack!" she said again, very firmly. She could just make out the shape of him, and of the tub, in the gloom. The lantern she'd left for him had gone out.

He continued to snore.

"Jack McLaughlin," she hissed, inching closer to the tub. She couldn't look, wouldn't look. Not for anything.

He made a burbling sound, and she dropped to her knees in panic beside the tub, certain that he was about to suck water into his lungs. When she reached out to grab his head and save him from drowning, he laughed, and even in that lightless room, she could see his blue eyes sparkling with mischief. Just when she would have slapped him right across the face, he caught hold of both her wrists and drew her closer.

Her heart was pounding like the hooves of a runaway horse, but she didn't try to pull away. "Why did you do that?"

"I guess I wanted to see if you would risk your virtue to save me." He had stopped grinning, but his eyes were still dancing. "Sure enough, you did."

"That was a reprehensible thing to do!"

He ran his lips across her knuckles, first on one hand, then the other. A shudder of exquisite pleasure caused Olivia's breath to catch sharply, and her body took up a pagan chorus all its own, complete with drumbeat. "But you're glad I did it," he said. "Aren't you?"

She couldn't speak up, even to deny his assertion. She couldn't even move.

"I've done my best to stay away from you, Olivia," he confided, in a low tone of voice, pitched to carry no further. "Damn if you aren't flat-out irresistible, though." With that, he put his free hand on her nape and pressed her head downward, until their mouths met.

The kiss awakened all the needs that had slept so long within Olivia; she forgot all her doubts for the moment, gave in to impulse, and surrendered herself to sweet sensation.

MARSHAL JOHN HENRY Spencer was a handsome man, Olivia supposed, barely thirty, with light brown hair and eyes the color of faded dungarees. He'd been in Springwater only a little longer than Olivia herself, but somehow he'd skipped over the outsider stage and fit right in with the community from the very first. In the way of so many people who traveled west, leaving behind other places and other lives, he seemed to possess no personal history at all.

"There's a dead man lying out there somewhere," Olivia announced, gesturing to indicate the rest of the universe, that icy morning in his office, a fairly new building with one cell, a desk and a potbellied stove. The weather was downright frigid, the wind bitingly cold. At least a foot of snow already covered the ground, more was promised by a low and brooding sky.

Understandably, the marshal looked surprised,

though whether by her announcement or the simple fact of her appearance at his threshold, she could not have said. Whatever his feelings, this attitude was an improvement over the expression of amusement that had crossed his face when she blew in from the street; no doubt, he'd thought she meant to lodge another fuss-and-bother complaint about the Brimstone Saloon.

He took a sip from a metal mug of coffee—to his credit, he had offered Olivia a cup as well, and she had politely declined—and regarded her over the brim. He took his time swallowing, and even then, there was a long interval before he spoke. "That so?"

Olivia was exasperated—she had other things to do, after all, of a Saturday morning—and Jamie was home alone, up to heaven only knew what. Jack had left for the mine well before dawn. "Yes, Marshal," she said, with patience honed to a fine point, "that is so. I've taken in an orphan—I have no doubt you've heard about her—a little girl named Jamie. Last night, she told me what happened. She was traveling with a man she refers to as Axel—I have no idea whether he was her father, uncle or simply an acquaintance of her mother's— and he was apparently fond of his liquor." She glanced, unwillingly, at the windows, through which she could make out the shadow of the saloon across the street. "In any case, he lay down by the fire one night, almost certainly intoxicated, and when the child tried to awaken him in the morning, he didn't stir. As far as she knows, he's still lying just where she left him."

"I hope you'll pardon me for saying so, ma'am, but that's unlikely," the marshal commented, without particular emotion. "By now, the animals will have gotten to him and scattered what remained of the poor bas—er—the body over half the territory."

Olivia cringed. The picture was a gruesome one; she had imagined a great many details on her own, and required no further prompting. "Be that as it may, I felt compelled to do my duty as a citizen and report the matter." Her glance strayed to the yellowed, tattered bills pinned to a nearby wall; wanted posters. Would she find Jack McLaughlin's face there among them, if she looked closely enough? She turned her gaze back to the marshal, but not soon enough. She knew, by his quietly shrewd expression, that she'd betrayed at least the shadow of her thoughts. There probably wasn't a person in Springwater or within a twenty-mile radius of the place who hadn't heard about the secretive stranger boarding at Miss Olivia Darling's place, and speculated as to his business in their town.

"Yes, ma'am," he agreed, "you've done your duty. I'll look into the matter. I'll need to know where they were camped, o' course." The lawman set aside his mug of coffee and hooked his thumbs in the gunbelt slung low on his hips. "Meantime, I've got a question or two for you."

Suddenly, Olivia wanted to flee, but she found

she was rooted to the spot, like a green and reedy cornstalk in a fertile field.

"Please," the marshal said. "Sit down. I should have said something before." He slanted a grin at her, and she felt some of her reserve melting. He was, she reflected, as much a stranger as Jack was, and he probably had just as many secrets, but the badge on his coat lent him considerable authority.

Olivia took the offered seat, as much because her knees felt unsteady as anything. Up until then, she'd preferred to stand. "I really don't know much about Mr. McLaughlin," she said, and immediately blushed, realizing that Jack's name hadn't been mentioned. All the marshal had actually said was that he had some questions to ask.

He sat down in his desk chair and regarded her thoughtfully for several long moments. "You can relax, Miss Darling," he said, at last. "Far as I know, your boarder hasn't broken any laws. Seems like he's bent on staying out of folks' way as much as he can, that's all. I was just wondering if everything was all right over there at your place—you being alone with that fellow, for all practical intents and purposes, I mean. You have any problems, you get word to me right away. I'm close by most of the time, but if something worries you, you just leave me a message on that slate board there by the door."

Olivia swallowed. She was moved by the marshal's concern for her well-being, aware though she was that he was merely doing his job. "All right," she managed, at some length.

The marshal sat with his fingers interwoven. "First time there's a thaw," he said calmly, "I'll go out looking for that Axel feller."

Olivia nodded, tugged at her gloves, and rose to her feet. "Thank you," she said, ready to take her leave.

The lawman rose to walk her to the door, shivered at the cold when he opened it. "Hurry on home," he said, as if they'd been friends for years. "This weather's enough to turn your ears brittle."

Olivia smiled, a bit uncertainly, perhaps, and nodded again. Her gaze strayed to the wanted posters again, and the marshal undoubtedly noticed, but he offered no comment. After all, they were standing there with the door wide open.

"Good day, Marshal," she said.

"Miss Olivia," he responded.

The Montana wind struck her hard as he closed the door; she felt the bite of it in every scrap and void of her being, and trembled.

The rumble was a distant sound, coming from deep within the earth, but Jack heard it even over the clang and clank of the pickaxes all around him. It sent a chill rolling down his backbone.

"What was that?" asked Williams, digging beside him as he usually did. He was about the hardest working fellow Jack had ever run across.

"I don't reckon it's anything unusual," Jack

replied, despite his initial trepidation, dragging a forearm across his brow. It beat hell how a man could sweat like they did, down there in that pit, where it was half again as cold as a congressman's heart. "Probably just a shift in the timbers somewhere."

Ben glanced around—and especially up—uneasily. "It worries me some, all the same. If I were to get myself killed, my wife and daughters wouldn't have a soul to look after them."

On impulse, Jack laid a hand to the other man's shoulder. "Nothing's going to happen to you," he said, hoping God would make good on the statement. Ben Williams was a decent, steady man, but virtue didn't seem to be high on the Good Lord's list of reasons for keeping somebody above the grass. Over and over again, he'd seen the best men take bullets and cannonballs and bayonets, while the sneaks and pillagers and slackers, who far outnumbered the heroes anyhow, not only lived on, but thrived, getting through the damnedest scrapes without a scratch.

Ben's grin flashed in the gloom, reminding Jack how young the man really was; probably not out of his twenties yet, even though he already had a family in full swing. "My little girls are sure excited about that Christmas pageant over at the church," he said. "That was all they talked about, either one of 'em, yesterday evening. Miss June-bug said she'd do up their costumes—my Sally doesn't favor sewing, if she can get out of doing it."

Jack chuckled, but a part of him was listening for another shudder in the earth around, below, and above them. The two of them were already wielding their pickaxes again, and the steel threw occasional blue sparks as it struck the hard stone.

"Miss Olivia is bound and determined to put on the best show she can. Almost makes me want to stay on and see what happens." He hadn't meant to mention his departure; for one thing, he went back and forth on the idea—go, stay. Tell, don't tell. Let himself fall the rest of the way in love with Olivia Darling, or get out while the getting was good.

Ben stopped swinging his pick. "You lighting out for someplace else?"

Jack thought of the blanket of snow covering the land in all directions. In some places, it was probably as much as six feet deep, and a man could ride straight into a gully and smother himself and his horse without going to any trouble at all. "I reckon," he said, somewhat reluctantly. "Next time we get a spell of good weather, that is."

"Why?"

Jack hesitated. Except for Miss Olivia, Ben was the closest thing he'd had to a real friend in a long time, and he would have liked to confide in him. Given that Ben and his family shared lodgings with Jacob and June-bug, though, he didn't see how he could. "I never meant to stay," he said. It was a weak answer, he knew, but it was the best he had to offer, for the moment.

"This is a good place. I've been thinking I'll stake me a claim to some land, come spring. Maybe it was God's will, our wagon breaking down and our food running out, bad as it seemed at the time."

Jack suppressed a sigh and kept on working. It gave vent to some of the anger he felt, though not all. If something bad happened, it seemed to him, then God might have had a hand in it. Anything good, well, that was pure luck. What was his surviving, while better men died all around him—and the best of them all in his arms—if not some kind of celestial joke? "Maybe," he allowed, for that was all the answer he dared give just then. He plied the pick harder, faster.

Finally, Ben laid a hand on his arm. "Easy," he said.

Jack stopped, breathing hard. He ran a hand across his mouth and, glad of the relative gloom, took care not to face his friend straight on.

"What'd you come here for, Jack, if you wasn't planning to stay on? I mean, you don't have a wife and kids to look out for the way I do, and there's more exciting places for a man on his own to light than Springwater."

"A lot of men drift," Jack replied, a little shortly. He still wouldn't look at Ben, and the morning's work had left him ravenous. He wanted the conversation—indeed, the whole shift—to be over.

"A lot of men do," Ben agreed. "But you aren't 'a lot of men.' There's something real different about you."

Fortunately, somebody took to clanging the dinner bell just then, and Jack was spared having to answer. He fetched his lunchpail, packed that morning by Miss Olivia, in a kitchen awash in warmth from the stove, light from the lanterns, and the subtle, fresh smell of a woman's flesh. He ached, recalling the way he'd kissed her, in the pantry the night before, him stretched out in his bathwater, her scandalized and, at the same time, sweetly responsive. If he could have done anything on earth that he wanted to, just then, he'd have gone back to Miss Olivia Darling's house, swept her up into his arms, carried her off to his bed, and made love to her until the sun split in half and made a partner for itself.

Impossible, he reminded himself. A decent man didn't bed a woman like Olivia without putting a wedding ring on her finger first and he couldn't do that.

Could he?

He shook his head. Once he'd faced Jacob and June-bug and told them the whole sorry story—by God, he *would* do that much, he owed them that and a lot more—he'd be lucky if he wasn't tarred, feathered, and run out of town on a rail. Miss Olivia, knowing only half the truth and thus inclined toward a certain fondness for him, judging by her reaction to his kiss, would probably lead the procession.

* * *

Jamie had already eaten and gone to bed by the time Jack came home that night; Olivia had kept his supper of chicken and dumplings warm, and set out the copper tub in the pantry. The memory of the kiss they'd exchanged rattled inside her, refusing to be forgotten, ignored, or discounted.

A virgin at thirty-two, Olivia knew little or nothing about kissing, and even less about the things that happened afterward, when the affections of a man and woman were allowed to take their natural course. All she was really sure of was that she wanted Jack to kiss her again, wanted what lay beyond still more.

Jack looked dirty and cold and unbearably handsome, as he stood there in the warm kitchen; it seemed as though he wanted to say something, do something, and couldn't think what.

"I've made chicken and dumplings," she said, to break the silence, and immediately felt foolish because her voice came out sounding high-pitched and perhaps a little breathless.

He cleared his throat, attempted a grin, failed at the effort. "I guess the population out there in the henhouse must be in serious decline," he said.

She laughed, grateful for the remark because it dissipated some if not all of the strange charge in the air. "I'll have some chicks in the spring," she said. "Meantime, I've got plenty of hens to spare. A good three-quarters of them won't lay anyway, thanks to Trey Hargreaves and the Brimstone Saloon."

He seemed to be keeping his distance. "About last night—"

Olivia turned her back, closed her eyes. If he expressed regret over that exchange, she would not be able to bear it. Life was unpredictable; that kiss might well turn out to be all she would ever know of love, and she intended to honor the memory. "Don't apologize," she said, and was mortified because the words came out sounding like a plea.

"I wasn't about to do that," he replied gently. "I probably ought to, though."

She turned back to him, couldn't keep herself from looking into his face, trying to read his expression. "It's true that it wasn't precisely proper," she allowed. Her voice was shaking a little, and so was the warm plate of food clasped in her hand. "Here, sit down and have your supper."

"Look at me," he said, and offered a faltering, boyish grin. "I've got half of the Jupiter and Zeus ground into my clothes. I was raised to respect a lady's kitchen."

"Were you?" she asked, very quietly. Perhaps now, in this delicate interlude, he would tell her the full truth about himself, set aside the barrier of secrets that kept them apart.

Again, she was disappointed, for he merely looked away.

Five minutes later, with his face and hands scrubbed clean at the basin—it had taken several changes of water and much soap to accomplish even that much—Jack sat down at Olivia's table and tucked into the food she'd cooked for him earlier. His shorter hair and lack of a beard lent him a sort of vulnerability that pressed a thumbprint-sized bruise into the very center of Olivia's heart.

When the meal was over, he lugged water into the pantry, bucket by bucket, and took a bath. Olivia lingered in the kitchen, taking far longer than necessary to wash the few dishes he'd used, but had anyone asked if she was hoping he would somehow contrive to woo her in there and kiss her again, she would have denied it fervently.

He did not summon her, nor did he pretend to be asleep, and apt to drown ignobly in his own bathwater. Indeed, he was whistling cheerfully and doing a great deal of splashing.

She finally retreated to the parlor, where she spent a half hour at the piano, playing softly lest she awaken Jamie. With every note, every heartbeat and breath, however, she was aware of Jack McLaughlin in her pantry, wearing not a stitch.

Finally, she took herself to bed, where she lay staring at the ceiling, waiting for the morning.

Jack was still asleep when she passed his room an hour or so after sunrise; she sensed his presence there, heard the springs creak as he turned over. She smiled a little and proceeded along the corridor to the back stairs, continuing down to the kitchen.

Jamie was already there, fully dressed, studying her reading primer as though it were some important historic artifact that must be deciphered at all costs.

"I *still* can't read," she said, looking at Olivia with an endearing expression of weary surprise. Perhaps she thought the skill was something that came unexpectedly in the night, like an idea or a spring snowfall or an earache.

Olivia was careful not to laugh, though she could not help smiling a little. "You will," she said, and began putting on her cloak. Before she could make breakfast, she had to feed the chickens and gather whatever eggs they might have laid. After the meal, it would be time to leave for church.

It didn't seem possible that a full week had passed since she'd brought June-bug and the others home for tea following the services. The weather had worsened, if that was possible, and December would soon be upon them, bringing Christmas and the pageant.

It caused her a curious combination of exhilaration and sorrow, contemplating what lay ahead. Before Jack, before Jamie, she might have been untouched, might have gone on as she had always done, making the best of things, never really daring to dream. But they'd changed her, the pair of them. Even if they went away, each in their turn, the miracle they had worked would not be undone. Olivia was now, for the first time in her life, a bona-fide, participating member of a community. There was indeed a place for her in Springwater, a home; perhaps she had truly buried Aunt Eloise, once and for all.

Small consolation, she thought, if she had to

spend the rest of her life alone, but there was no sense in trying to cross that bridge before she reached it.

She had changed into her Sunday clothes and was just leaving her room when Jack appeared in his doorway, wearing trousers and the shirt to his long underwear. He hadn't combed his hair, but the disarray only heightened his appeal.

"Mornin'," he said, and yawned expansively.

"Good morning," Olivia replied, as briskly as she could. There was something so sensual about seeing him this way, barely out of bed and only half dressed. "You're planning to stay at home again this week, I see," she added.

His grin tilted up at one side, giving him a rascally aspect. "Yes, ma'am," he said, with a little salute. "I won't detain you. I just wanted to know if you were going to bring another flock of women home to inspect me, like you did last week."

Olivia flushed. She tried to think of an excuse for what she'd done, but the truth was, she didn't have one to offer. "I believe I apologized for that."

"I've apologized for plenty of things in my life," he answered, folding his arms and leaning a little, one shoulder braced against the door frame. "Didn't necessarily mean I wouldn't do it again, though. Just that I was sorry at the time."

"Perhaps your word can be stretched and reshaped to suit the purpose at hand, Mr. McLaughlin," she said. "When I speak, however, I mean what I say."

"Jack," he corrected her. "And I notice you haven't answered yet."

She raised her chin a little. "I have no intention of inviting anyone back to the house. On the other hand, I most certainly do reserve the right to entertain acquaintances in my own home."

Once more, he touched the tips of two fingers to the side of his forehead, then he grinned again and stepped back into his room, closing the door quietly in Olivia's face.

She was not able to concentrate on the sermon that Sunday morning and had forgotten the heart of the message by the time she shook hands with the pastor, out on the church steps.

It was ironic, perhaps, that she found the wanted poster first thing after breakfast, on Monday, not more than half an hour after Jack had left the house for the mine. She'd gone to his room to put fresh sheets on his bed.

She wouldn't have searched through his belongings, curious though she was, but the tattered paper, folded in quarters, was lying on the floor, partway beneath the bedside table, and she'd already bent and picked it up before she had the first inkling of what she'd discovered.

A section of the word "Wanted" showed, along with a corner of a sketch.

With trembling fingers, Olivia unfolded the worn bill and felt her stomach drop like a stone pitched off a high bridge.

Wanted for a Variety of Crimes
William J. "Will" McCaffrey

The face looking back at Olivia, though drawn years before, was unquestionably Jack's.

She shouldn't have been surprised, she supposed; Jack had made it plain enough that he'd come to Springwater to see Jacob and June-bug, once she'd cornered him, but the realization left her thunderstruck, all the same.

Her first impulse was to bolt to her feet and dash to the station, bursting with the news that one of the McCaffreys' sons, at least, was alive. Only a moment passed before she realized, though, that she couldn't do that. It was Jack's—Will's—place to break this news; he would do so when he was ready.

In the meantime, she thought, folding the poster again and replacing it beneath the bedside table, she would keep her own counsel, in so far as possible. She did mean to confront her boarder with what she'd learned.

When he arrived home that night, she shoved the worn sheet of paper under his nose immediately.

"Will," she accused. "You are Will McCaffrey."

His face went stony. "You've been going through my things." The words were flat, containing neither confession nor denial.

"I found this on the floor," she replied. "The floor, I might add, of *my* house."

"Leave this alone, Olivia," he said, his voice even and cold, as he took the poster from her hand. "Just leave it alone. You can't possibly understand what it means."

She said nothing, and after that, there was a silent, uneasy truce between them.

The following afternoon, Olivia returned to the church, having made a sort of peace with her uncomfortable knowledge, and determined to mind her own business. She was gratified when half the children of Springwater appeared, seeking parts in the pageant. The cast would be a large one, for no one would be turned away, and as the process dragged on, she was doubly grateful for Emma Hargreaves's help. Tired from a day at school, excited and probably hungry, the future shepherds, Wise Men, and angels were somewhat unruly.

All the same, Olivia managed to complete the task at hand, assigning parts to everyone. Millicent, a shy girl from one of the outlying ranches, would play Mary, and Isaiah Kildare, big for his age, was given the part of Joseph. There were no less than seven shepherds, some of them female, and one of the Wise Men was a girl as well. It would be no small challenge, she thought, resigned, to find lines for the donkey and the oxen, the camel and the sheep, but somehow she would manage. Jamie insisted upon proving herself worthy before accepting an angel's role and a solo rendering of "Silent Night," perhaps afraid some of the others would be envious, and when she sang, "O, Little Town of Bethlehem," by way of an audition, even the smallest children went still and listened. Another member of the heavenly host, probably Daisy or Rose Williams, would announce the Holy Birth to the shepherds.

She and Jamie were walking home, hand in hand, through brittle snow, the sun already gone for the day, when the child raised eager, hopeful eyes to Olivia's face. "I sang good, didn't I?" she asked. "Good enough to be an angel, even if I'm not really your little girl?"

"You will make a splendid angel," Olivia said, after a moment spent gathering her composure. "Where did you learn the words to that song? I didn't think you'd ever gone to Sunday School."

"Jack taught me," Jamie said, pleased with herself and with him. "We practiced and practiced, while you were at church yesterday. I told him I wanted to be an angel in the worst way, but not if you were going to give me the part like a present."

"Is that what you thought I would do?" Olivia asked gently. They had reached the front gate, and the weather was bone-chilling, but she paused, waiting for Jamie's answer. She was deeply impressed that a child so young, with so little guidance, had developed such a profound sense of honor.

"Maybe you feel sorry for me," Jamie said. Her voice was small, and Olivia knelt right down, there in the snow, heedless of her skirts and her poor frozen knees, and pulled the child close. When she drew back and looked into that earnest little face, Olivia sniffled and gave a watery smile.

"I am very sorry that you've had such a hard time, darling. But I couldn't pity you, not ever. I admire you too much."

"Are you still going to adopt me?" The question was hopeful, and frail enough to blow away on the night wind.

Olivia gripped the child's bony shoulders. "I'll see Mr. Calloway tomorrow, I promise. Then we'll sit down and discuss the situation, you and I. Fair enough?"

Jamie nodded. "You'd better get up, then, before you get your drawers wet," she said sagely.

Olivia laughed and got to her feet, and they went into the house, where a fire was crackling cheerily on the parlor hearth. A few lamps burned, here and there, spilling a golden, glowing welcome through their ornate china globes. A savory aroma filled the air.

She and Jamie hurried to the kitchen, where they found Jack standing in front of the stove, with a blue-checked dish towel tied around his middle for an apron, stirring something in a pot. He smiled when he saw them.

"I'm an angel!" Jamie whooped, in an explosion of delighted energy.

"That," Jack replied, "could be debated."

"You're—cooking?" Olivia asked, still a bit behind. She had never seen a man prepare a meal before; had never even imagined such a spectacle.

He shrugged. "I got home from the mine early today, while you two were at the church, so I went out and shot a rabbit. This is pretty much all I know how to make—stew."

"It smells wonderful," Olivia said.

Jamie looked less certain. "Did you take the hide off?"

Jack reached out and lightly rubbed his knuckles across the top of her head. "Yes, Smidge. Ears and eyeballs, too."

Olivia made a disapproving face, but the truth was, she was enjoying the very ordinariness of the exchange, the warmth, and the sense of being part of a family.

She brought herself up short, and a familiar voice echoed, however faintly, in her mind. *Don't care too much.*

The next morning, after making breakfast, packing lunchpails for both Jack and Jamie, feeding the chickens, gathering the eggs, and making up the beds, Olivia put on her best and most businesslike dress, a green velvet skirt and jacket with black cord piping, worn over a starched white shirtwaist, donned her cloak, and set out for Mr. Calloway's office.

He greeted her with startled interest, much the way the marshal had done when she called upon him. It galled her only a little, she found, to recall how obviously Mr. Calloway had enjoyed her futile visit to the town council meeting. She had not intended, after all, to provide entertainment.

He offered a chair with a gentlemanly gesture, and Olivia sat down, clutching her handbag in her lap.

"How can I help you?" he asked, seating himself behind his broad, cluttered desk.

"I suppose you've heard about Jamie—she was found robbing our—my chicken coop." She paused, aware that she was prattling, but determined to explain the situation clearly. "It appears that the child is completely alone in the world. She doesn't know where her mother is, and she was traveling with a man she called Axel before she came to us—me."

Mr. Calloway regarded her in silence for a long moment, his expression as unreadable as if he were playing a pivotal hand of cards or trying to divine the thoughts of a judge and jury. Then, tenting his fingers beneath his chin, he asked, "And you want—?"

"I want to adopt Jamie."

He was quiet again, and for such a long time that Olivia's worry deepened. "I see."

"Mr. Calloway?" she prompted.

"I don't have the power to make the final decision, of course. You'd need a judge for that. You'll most likely be asked to wait a year, in case someone comes forward to claim the little girl. And—" His voice fell away again, and he appeared to be genuinely dismayed, though it might have been a lawyer's ruse.

Olivia had to remind herself to breathe. "And?"

"You don't have a husband, Miss Darling."

"I am well aware of that, Mr. Calloway," she responded, but her head swam a little as the truth of the matter sank in. "I wouldn't be *allowed* to adopt Jamie on my own. Is that what you're saying?"

"If you were a blood relative, or the child's stepmother, there would probably be little or no difficulty. However—"

"And if I were married?"

"You could petition a judge in Choteau, and you'd very likely be given custody, after the waiting period had ended."

She opened her handbag. "Thank you," she said. "What do I owe you for your time, Mr. Calloway?"

He held up a hand, as if to swear an oath. "Nothing, Miss Darling. After all, I wasn't much help."

She sighed, rose to her feet. She had a great many things to ponder, and she needed to be alone in a quiet place to concentrate properly. "On the contrary, Mr. Calloway, I insist that you send me an invoice."

He smiled, spread his hands in silent surrender.

Olivia stepped out into the street and, leaning into the wind, made her way toward home.

CHAPTER

❧ 11 ❧

IT WAS HEARTENING to Olivia, the way the townspeople rallied round to help with the Christmas
pageant, once she had been roped into heading up
the project. Perhaps they had merely been waiting,
the men and women and children of Springwater,
for a nod from her. Now they behaved, from Jacob
and June-bug McCaffrey right on down through
the benevolent hierarchy to the smallest children,
as though she had always been an integral part of
all their doings.

The men set to building a simple but remarkably
authentic manger scene right away, behind the rustic pulpit, hammering and whistling under their
breaths when they weren't busy with their own
ranch work or the like. Even Trey Hargreaves and
Gage Calloway lent a hand, wearing their fancy
suits and coats. The women sewed costumes, helped
with the singing, and provided cookies and other
refreshments to the small, ravenous performers.

The exception to all this community harmony, of course, was "Jack McLaughlin"; he avoided the locals, those who lived and worked aboveground, at least, as assiduously as ever. He worked in the mine from before first light, he came home to bathe and eat, and then he either played checkers with Jamie or stumbled off to bed, depending upon the sort of day he'd had. He cried out at night, in his sleep, more and more often and, correspondingly, said less and less to Olivia when they encountered each other somewhere in the house. She guessed, on some level, that it had something to do with her learning his secret.

The chaos of putting on a small-town Nativity program almost certainly kept Olivia from tumbling headlong into the well of sorrow rising within her heart like the waters of some subterranean river.

One afternoon, in mid-December, when a particularly tiring rehearsal had just ended, and Olivia was gathering her music to leave for home, where she had yet to make supper and oversee Jamie's continuing struggle with the alphabet, June-bug approached. Mrs. McCaffrey had been an almost constant presence during the proceedings, having a lovely and powerful singing voice herself, but lately she'd seemed distracted, less substantial somehow. Her gaze had turned inward, as though she were experiencing some private twilight, and Olivia was filled with guilt.

Olivia's throat tightened, for she could not help

thinking of Jack, and of loss, and of all this good woman and her equally good husband had endured over the years, believing both their sons were dead. She had never been a mother herself, of course, and maybe she never would be, but she understood that the loss of a child was a fierce and consuming misery, one that could bring even the strongest men and women to their knees.

On impulse, she reached out, took June-bug's cool, surprisingly smooth hand in her own. "What is it?" she asked softly. "June-bug—Mrs. McCaffrey, are you ill? Shall I send for Jacob, or for Dr. Parrish?"

June-bug shook her head and gave a rueful little laugh that contained none of her usual liveliness. "You call me June-bug, or I won't answer," she said, and Olivia glimpsed a wisp of the old spirit in those blue, blue eyes. Eyes precisely the same color, now that sadness had settled in, as Jack McLaughlin's. It was a shock to notice that, though it shouldn't have been, given her discovery. "No," June-bug went on. "I ain't sick. Just feelin' a little raveled around the edges, that's all."

Olivia wanted to blurt out what she'd learned, but therein lay the problem. She knew so very little, after all, and Jack had never actually admitted anything where his identity was concerned. To interfere, to say she had good reason to believe that Jack McLaughlin was really Will McCaffrey, could only cause harm. Painful as it was to watch the drama unfold without helping things along, that was unquestionably the right thing to do. "Is there anything I can do to help?" she asked, very softly.

"Well, yes," June-bug answered, bracing up and flashing a brief, tentative smile so like Jack's that it nearly took Olivia's breath away, "there is. We're goin' to be quiltin' on Sunday afternoon, over at the station house. We'd admire for you to join in."

Olivia was inordinately pleased. It was still new to her, still precious, the acceptance, the sense of belonging, that she had found in Springwater. If only Jack would stay, and be part of it all. "I would like that," she said, and meant it.

June-bug raised her chin, summoned up another smile, and squeezed Olivia's hands between her own. "Good. We'll be gatherin' together directly after church. Bring the little one, if you'd like. There'll be plenty to eat."

"Thank you," Olivia said, deeply moved. Jack's name hung between them, unspoken, and not for the first time, Olivia wondered how much June-bug had already sensed. Did she know, in some deep and hitherto unexplored region of her being, that the stranger hiding out at the local rooming house might be her own son?

The two women parted then, and Olivia closed up the church and made for home, Jamie skipping along beside her. The snow was deep, and already splashed with the light of a winter moon, but the sky had been clear for nearly a week, blue-on-blue in the daytime, splattered with silvery stars at night. How, Olivia asked herself, had she reached her age without noticing how beautiful the day-to-day world could be? For all its war and sorrow and disease, or more properly in spite of those things, *here* was the best place to be, and *now* was the finest time to live.

Lights glowing in the kitchen windows revealed that Jack was home from the mine, and moving about the house instead of brooding in his room the way he too often did. Olivia's foolish heart leaped at the prospect of merely seeing him, seeing the lantern light catch in his fair hair, admiring the unconscious grace of his movements, memorizing the unique combination of mischief and character etched into his features.

He was there, all right, bathed and dressed in the simple trousers and shirt he generally wore in the evening. There was none of the old merriment in his eyes, however, as he stood near the sink, arms folded, watching Olivia bustle about the kitchen, starting supper. Jamie, full of chatter, rattled through the day's experiences, one by one but at top speed, like a runaway train hurtling down a steep grade. Olivia was not really listening, and she sensed that Jack wasn't either.

Jamie talked through supper, and through her bath afterward. Only when she was snuggled in bed, wearing one of her new flannel nightgowns, did she settle into an exhausted silence. She listened to the story Olivia told, one she'd made up herself, about a lost princess who finally finds a home in a fine castle, and fell asleep.

Jack was waiting downstairs. He'd moved to the parlor, and stood gazing out at the moon-bright snow, a fire crackling on the hearth.

"You're thinking of leaving again?" Olivia said, without planning to, and saw his answer in the sudden rigidity of his backbone. It was on the tip of her tongue, his true name, but she withheld it.

He turned to meet her eyes straight on, she had to give him credit for that, but in the end, he merely shrugged.

Olivia put out a hand, pressed her palm to the doorjamb to steady herself. She would not beg or argue, she had decided that long since. "Where would you go if—if you left?"

Again, those wonderful, Jacob McCaffrey shoulders of his moved in a shrug. "I don't rightly know. California, Mexico—maybe Australia."

A feeling of such bleakness swept over Olivia that she swayed ever so slightly on her feet, and had to tighten her grasp on the framework of the door to remain upright. "I see," she said, and then the words tumbled out, past all her lofty resolutions. "You're just going to let Jacob and June-bug go on believing you're dead."

To her surprise, he shook his head. "No," he ground out. "I'll let them know what happened. Most likely, Miss Darling, you won't want me around, once you know all of it, and I'm pretty sure they won't, either." He'd put the slightest caress into her surname, damn him. Was he *trying* to torture her? Wasn't it enough that he had the power to break her heart so badly that she'd never be able to find all the tiny pieces, let alone fit them back together?

"When?" she whispered. "If—if you went, I mean, when would you go?" When would the sun go dark, when would the sky crack like an eggshell.

"I've already finished out the time I promised Hargreaves. He asked me to stay on another week—we're close to hitting a new vein—and I said I would." He fished in his shirt pocket with two fingers, drew out a coin. "This will cover my board and room, won't it?"

It was a five-dollar gold piece. "Quite nicely," she managed to say. She might have had a whole chicken stuck in her throat, feathers, spurs, and poor disposition included, so difficult was it to push out those two simple words.

He shoved a hand through his hair. "You've been good to me, Miss Olivia. Good *for* me, too. I'm grateful."

Don't go, she thought, but she was still choked up and could only nod her head.

Perhaps it would have been bearable if he hadn't crossed to her then, taken her into his arms, held her against that lean, work-hardened chest.

"I'm sorry, sweetheart," he murmured.

No one had ever called her by that endearment, in the whole length of her memory, not her mother or father and certainly not Aunt Eloise. A wretched sob escaped her, because finding Jack only to lose him again seemed so much worse than never knowing him at all.

"Shhh," he said, and kissed the top of her head.

She turned her face into his shoulder and made a heroic effort to stop crying, but she couldn't. It shamed her terribly, carrying on that way, but the sobs kept coming, shuddering their way up from somewhere in her depths and bursting out. She was grieving over a great deal more than the very real prospect of losing Jack McLaughlin, even in her semihysterical state she knew that, but knowing didn't seem to make a difference.

He curled a finger under her chin and caused her to look up at him. "Olivia," he said. "What's this about? All these tears can't be for me."

She sniffled, and her chin wobbled, but she still had *some* dignity left, and she met his gaze directly. "Of course I'm not crying over you." She paused. Although she did not personally believe in eternal damnation, Aunt Eloise had spoken often enough of the multitudes of liars stewing in the fires of hell, alongside heretics, murderers, and politicians. Best not to take chances. "At least, not much."

He laughed, though from the look in those Junebug–blue eyes, she suspected he wanted to cry, too. Cupping both her cheeks in his hands, he ran a callused thumb very lightly across her lower lip. "Say you don't want me to go, Olivia," he said. "That's all it would take."

She stared at him. Hot shivers went through her with every pass of his thumb across her mouth.

"Well?" he prompted, when the silence lengthened uncomfortably.

"You'd stay? Just because I asked you to?"

He nodded. "You'd have to marry me, though," he said, "because I can't go on sleeping under the same roof with you for much longer without going crazy." He paused. "I've been saving my money for years, Olivia. Didn't have much to spend it on." His eyes were on her lips now; he studied them as though fascinated, and she wished he would just go ahead and kiss her. "If I stayed on here, I'd start my own livery stable and blacksmith shop."

She began to tremble. He bent his head, tasted her mouth, and she felt all sorts of things happening within her—tumbling spills of fire, sweet tugging sensations, small, delicious aches, scattered throughout her being and yet all of a piece. "And Jacob and June-bug?" She almost whispered the question. "What about them? What about—?"

Jack sighed. "I'll talk to them in a day or so. Maybe after you're all through with church on Sunday." He brushed his lips across hers again, touched them with just the tip of his tongue. "Being with you makes me think that—well— things might not be so impossible after all. But none of this is going to be easy, Olivia. Not for me, and not for you, either."

Olivia groaned, caught up in the promise of a kiss. She had always been critical of people who stepped off the straight and narrow path, but now she understood at least one of the attractions of sin.

"Shall I stay, Olivia?" he asked. His voice was throaty and low; she knew he had not planned to say what he had, that all of this had been locked away somewhere inside him, and found its way out against his better judgment.

She thought of the long and lonely years ahead. She thought of the children she yearned to carry in her womb and nurse at her breasts, to love and teach and raise. This man's children. Adopting Jamie, virtually impossible for a spinster, would probably be easy, if only she had a husband.

Besides, she loved this complex stranger. More than her next breath, her next heartbeat.

"Stay," she said, at long last.

He kissed her then, a long, thorough, ravishing kiss that weakened her knees and made her head seem to float loose from her neck. Her whole body strained to arch against him, and she held the instinct in check only by the most assiduous of efforts.

When he finally drew back, she was dazed, even dumbfounded. He smiled down at her. "You'll marry me, then?" he asked. "Right away?"

She wanted so much to say yes. Not just for Jamie, but for herself. She knew what she felt for this man *must* be love, it was so powerful, so utterly all-encompassing. However, if she took him for a husband, she would be marrying a shadow, a lie. She wanted the matters of his identity and his past settled first. "After you've spoken to the McCaffreys," she said, with all the firmness she could muster.

She saw him withdraw into himself, just a little, even though he didn't actually move. He was still standing ever so close, with his hands resting loosely now at the sides of her waist, and yet he had established a distinct distance between them. At the same time, he seemed to have come back to himself from somewhere far away, and to be remembering things he would have preferred to forget.

He shoved a hand through his hair and turned back to the window. She wondered what he saw out there, in that cold night, what he was watching for.

Olivia waited in vain for him to speak again, but he did not. In time, she left the parlor and mounted the stairs.

He saw the doctor pause at his front gate, and glance in the direction of Miss Olivia's house, as if he knew that someone was watching him. It wouldn't have surprised Jack; according to Ben, Parrish had been a Union surgeon. War developed new and mysterious senses in those who survived it, things that went well beyond seeing and hearing and the rest.

On impulse, he snatched open the door and went out, not even bothering to collect his coat first.

Doc Parrish approached, the ever-present black bag dangling from one hand. "Evening," he said. His eyes were watchful.

"Evenin'," Jack replied, and waited. Their breaths made fog in the evening air, and blended.

Parrish sighed. "I've been racking my brain ever since you came here, trying to figure out where I'd seen you before."

"Maybe the war," Jack suggested. Dodging the truth was such a habit with him that he did it automatically.

"No," the doctor said, with grim certainty. "I considered that. I can tell by the way you talk that you were a Reb, but that isn't why I recognized you."

Jack waited. He wasn't sure he could have spoken if he'd tried.

"Except for your coloring," Parrish went on, "you're the image of Jacob McCaffrey. You're one of his sons, unless I miss my guess."

Still, Jack said nothing. His throat felt as if it had rusted shut.

Parrish would not be turned aside. "Are you going to tell them?"

At last, Jack managed a nod and a ground-out, "Yes."

"The resemblance is pretty amazing," Parrish ruminated. He sounded tired enough to go to sleep standing up, like an old horse. "You move like Jacob. You're built like him, too. You even sound a little like him."

Jack made no response.

"You be careful how you approach this," the doctor said. "They'll be glad to see you, I can't imagine how they could be anything else, but I'm a little concerned about Jacob's reaction when he finds out. As his friend and as his doctor."

Jack felt a muscle tighten painfully in the pit of his stomach. "As his doctor?"

"He had an episode with his heart a few years back. Nearly died. He's fine now, but I don't think a lot of high emotion would be good for him."

Jack digested this information with no little difficulty; Jacob had always been as strong as the proverbial ox. "My God."

"I care about Jacob and June-bug," Parrish went on. He glanced toward the imperious house behind Jack. "Miss Olivia, too, prickly as she is. It's only fair to tell you: I won't take kindly to it if you do harm to any of these people, and neither will anybody else in Springwater."

"Is that a warning?"

"I guess that's up to you," Parrish answered. "The people of this town have their squabbles, but they're close-knit. In a very real way, the McCaffreys are the heart of the place. Most of us would do just about anything for either one of them."

Jack understood that; he would have done anything for Jacob and June-bug too—anything but spare them the all too many years of grief they'd endured on his account. "Maybe it's better just to leave things as they are," he said, speaking partly to the doctor, but mostly to himself. It was just habit, mostly; he had no intention of backing down now. There was too much at stake.

"It's a little too late for that," Parrish said,

revealing no emotion at all, unless weariness could be counted as such. He glanced toward his house, where lights burned in the windows, where a loving wife and children waited to greet him. "I guess we'd best put an end to this little chat before I have to treat the pair of us for frostbite."

Jack might have smiled, under other circumstances. He liked the doctor, had him pegged as a kindly man, good at his work. " 'Night," he said.

Parrish raised a hand in farewell as he turned away.

He'd waited long enough, Jack decided. He opened the gate and walked out into the street; got halfway to the Springwater Station before thinking of Jacob's weak heart, turning around, and heading back to Olivia's place.

Furious with himself, he mounted the stairs to his room, dragged his valise out from under the bed, and then just stood there, staring at it, making no move to pack. He didn't deserve folks like Jacob and June-bug, didn't deserve Olivia, either, or that little girl who so obviously wanted to nominate him for the high and honorable office of daddy. He wouldn't be doing any of them a favor by staying, yet he couldn't quite make himself go.

He didn't realize he'd left the door open until it was too late.

"Your resolve didn't last long, did it?" Olivia asked quietly. Seeing the open satchel on his bed, she'd drawn the obvious conclusion.

He turned his head, saw her standing there on

the threshold in a high-necked nightdress, her lovely rosewood hair braided, eyes the size of stove lids and full of feeling.

"What if it kills him?" he said miserably. "What if it hurts them both so badly that—?"

She knew, of course, that he was referring to Jacob and June-bug. "More than losing both their sons, you mean, and never even having bodies to bury?" she asked gently. For all her soft tone, those words went through him like spears.

"It's time to stop running," she went on. "Whatever happens between you and me after this, Jack, you've got to set your jaw and tell the truth."

"I'm not even sure I know what that is anymore," he said, and he meant it. He'd learned a long time ago that you could see things, touch them with your hands, believe with all your heart and soul that they were real, only to find out that you'd been mistaken right along.

"For your own sake, as well as theirs—and mine—you'd better sort that out once and for all. Claim your life, Jack. Take it back."

He stood stiffly, listening to her, knowing she was right, knowing too that that didn't mean he'd be able to take her advice. Without replying, he set the satchel on the floor again, and kicked it under the bed.

Olivia didn't say anything further. Out of the corner of his eye, he saw her move out of the doorway. A few moments later, her bedroom door closed softly in the distance.

A hopeless yearning came over him; he wanted to join her, take refuge in her arms, in her heart, in her body. But he had no right, not yet.

In time, he undressed, blew out the lamp, and climbed into his cold bed. Moonlight spilled in through the window, bright enough to read by, and he lay with his hands behind his head, staring up at the ceiling.

Remembering.

Wes acted downright cocky after the victory at Chickamauga; you'd have thought he'd turned back those Yankees all by himself, the way he crowed over it. He didn't have the horse sense to be scared, even with men splintering like bottles left in the sun all around them. Will, on the other hand, was more than scared, more than just uneasy. He would have given just about anything, including an arm or a leg, to get back home to the farm, and if he never heard another word about the war again, why, that would be just fine with him.

Wes, now, he'd taken to gambling with some of the boys from Virginia—they couldn't have scared up five cents between them, Wes included, even if they turned out all their pockets—and while he admitted to missing home, he'd made it clear he wasn't going back anytime soon. Not now, and not when they'd put the blue-bellies on the run, once and for all.

Will wondered, gazing into the campfire that

night in September of 1863, when—and if—he'd ever see home again, ever marry, and work the cotton fields alongside his daddy. Would his responsibility to Wes be fulfilled if he just got him safely through the war? Surely nobody expected him to traipse all over kingdom come for the rest of his life, just in case Wes scraped a knee or chipped a tooth.

An elbow to the ribs, though painless, jolted him out of his reflections. "Quit your broodin'," Wes jibed, sitting beside him on the ground, legs crossed like a red Indian. "We got those bastards right where we want them now. Why, by summer, you'll be married and settled in, farming with Daddy."

Will tried to smile, but he couldn't. These days it seemed like he was always torn between laughing at Wes and grabbing him around the throat and choking the life out of him. These days? Hell, it had been like this for as long as he could recall, from the cradle probably. Maybe from the womb.

"This war could run on for years, Wes. With or without you and me."

Wes's azure eyes glinted in the firelight, and his grin was both crooked and slightly stiff. "You're wrong, brother. But even if you're right, that just gives me more time to win that medal for Mama."

Will had been chewing on a blade of grass; now, he tossed it into the fire, disgusted. He felt about a hundred years old. "You know, God must have been in a mood to make idiots when He drew up the plan for you. People are getting *killed*, Wes, all around us, every single day of the week. Yankee, Confederate, it doesn't matter. They're human beings, with farms and hound dogs and folks and sweethearts. One hell of a lot of them are never going to get home. And for what?" He suppressed an urge to grab up the front of Wes's soiled shirt in both hands and shake him hard. His fingers flexed spasmodically. "*For what?*"

Wes was flushed, even in that chilly night, where the fire warmed only the half of a man's body that happened to be facing in that direction and left the rest to freeze. "For the honor of the Confederacy," he hissed. "Or doesn't that mean anything to you anymore?"

Will couldn't rightly figure what honor had to do with all this slaughter and destruction, but he'd worn himself out trying to get through to Wes. He needed his strength just to keep the damn fool from running ahead of the rest of the army, looking to make himself a hero. "If there's anything commendable in all this," he said, "I can't see it. I guess you can, and that's your business. Just don't ask me to agree with you."

Wes grinned and laid a hand on his brother's shoulder. "We're gonna take Lookout Mountain and hold it. Just you wait and see. I'll get me a medal, for sure, and maybe one for you, too."

Lookout Mountain. Will glanced toward the shadowy peak, looming against the night sky and rimmed in moonlight. "This isn't the county fair,

Wes," he said, though he knew he was wasting his breath, and an all-too-familiar passage of Scripture rose up to haunt him, as it had so many times since all this had begun. *Nation shall rise against nation, brother against brother—*

A chill snaked down his backbone. God, if only he'd wake up in his old room at home, with Wes in the bed across from his, with Mama singing in the kitchen and Daddy booming out that the fields weren't going to plow themselves. None of that was going to happen, of course. This was a nightmare, all right, but it was all too real.

"We've got a game of faro goin' over here," Wes confided, eyes shining. One thing you had to say for him: he enjoyed most every moment as it came, even smack in the middle of a goddamned war. "You ought to join in. Win yourself a pair of boots. You could use 'em."

That, Will thought ruefully, looking down at his feet, was true enough. The soles were so loose that he tripped on them a dozen times a day, and come winter, he'd be lucky if he didn't lose half his toes. Wes had won various things since their enlistment—a pocketknife, a plug of tobacco that had sent him running into the brush to vomit, when he planted a chaw in one cheek, a dented canteen, and a deck of playing cards missing two eights and a king. Yes, sir, he was making his mark in the world, Wes McCaffrey was.

Will shook his head in benign wonderment, gave a hoarse laugh, and joined the game. By the time it was over, he'd not only seen the last of his comb and his spare pair of socks, he'd obligated himself to walk two nights' guard duty for another soldier.

Maybe it was that, the lack of sleep. Maybe it was fate, or the will of God, or just plain sorry luck. Whatever the reason, it came the next morning, that bullet he'd been expecting, came whistling through the September air as surely and as deliberately as if it had been fired the day the both of them were born.

There was blood everywhere, his own, his brother's, it ran together and mingled, and he couldn't tell whose was whose. All he knew was that his twin was lying in his arms, staring upward at his face with eyes that reflected disbelieving protest.

"You tell—Mama—I tried—"

"Don't," he pleaded, wailing the word, rocking his brother back and forth, as though to jolt him into holding on. "Damn it, don't you go and leave me!"

There was no answer. Just a gurgling sound, and more blood. A fount of it.

He let out another sky-rending bellow—of protest, of grief, of fathomless rage.

Cap'n Jack McLaughlin crawled through smoke and rifle fire to reach them.

"He's gone, McCaffrey," the officer said. "You've got to leave him now."

"No. *No.*"

"Yes, damn it. You're goin' to get your head blown off, and mine, too. Now, come on!"

In the next instant, Cap'n McLaughlin seemed to explode from the inside, in all directions. There only a moment before, whole and breathing, he was gone now, forever. Scattered over the earth like seed.

Pain. There was pain, abrupt and cruel and completely, utterly welcome. Then blood, so much blood that he couldn't tell whose was whose. Sounds receded, like water ebbing into the depths of a cave, and so did the terrible stench of death. His vision narrowed with sickening suddenness, and he felt himself falling forward, to lie sprawled across his brother's body.

Chapter 12

THE DREAM AWAKENED him, brought him bolt upright in bed, drenched in sweat and gasping for breath. How many times had he relived that anguish—a hundred? A thousand?

He tossed back the blankets and went to the window to look out at the sky. It was still full dark, and the moon was high. He stood there, drawing slow, deep swallows of air, until he'd settled down a little. In the near distance, he could just make out the shadowy hulk of the Springwater Station. Was that a light he saw?

The rest of the town was sound asleep; even the Brimstone Saloon had hunkered down, like a big, awkward dog, to wait for morning.

Jack squinted. It *was* a light, faint but nonetheless there.

He groped for his trousers, last night's shirt, socks and boots, fetched his coat from the peg in the kitchen as he passed, and then he was out of the house and striding down the center of Main Street, his shoulders hunched against the cold. Against what was to come.

His hour of reckoning had arrived at last, and he would not turn away from it. Not again.

Drawing nearer to the station, he realized that the lamp was coming from the front part of the building where, presumably, meals were served to passengers and other wanderers. It must have been one in the morning—was somebody sick?

Recalling what the Doc had said about Jacob's heart, he quickened his pace.

Reaching the station door, he found himself at a loss. He raised his hand to knock, let it fall to his side, and was getting ready to try again when the thick panel creaked open on its hinges and Jacob McCaffrey loomed in the chasm, looking as big and forbidding as any mountain.

Not a flicker of recognition showed in the dark eyes, or the rugged, time-weathered face. Jacob's voice was deeper than ever, and void of either welcome or rebuke. "Come in," the older man said, as though it were an ordinary thing to greet a visitor in the middle of the night.

He stepped over the threshold when Jacob made room—Jack was as tall and as broad in the shoulders as Jacob, though he felt a lot smaller just then—and kept his hands wedged into the pockets of his coat. He could not quite meet that fierce, questioning gaze, but he could feel it, all right, searing his hide like a branding iron.

"What—?" It was June-bug's voice; she appeared in an inner doorway, holding a glass of water in one hand. At the sight of the visitor, she let go, and the glass shattered at her feet.

For a long moment, she simply stared at him, as though afraid to trust her eyes. Her lips moved, once, twice, without sound, before she finally managed to speak.

"*Wesley*," she whispered. She put a hand to her mouth. "Wesley?"

His heartbeat pounded in his ears. He couldn't speak, couldn't look at his father. Not yet. But he held his mother's gaze. Or was she the one doing the holding?

The door closed quietly behind them. He sensed Jacob's presence there, and was reminded of a steam boiler on the verge of blowing.

"Dear God in heaven," June-bug cried, half strangling on her joy, and hurled herself toward him, heedless of her bare feet and the broken glass. "Wesley!"

He grabbed her up, held her close, spun her around once, as he had yearned to do so often over the years. His eyes were full of tears when he stopped and looked down into her beloved face, and so were hers.

"I just don't know what to say," she whispered.

Jacob spoke at last, and his tone did not bode well. "I do." He took hold of Wesley's shoulder and turned him around hard. "Where in *hell* have you been all these years?" he rasped.

Wes swallowed. "That's a long story, Daddy," he answered. He was a man, long-since grown and wholly responsible for himself, but the words came out sounding small.

"Jacob," June-bug protested. It was plain from the way she spoke that she was afraid her son, just back from the grave, would vanish again.

Jacob did not even glance in her direction. His gaze bored into Wes, molten with fury. "You'll have your say, woman," he said. "Just now, I mean to have mine. We sorrowed over you, boy. We grieved. We wept and we walked the floor and we shook our fists at Almighty God, and the pictures we carried in our minds were too terrible to speak of, even with each other. That's how it was—for almost twenty years. So I will ask you once again—*where have you been?*"

Wes ran the tip of his tongue over his lips, which had gone dry, like his throat.

"At least let him sit down," June-bug interceded, and although her words had an edge, it was plain enough that she wasn't going to step between her husband and son.

With a gesture of one massive hand, Jacob indicated the two chairs facing the banked fire.

Wes crossed the room and waited while his father tossed a couple of logs onto the grate. Only when Jacob had seated himself did Wes take a chair of his own. June-bug, meanwhile, stood behind her husband, her hands resting lightly on his shoulders. If it hadn't been for the situation, and the fact that Jacob was wearing pants and a woolen undershirt, in perfect complement to his wife's nightdress, they'd have looked like they were posing for a formal likeness.

Gazing into the fire, Wes saw himself, kneeling on the rocky ground, holding Will in his arms and bellowing at the sky. He was silent for a long time, and neither of his parents prodded him to speak before he was ready. Their solemn regard was urging enough, all the same.

"Will died on Lookout Mountain," he said, at long last. He made himself meet his mama's eyes, then his daddy's, each in turn. "It was quick. Real quick. A lot of men weren't so lucky." *All the same,* he thought to himself, *I'd have traded places with any one of them. But especially Will.*

He saw his mother's lips move, knew she was offering some private prayer.

Jacob said nothing. He just waited, sitting there like Moses watching his people bow down to the golden calf. His eyes blazed, and his jaw might have been chiseled from a Tennessee field rock.

"For a while," Wes went on, after another interval of reflection, "I didn't know who I was. Then I started thinking I must be Will, because he was the one that deserved to live. I spent a day or two in a Yankee field hospital—just a flesh wound, though I did my share of bleeding—then they marched me and a lot of other men north for two or three days, till we came to a railroad platform. I was in prison in Washington City until after Appomattox."

Jacob applied a spur. There was a long gap between the end of the war and the here-and-now, and he wasn't going to pretend it didn't matter. "And then?"

He looked away, made himself look back. "I led a raiding party for a while."

"You were a thief," Jacob said flatly. He'd still revealed little or no emotion.

Wes swallowed hard. "A man was killed."

June-bug drew in a sharp breath, and Jacob closed his eyes. "You did murder? On top of everything else, *you did murder?*"

"No, sir," Wes answered, sick at his stomach but determined to get it all out in the open. He felt like he was sixteen again. "I swear to you, I did not. But there is something else."

"What?" Jacob demanded. His voice was like a thunderstorm, brewing on a hot day. It was distant, and full of suppressed sound and fury.

"I used Will's name. I figured on taking revenge on the Yankees, and I guess I thought he'd want to be part of it. So I called myself Will McCaffrey, and that's the name they put on the wanted poster." He took the sheet of paper he'd been carrying for so many years, as a sort of penance, he guessed, from his shirt pocket. Held it out.

Jacob didn't take it. His face was cold and quiet.

"Go on," June-bug urged, when the silence lengthened still further.

Wes gazed into the fire. "I started for home. Once—twice, who knows how many times I set my face for Tennessee and made up my mind to keep moving until I got there. One time, I came within five miles of the farm, but I always got to thinking of Will, and how it should have been him coming back, instead of me. How I'd taken away all he had left after Lookout Mountain—his good name." His eyes burned. In a sidelong glance, he saw June-bug bite her lower lip, while Jacob's right temple was pounding visibly.

"I know it's all my fault," he went on. "Will wouldn't have gone to war if it hadn't been for me. He wanted to stay put and farm. Take himself a pretty wife." He smiled bitterly at the memory of his younger self, so thoughtless and full of vainglory, so blind to the sacrifices his brother was making.

June-bug made a muted, moanlike sound in her throat, but said nothing. Her back was rigidly straight, her skin pale as the untouched snow blanketing the plains for miles around.

"My fault," Wes repeated. "Will was looking to protect me, and he did a good job. Too damned good."

"Oh, Wesley," his mama whispered. Then she came to him, smoothed his hair with one hand. How many times had he secretly yearned to feel her touch again, especially during the days when he was either starving and sweltering in prison, or starving and freezing. "You're our son, and we love you. No matter what you've done. We've got to work it through, that's all."

The legs of Jacob's chair scraped the floor loudly

as he stood up. Wesley rose too; the least he could do was face the man.

"Now, Jacob," June-bug fretted, "don't you go makin' a scene and wakin' up Ben and Sally and their little ones."

Jacob's gaze never left Wes's. Without any warning whatsoever, he brought up his arm and backhanded Wes so hard that he almost fell into the fire.

"You had twenty years," the old man growled. "Twenty years to make peace with the truth. And you left your mother and me to suffer all the while. I don't know that I can forgive you for that." With those words, Jacob turned his back and walked away, passing through the outside door into the snow.

June-bug touched Wes's arm. "He'll come to terms with things in a while, Wesley. You just give him a little time."

He heaved a sigh. "Twenty years, maybe?" he countered grimly. He'd been paying the price for his part in Will's death for a long while, but the debt was never diminished by so much as a whit. "Mama, I'm sorry," he said. "I'm sorry for all of it— sorry Will had to go to war to look after me. Sorry he died—oh, God, you'll never know how sorry I am for that—"

She reached up and cupped his face with both hands. "Hush, now, Wesley. It wasn't your doin', what happened to your brother. And maybe you could have come home sooner than you did, and not done some of those things. But all that's in the past and there ain't nothin' much we can do about it, any of us. We got to go right on." She paused. She reached, with an unsteady hand, for the wanted poster he'd tried to give to Jacob. "It is in the past, isn't it? You're not still on the run?"

He took one of her hands in his and kissed the palm lightly. "I'm not on the run, Mama. As for whether or not I'm wanted, I guess I'll have to ask the marshal about that." He looked toward the door, which was probably still shuddering imperceptibly on its hinges. "Right now, I'm more concerned about you and Daddy. Somehow, I don't think he's out there killing the fatted calf." He tried to smile, but the attempt was a failure. At least he could credit himself with the effort. "I keep thinking I ought to leave—"

"No," she murmured, and shook her head. "I just got you back. I can't lose you again. I *won't*." She paused and took a breath. "As for your daddy, he's just afraid this is all some sort of mistake. That you aren't really back at all." She studied him. "What about Olivia?"

Somehow, he felt that question even more keenly than the force of the blow Jacob had dealt him before storming out of the station, and his jawbone was still reverberating from that. "What about her?"

"She loves you, you derned fool," June-bug said, smiling up at him through another wash of tears. How many tears had she cried, for him and for Will, over the years?

"I love her, too," he admitted, with an ease that surprised him. "But Olivia thinks I'm Will."

"You told her that? That you were Will?"

He shook his head. "No. She just worked it out for herself, after she found the poster. I don't imagine she's going to be able to forgive me, any more than Daddy will. Once she knows the whole truth, she'll realize she's got the wrong brother."

"That's nonsense."

"Will was far the better of the two of us, Mama, and you know that, whether you'll own up to it or not."

"You're not being fair to your brother, tryin' to make him out to be somethin' more than a man. You're placin' a burden on him, even in death." Her voice trembled. "Now, let me hold you in my arms for a moment, Wesley McCaffrey. I've ached to do it, and so has your daddy."

They stood that way, in silence, for a little while, and then June-bug turned briskly away and went to the stove. When he was a boy, she'd always taken refuge in her cooking, when she was trying to make sense of something, and obviously that was one thing that hadn't changed.

"I'll make some coffee. You sit down at one of them tables, Wesley, and get yourself readied up to tell me every single thing that's happened to you since you left home all them years ago."

He chuckled, without humor, and sat. It wasn't until then that he realized he was still wearing his coat and took it off. "That's a powerful lot of telling, Mama."

"I got all the time in the world."

He began to talk then, the memories welling up behind his eyes and at the back of his throat, flowing free all of the sudden, after being locked away for so long.

His mother brought the coffeepot to the table where he sat, brought too a slice of dried apple pie. Then she sat down across from him and listened the way she did everything—with mind, body, and soul.

He told her how it was for him and Will, being in the army, and admitted that he'd oftentimes put on a front, not wanting to confess to his brother that he was homesick, that he was scared, that he wished to God the killing and the dying and the screaming would stop. Once and for all, just stop. Instead, though, he'd acted cocksure, running off at the mouth about how he was going to win a medal for their mama, to make her proud, and head for California when the war was over, to dig for gold. Will had been dead a month before Wes realized that his brother had believed everything he said, and that had torn him up all the more, because all that precious time, the last they would ever share, had been lived as a lie, on his side, at least. Will, he couldn't be tarred with that brush; he'd told the blunt truth all along, and that had taken one hell of a lot more courage than just playing soldier, like Wes had done.

He spoke of the raids he'd made, harassing occupation troops after the war ended, and described his time in the Yankee prison, though not in quite the same way he would have done if he'd been talking to his daddy. There was no need for June-bug to know about the hunger and the filth, the cold of winter and the suffocating heat of summer, the rats shimmying through the fetid straw on the floors.

"I saw Mr. Abraham Lincoln one day," he said, wishing he could say he'd encountered Robert E. Lee instead, or old Jeff Davis. The tall and unmercifully homely man from Illinois had come to the prison one Sunday afternoon and walked through every inch of the place, big hands clasped behind his back, dark, somber eyes missing little. With a half-dozen blue-coats guarding him, the Union president had inspected the conditions and spoken kindly to the prisoners he passed. As he went, he murmured things to a spindly little clerk trotting along beside him, trying to keep up with those stilt-long strides, and the clerk scribbled notes onto a pad of paper. For a while after that, things were better, but the Federals, while not in the same dire straits as the Confederates, were running short on food, medicine, and guns for their own troops, and that meant thin charity for captured Rebels.

He told about the years he'd spent wandering, after he'd gotten back on the straight and narrow, about his unsuccessful attempts to go home. Said how he'd herded cattle on ranches and driven spikes for the railroad, spent time in Mexico, and learned the blacksmith's trade down in Denver. Finally, just about six months before, he'd traveled north to Montana Territory, and heard by chance of Springwater, and the man and woman who ran the stagecoach station there.

June-bug brought him more coffee and another piece of pie, and he kept right on talking. He hadn't figured on it being such a relief, all that confession, but it was as if he'd had a broken bone set, and could now begin to heal.

The sky was pink and gold and Toby was stirring, along with Ben, when he finished. They went about their business, Toby and Ben, and didn't ask any questions. Ben headed out for the mine, just as he did every day, and Toby put on a heavy coat and went to look for Jacob.

"Your daddy and me," June-bug said, when her turn came at last, "we stayed put in Tennessee as long as we could. Then Tommy Collins—you remember him, that little feller with the bad teeth—came home and said he'd seen you and Will fall together, at Chattanooga. We waited some more, all the same, hopin' he might be mistaken. A battle's got to be a mighty confusin' thing, with all that noise and smoke and the like. Then some deserters came through and burned the home place right down to the ground. So your daddy and me, we gathered up what we had left and came out west. We spent some time in Nebraska, and a few years out in Kansas, too, but our feet was itchin', so we lit out again. Got as far as

Choteau, that last time, and heard the stage line was fixin' to put in a way station out here. Course they needed folks to run it, and they hired us on. We long since bought the station for ourselves, o' course. Been here ever since the place was built, goin' on fifteen years ago, now." She sighed, took a sip from her coffee, which must, by then, have grown cold. "More'n once, we wondered if we'd got the worst of the bargain. It was lonely out here, and we had some trouble with the Indians. Then Landry Kildare came and settled his place, with his first wife, Caroline, God rest her soul, and that gave us some company. Not too long after, Big John Keating and his partner, Scully Wainwright, staked themselves a claim to some ranch land and started bringin' cattle up from Texas and Colorado." She laughed. "Seemed like a regular party, then. Trey Hargreaves showed up, too, 'bout that time, but he didn't socialize much in those days. He's had himself a hard life, Trey has, however fancified it seems now—he was a different man entirely afore he took up with Rachel."

Sunlight filled the room, and June-bug extinguished the lamps.

Toby came back inside, stamping the snow off his feet on the rug in front of the door and slanting narrow looks in Wes's direction. No doubt Jacob had told him all about the prodigal, and it was plain that he shared his adoptive father's sentiments. *You still here?* his glance asked, even though he didn't say a word out loud.

Ben's wife, Sally, appeared, and then the little girls, chattering like birds about the pageant scheduled for Christmas Eve. The point of their conversation seemed to be the greater likelihood of St. Nicholas finding them after all, what with the Nativity program surely drawing attention far and wide.

Wes smiled to himself, and wondered if Jamie was thinking along similar lines.

"I'd best go, Mama," he said, in good time, and got to his feet. He'd probably be shown the road at the mine, late as he was, but he meant to show up, all the same.

She stood and rose on tiptoe to kiss him on the cheek. "You been runnin' for a long time, Wes. Time you planted your feet someplace and built yourself a life. Springwater's as good a place for that as any, and Miss Olivia's as good a woman as you'll find anywhere on God's earth."

He smiled, placed a responding kiss on her forehead. "I'll keep that in mind," he promised. A few moments later, he collected his horse from the barn without encountering Jacob—no accident, he figured—and headed back to the rooming house.

Olivia wasn't at home; no doubt, she'd taken Jamie to school. He changed into his work clothes and rode out to the mine. Instead of paying him off and showing him the road, however, old Smiley, the foreman, sent him right down into the pit.

Ben was already there, wielding his pickax fit to chip his way right through to China, and a grin streaked across his dirt-blackened face when he saw Wes. "Well, then," he said, "I don't suppose you want to tell me what you were doing at the station in the middle of the night?"

Wes reached for an ax of his own. "They're my folks," he said. It felt good to be Wesley J. McCaffrey again; whatever happened, he had his right name back. Telling the truth had lifted a weight off his spirit, but he still wasn't sure whether he wanted to laugh or weep. Both, maybe.

Ben looked downright amazed. "But their boys were killed, except for Toby of course—"

"My brother Will was killed at Lookout Mountain," Wes said. He'd established a rhythm with the ax, and that was soothing, in an odd sort of way, even though it made the muscles in his arms, shoulders and chest burn like they'd been doused in kerosene and set afire.

Ben remembered that he was there to work and began swinging again. "I'll be," he marveled. "All this time, they thought you were six feet under. They must be about the happiest folks drawin' breath this morning."

Wes didn't even slow down. "My mama is real pleased. My daddy, on the other hand, takes a whole different view."

"How can that be? You're his son."

"Yeah, the one who was always in trouble. If Daddy had been given the choice, Will would be the one standing here right now, not me."

Ben spat. "That's pure foolishness. Jacob isn't

the sort of man to favor one son over another. If he's out of sorts right now, it's just because he's had himself a shock."

Out of sorts, Wes thought, and smiled a little. He could still feel the blow Jacob had struck him back there at the Springwater Station; it had all but loosened his teeth, and his ears probably wouldn't stop ringing for a week. Not that he blamed the old man; he'd probably have done the same thing, in his place.

"You still leaving town?" Ben persisted.

A muscle tightened in Wes's jaw. "Depends," he said, thinking of Olivia.

"Well, if that doesn't beat everything," the other man said, and flung down his pickax. It rang against the bedrock beneath their feet. "Here you've got yourself a fine family, and a good woman to boot, and you'd rather hit the trail. That's just downright ungrateful, if you ask me."

"I didn't ask you," Wes pointed out.

Ben was unfazed. "What are you punishing yourself for, Jack?" he demanded.

"Name's Wes," Wes answered. "Wesley J. McCaffrey. The J stands for Jacob. That was my brother's middle name, too. We were twins."

Ben just stood there, staring at him, and Wes figured the other man must have thought his partner had gone loco from the darkness and the cold and constant clash of steel and stone. He had no way of knowing, poor Ben, that he'd struck his mark, dead-center. Wes *had* banished himself to wander the earth; the loneliness, the longing, all of it was penance for living when he should have died. A just penance, into the bargain.

"Shut up and work, Ben," he said. "You're not being paid to gawk at me."

Ben didn't move. "I ought to slug you one," he said.

Wes grinned. One whole side of his face ought to be good and swollen up pretty soon. "Someone beat you to it," he replied.

Priscilla Turnbull arrived that very day, on the afternoon stagecoach, and took a room at the Springwater Station. It seemed to her that there was entirely too much activity in that place, folks running hither and yon, children coming and going with no respect for their elders or for civility itself, but she had to stay someplace.

Miss Turnbull, forty-seven and relatively comfortable, if not wealthy, didn't plan to spend any more time in that backwoods town than it would take to find and collect her feather-brained sister's ragamuffin child. Heaven only knew what name the little heathen was going by—she'd been christened Martha Sue Swain at birth, but she wouldn't answer to that. Oh, no. That was too solid a name, too plain and practical. Martha Sue had once called herself Isabelle for an entire year, according to Julia, and since then, she'd gone through a number of other monikers as well, just appropriating Jane or Mary or Elizabeth or whatever took her fancy. She was a liar, all right, and now that she'd spent six months with her no-good stepfather, Axel Carruthers, probably a thief as well—but what could one expect? Why, that child could stand flat-footed and lie to the Angel Gabriel himself without raising a hair.

Not that it was Martha Sue's fault, entirely. Julia hadn't looked after her; had dragged her from place to place and man to man, never even letting her get settled in a proper school, never mind a Sunday School class.

Well, it was time and past that someone took the poor, ignorant little creature in hand. Julia was long gone, having taken up with yet another smooth-talking man, but she'd come to Priscilla before she left Choteau, all weepy and remorseful, saying she'd given Martha Sue to Axel—she just couldn't look after her any longer, she'd snuffled—and now she wished she hadn't. Quite by accident, through the offices of a talkative peddler, Julia had learned that her remarkably resourceful young daughter had found her way to a place called Springwater, though whether Axel was still around she could not—or would not—say. Martha Sue was, according to the peddler, who traveled down that way regularly, living the high life in some spinster's big house.

Priscilla would put an end to that nonsense, that was for certain. Not that she really wanted to be bothered with a child, especially a difficult one like her niece. Her last effort to provide a home for

Martha Sue had been disastrous. Her gout was getting worse by the day and, besides, she had her clubs, her friends, and her needlework, and, in the summer, her rose garden. Perhaps it would be best for all concerned if she simply took Martha Sue straight on from there to Denver, or even San Francisco, and enrolled her in the strictest boarding school she could find. A product of such institutions herself, Priscilla knew them to be efficiently run, though she was at a loss to explain the way Julia had turned out, given that they'd been educated together. She liked to remind herself, whenever Julia came to mind, that they were actually *half* sisters; Papa had taken Julia's mother to wife barely six months after Priscilla's own beloved *Maman* was buried.

Lumbering down the middle of Springwater's rutted main street, parasol in hand, Priscilla guided her thoughts firmly in another direction. Best to concentrate on the business at hand. Hadn't Papa always said so?

The man in the telegraph office pointed out the spinster's house, not that she could have missed it. Martha Sue had feathered herself quite a nest this time.

In the side yard, chickens squawked and pecked and ruffled their wings. Imagine. A grand house like that, with *chickens* wandering about loose, ranging over the grounds as if they were peacocks.

She had not arrived a moment too soon.

Priscilla mounted creaking front steps, stomped

across the porch, and gave the bell a vigorous twist. When no one came, she knocked briskly and called out, "Halloo! Halloo!"

A small hand pushed aside the lace curtain covering the oval window in the front door, and Martha Sue's urchin face peered out at her.

"Martha Sue Swain," she cried, "you let me in, this instant!"

Martha Sue gave a little shriek, audible even through the door, and then turned around and fled. Priscilla heard retreating footsteps, and her frustration mounted. She began to knock again, this time with true industry.

She almost fell into the house when the door was suddenly opened, and a tall, slender woman stood before her. With her bountiful, reddish-brown hair and dark eyes, this person was certainly not Priscilla's idea of a spinster. But then, she did not feel that the word described her adequately, either. Most of her friends and acquaintances, she was quite sure, would readily agree.

"Yes?" the woman asked coolly. She was probably a hussy, Priscilla decided. Hair that color was a sure sign of an unruly nature. And this was a rooming house, after all, she'd learned that at the stagecoach station, and what were rooming houses if not havens of debauchery and sin?

After all, what *decent* woman would be willing to take in strangers for money?

Priscilla gave the porch floor an eloquent little thump with the handle of her parasol. It was a constant challenge to be a lady in this godforsaken wilderness, but she was nothing if not persistent. "My name," she said, "is Miss Priscilla Turnbull. I am Martha Sue's aunt, and I have come to take her home."

The woman's otherwise smooth brow crinkled slightly. "Martha Sue?" she asked.

Priscilla nodded, taking a certain satisfaction in knowing something the rooming house woman so obviously didn't. "No doubt she's given you another name, and told a pack of wild stories into the bargain," she said. "Let me assure you, Miss—er—"

"Darling," came the reluctant response. "Olivia Darling. Won't you—won't you come in?"

It was, Priscilla thought, about time the invitation was put forward. Of course, these ill-mannered bumpkins might be expected to leave a guest standing on the veranda to catch her death. "Let me assure you, Miss Darling," she repeated, bustling into a spacious and airy entryway, "you will find little or no truth in anything Martha Sue says."

Miss Darling was pale, a fact that secretly pleased Priscilla. "Please—sit down, here in the parlor, by the fire, and I'll make tea."

Priscilla would have refused, if she hadn't been so enervated by her grueling travels. The child was out to run her ragged, that was plain. "Thank you," she said, and did not trouble herself to remove her cloak.

Miss Darling was gone a long while, longer by

far than it should have taken to brew a pot of tea, and by the time she returned, her entire countenance had altered. Nervous and startled before, she now seemed quietly determined, and quite unruffled by the news that she was harboring an incorrigible miscreant.

"Where," Priscilla asked pointedly, "if I may ask, is my niece?"

Miss Darling smiled. "She's hiding under her bed," she answered, "and vows she won't come out until you've gone away for good." She paused. "Will you take sugar in your tea? Milk, perhaps?"

CHAPTER
🌿 13 🌿

MISS PRISCILLA TURNBULL was, to Olivia, the embodiment of her late Aunt Eloise, and the very idea of turning a child over to the woman—especially when that child was her Jamie—was quite beyond bearing. Sitting there in her fancy parlor, with a new snow beginning to dust the ground, Olivia listened for the sound of Jack's footsteps in the kitchen with one ear, and to Miss Turnbull's rantings with the other.

The old tyrant didn't want Jamie—or Martha Sue, or whatever her true name was—any more than Aunt Eloise had wanted her, Olivia knew, but the matter had to be handled delicately all the same. If Miss Turnbull were to get her back up, no argument, however reasonable, would sway her.

In the distance, the back door opened and closed. Olivia's heart lifted.

"Miss Turnbull," she said, when an opening came. "I cannot believe that a woman of your means and caliber has nothing better to do than raise a young child."

The flattery struck home, as flattery so often does, human beings being what they are. The visitor lost some, if by no means all, of her pomposity, and fluttered one hand in front of her round face, as though to rouse herself from a swoon. "One does one's duty," she said, finally. It was precisely what Aunt Eloise would have said, *had* said, a thousand times.

Jack was moving about in the kitchen, and Olivia imagined him hanging up his coat, washing or getting ready for one of his pantry baths, pouring himself a cup of the coffee leftover from breakfast. Each time he came back, instead of leaving Springwater forever, she counted it as a small victory.

"Well, yes," Olivia agreed cautiously. "I myself was raised by an aunt. Poor dear. She sacrificed so much to give me a proper start in the world." *And never let me hear the end of it until they closed the lid on her coffin.* "I'm sure if she'd had any alternative—"

Miss Turnbull sighed heavily. She was a big woman, clad in fusty brown sateen and overlapping the sides of her chair. "I must admit that I doubt my own ability to cope with Martha Sue, being that she's so difficult," she said, watching the fire popping on the grate with a slight frown. "No doubt, a boarding school is the place for her."

Olivia was secretly horrified; such places were so

often loveless and cold, and Jamie would surely wilt in an environment like that. Still, she held her tongue long enough to regain her composure. "I would be happy to adopt Jamie," she said, quietly and carefully.

"Is that what she calls herself now?" Miss Turnbull asked, after a hefty *harumph*. "A boy's name, no less. Next she'll be going by 'Albert' or 'John.' I declare, that girl will be the finish of me one of these days."

Olivia waited. She felt like a tightrope walker; one false step and she would plummet to the earth and fracture the bones of her very soul.

"All the same," the older woman went on, following more glum reflection, "I am accountable for my niece, Miss—Darling. I should not be able to live with myself if I left my sister's child in the care of a—pardon me—a boardinghouse woman."

She said the words "boardinghouse woman" as though the occupation were comparable to prostitution or thievery. Olivia squared her shoulders and opened her mouth to speak, but before she could get a word out, Jack spoke from behind her.

"Miss Olivia will be a respectable married lady pretty soon, if I have anything to say about it," he announced, and when Olivia whirled to look at him, she saw a broad grin spreading across his just-scrubbed face, spectacular as dawn rising over a mountain range. "I'd be proud to have her for my wife."

Olivia's face went hot with surprise, and something much more private, and she glared, but Jack's expression remained mischievous. He looked like a winsome schoolboy standing there in the parlor doorway, instead of an erstwhile outlaw, headed in the general direction of forty.

"And who," Miss Turnbull intoned, bristling with disapproval and yet plainly charmed, "might you be?"

Jack crossed the room and put out one hand, at the same time executing a slight but nonetheless princely bow before Miss Turnbull's chair. "Wesley J. McCaffrey," he said. "The J stands for Jacob."

Wesley McCaffrey? Not Will?

Olivia's mouth dropped open. Between Jamie, who was really Martha Sue, and Jack McLaughlin, who wasn't Jack McLaughlin at all, she was getting more confused with every passing moment.

When Miss Turnbull gave Jack—*Wesley*—her hand, he bent his head and kissed it lightly. When he released his hold, long moments later, there was a suave reluctance in the move that caused Olivia a pang of envy and made her want to kick him for it.

Miss Turnbull, on the other hand, batted her eyes in a fashion that could only be called coquettish, and laid the splayed fingers of one hand to her bosom. "My goodness," she said.

"My goodness indeed," added Olivia, with a tart note in her voice. How dare he bandy about the subject of marriage? It was a sacred matter.

Wesley gave her a sidelong, teasing glance. The intimacy in that look made things twist and spill and tug deep within Olivia, and only by the greatest discipline did she avoid squirming in her chair. "We can provide a fine home for the little girl, can't we, dearest?"

Olivia swallowed. Had the man lost his mind? Miss Turnbull would never sign her niece away to strangers, just because they were going to get married—would she? Besides, they *weren't* getting married.

Were they?

"Yes," she agreed finally. "*Dearest.*"

His blue eyes were full of laughter; he knew *exactly* what he was about, of course, although she was still in the dark. "Well," he said, "I'd better excuse myself. I'm not fit for the company of ladies, as you can see." Ruefully, he indicated his grimy clothes, and once again there was something endearing in the gesture, something reminiscent of a small boy who has tried very hard to be good and still managed to ruin his Sunday best.

"I'll need some time to think about this," Miss Turnbull fluttered.

You will? Olivia thought dryly. *Just imagine how the "bride" feels.*

"All the more opportunity for us to enjoy your company," this stranger, this Wesley McCaffrey, said, in parting.

It took all the self-control Olivia possessed to keep from bolting to her feet and dashing after him, demanding an explanation for the outrageous things he'd said.

When Wesley was gone, and only then, Miss Turnbull got to her feet. "A night's rest will clear my mind," she said, with a philosophical sigh.

I wish I could say the same, Olivia thought. She probably wouldn't sleep a wink. Had Jack— Wesley—meant what he'd said, about making her his wife? Did she truly *want* to exchange vows with him?

He'd left the house that morning as Jack McLaughlin, and come back with another name entirely. Did that mean he'd finally gone to Jacob and June-bug and told them who he was?

Olivia practically shoved Miss Turnbull out the front door, she was so anxious to find her boarder and pepper him with questions.

Miss Turnbull shook a gloved, sausagelike finger under Olivia's nose. "This matter is by no means decided," she warned. "*Saying* one's about to be married and actually going through with the ceremony are two very different things."

Don't I know it, Olivia thought, and nodded. "I understand," she said, in the sweetest tone she could manage. Then, after practically slamming the door in Priscilla Turnbull's face, she turned and hurried through the house to the kitchen.

She must see Jack. No, not Jack. *Wesley*.

She mounted the rear stairway and barreled down the corridor, intending to beat down his door if she had to, and insist on an accounting. On the way, however, she passed Jamie's room and saw him sitting cross-legged on the floor, with a checker game set up in front of him. A small hand reached out from under the bed to jump three of his men and deftly remove them from the board.

He looked at Olivia and winked.

Gazing back at him, Olivia thought what a remarkable paradox he represented; he was, at one and the same time, a total stranger and the only person in the world she felt she truly knew. She leaned one shoulder against the doorjamb and folded her arms, taking in the two people she loved, cherishing them in her heart.

Jack and Jamie.

Wesley and Martha Sue.

Her head felt light. Suddenly, her life was brimming with beloved strangers.

"So," Wesley was saying, "if I win, you'll come out of there, right?"

Jamie took more pieces off the board. "You don't really think you're going to beat me, do you?" she asked, in a tolerant tone.

He laughed. "You can't stay under there forever, you know. Christmas is coming for one thing. Last I heard, you were in line for a pair of cheesecloth wings with a tinsel fringe and scheduled to sing a solo. You planning to let all these good people down?"

"I ain't comin' out until *she's* gone."

" 'She' being your aunt," he mused, studying the board, which looked hopeless even from where Olivia stood, and she was certainly no authority on the game.

"Old witch," Jamie said.

"Now is that any way to talk about your own kith and kin?"

"She ain't my kin. You and Miss Olivia are."

Olivia's eyes brimmed with tears. It was a pretty dream, but a fragile one. Mr. McCaffrey had made a show of saying they'd be married soon, but he hadn't troubled himself even to consult her. Either he'd been teasing, she figured, or he'd just wanted to have some fun with Miss Priscilla Turnbull.

"According to her," Wesley said, as though the child hadn't spoken, "you aren't called Jamie at all. She says your name is Martha Sue."

"She don't know nothin'."

"Until you get your grammar straightened out, you shouldn't go around making statements like that. Is your name Martha Sue or not?"

"Is your name Jack, or not?" the little girl countered. Maybe it was true that kids just knew things like that somehow, through some extra, soon-lost sense.

He sighed. She had him there. "Nope," he confessed. "My mama and daddy called me Wesley."

"Well, I didn't have a daddy, and my mama couldn't think what to call me, so Miss Priss had me christened 'Martha Sue.'" She made a rude noise to show what she thought of that. "For Pete's sake. Anybody lookin' at me can tell I ain't a Martha Sue."

Wesley tilted his head, in order to see under the bed, and studied her thoughtfully. Olivia might have faded into the woodwork, for all the attention either of them paid her. She didn't mind, though, because in spite of everything, all the uncertainties, all the complications, she was perfectly happy in that moment.

"Well," he answered, after due consideration, "I guess that's true. I'd have pegged you for a Susan, myself. Or maybe a Margaret. But a Martha Sue? Not in a hundred years."

"I like Margaret," Jamie allowed. "If I were your little girl, would I be Margaret McLaughlin?"

Olivia swallowed hard.

"No," Wesley answered, "you'd be Margaret McCaffrey."

Olivia squeezed her eyes shut. *Please—don't give her false hopes. Or me.*

"One thing, though," he continued. "If you were going to be my daughter, you'd have to pick one name and stick with it." He glanced at Olivia again. "Otherwise, I might think you didn't really mean to stay around."

"McCaffrey?" asked Jamie/Martha Sue/Margaret. "You related to Miss June-bug and Jacob?"

He nodded. "They're my mama and daddy."

"You're a grown man, and you call them that? Mama and Daddy?"

He grinned. "Yep. It's something we do down South. That's where I'm from—Tennessee."

"You ain't goin' back there, are you? To Tennessee?"

Again, his gaze strayed to Olivia's face. "That

depends," he said. Then, in a master stroke, he picked up one of his few remaining men and jumped every single one of Jamie's. "I win. Come on out."

Jamie scooched backward, like a little hermit crab retreating into its shell. Her small voice echoed from beneath the mattress. "No."

"Now, that isn't fair," Wesley said reasonably, and without petulance. "When I lose at checkers, I always cover my bets."

"I didn't make no bet," came the stalwart response, "and I'm stayin' right where I am until *she's* gone."

Wesley sighed again, resigned. "All right, then," he said, gathering up the pieces and the game board, then getting to his feet. "We'll miss you at supper."

With that, he walked across the room, took Olivia gently by the elbow, and squired her out of the room with him, along the corridor, and down the back stairs.

"What am I going to do?" she whispered, in the safety of the kitchen. Snow was lining the lower edges of the windowpanes over the sink and practically blotting out the view beyond.

"About Jamie?" He shrugged. "Just wait. She'll come out when she gets too hungry or needs to use the privy."

"That isn't what I meant," Olivia replied, perhaps a bit snappishly. Her nerves were stretched to their limits; she, who had always governed her emotions so well, was spinning like a windmill run amok. "I know women like Priscilla Turnbull—my own aunt was just the same sort of person. All that mattered to her was being right. Not being kind. Not being fair. Just being *right*."

Wesley took her shoulders lightly in his hands. "I think we're talking about you now, aren't we, and not Jamie?"

She sidestepped the question, countering with one of her own. "Are you going to start calling yourself something else, just when I get used to your being Wesley instead of Jack?"

He smiled, kissed the tip of her nose. If Miss Turnbull were to see them spooning that way, it would probably be the end of Olivia's hopes of keeping the child, but she couldn't make herself pull back. Besides, it seemed unlikely that the woman would leave the warmth of the station to venture out into a rising snowstorm.

"Wesley is my name," he said. "I won't be changing it. My brother called me Wes, and so did my daddy, back when he was still speaking to me, that is. To Mama, the name she wrote in the family Bible is the name I ought to go by."

Olivia bit down hard on her lower lip. "Your father—he's angry?"

Wes nodded. "Madder'n a rooster with one foot stuck in a tar pit," he said. "And I can't say I blame him." He explained about using Will's name during the raiding, and told her he'd already been to see the marshal, who'd sent some wires back East, looking into the matter. "To Daddy's way of think-ing," he went on, while Olivia's head was still spin-ning, "I should have come right home when the war was through and told them both that Will was dead—because of me—but I just couldn't make myself do it." In that moment, there was a look of such ineffable sadness in his eyes that Olivia despaired of him. Her heart would be broken if he left; his had been shattered long, long ago.

He gave a great, shuddering sigh and leaned for-ward a little to rest his forehead against hers.

She held him. "Wesley, Jacob's a good man, but he's had a shock. He'll come around."

"Maybe," he replied. He sounded doubtful, though. "It must be like losing Will all over again, having me show up out of nowhere."

She reached up and ran a tentative fingertip across his mouth, much as he had done, once before, when he'd been about to kiss her. "Losing Will, yes," she agreed. "But *finding* you. Give him a little time, Wes. He's your father."

"I guess I owe him that much," he said. "On the other hand, something inside me keeps saying that no good can come of my staying on here—"

"So," she said, trying to speak lightly, "you were only dallying with my emotions when you told Miss Turnbull we were about to be married."

He chuckled. "Well, no, I wasn't dallying, Miss Olivia. I'd marry you in a moment, if you'd have me."

She was completely confused, and could no

longer pretend that the subject was of anything other than the most vital importance to her. "Why?" she asked seriously. It was too much to hope for, that he'd say he loved her, but she had to know.

"Why would you have me?" he teased. "Or why would I marry you?"

She prodded his chest once, with the heel of her palm.

He laughed and gave her a leisurely kiss that probably sealed her fate forever, all on its own. "Because I think I love you," he said, long, delicious moments later, when she was still reeling.

"You *think* you love me?"

He shrugged. "I've never been in love before," he said. "I'm not exactly an authority on the subject."

"Well," she said, "I've never been in love before, either. Maybe we're both mistaken."

He kissed her again. "And maybe not."

She drew back, while she could still breathe, while she still possessed a modicum of good sense. "If you think you can arrange a two-dollar wedding, have your way with me, and then move on when your feet start itching, Wesley McCaffrey, you're sorely mistaken."

He raised both eyebrows, clearly amused. "Oh? And what do you mean to do if I take to the trail, darling Olivia Darling?"

"Set Marshal Spencer on you," she said, but she was bluffing and they both knew it. She must think carefully now, for if he decided to leave her later on, of course she would not be able to stop him. She would be a long time, maybe forever, getting over the loss.

"As long as it isn't the Ladies' Quilting Society," he teased.

She gazed up at him, knowing her heart was showing in her eyes, unable to help revealing the innermost landscape of her very soul. "Don't marry me," she said, "not if you're going to turn around and leave. That—that would be worse than never knowing you at all."

"If I hitch up with you," he replied, utterly serious now, "I'll stay by your side until the day they put me in the ground. Now, Miss Olivia, what's your answer?"

She laid her forehead to his shoulder, and her reply, though muffled by the fabric of his shirt and the warm, solid flesh beneath, was clearly audible. "I'll ask the preacher to marry us as soon as he can."

"I want my father to do that," Wesley said firmly.

Looking up at him, she nodded. "When?"

"Now?"

She laughed and shook her head. "No, Wesley, not *now*. After Christmas, when Miss Turnbull is gone and the pageant is over. I won't be able to think straight until then."

"I won't either," Wesley agreed, "but for different reasons, I believe."

She blushed, and he let out a joyous whoop, all

of the sudden, grabbed her around the waist, and hoisted her high in the air, just as if she weighed nothing at all.

The next morning, Miss Priscilla Turnbull became Olivia's second boarder, saying she could not tolerate the constant distractions over at that stagecoach station for one more moment. Olivia wasn't fooled—Miss Turnbull wanted a closer look at the inner workings of the household where she might agree to leave her niece forever. From that standpoint, it seemed like a reasonable thing to do, and Olivia was determined that the woman's impression would be a positive one.

On the other hand, however, Miss Turnbull made a very demanding tenant.

She wanted to dine formally, not in the kitchen, but at the long table, set with fancy silver and china. She stayed in bed until ten every morning, at least, and then thumped on the floor with the handle of her parasol, her way of letting it be known that she wanted her breakfast tray brought forthwith. If her tea was not brewed to the exact strength she preferred, she would insist that it be made over again.

Olivia, busy with the pageant and an ever more difficult Jamie, called upon all her forbearance to avoid telling the old curmudgeon to either look after herself or move in with the chickens. Jamie came out from under the bed, by necessity, but gave her dreaded aunt the widest possible berth.

When she wasn't at school, or at the church practicing for the pageant, Jamie wouldn't even enter the same room with the woman she continued to refer to as "Miss Priss." Olivia was amused by the title, for it suited, but of course she dared not show it lest she encourage the child to treat her elders with disrespect.

Wes continued to work at the mine, and word of his true heritage spread like wildfire through the town. Jacob still hadn't softened any toward his son, though oftentimes Wes visited the Springwater Station after his shift ended, eating supper there now and again, and sometimes even taking a bath. Olivia understood, certainly, but she also missed him dreadfully. She had not known how much his presence truly meant to her, and this glimpse of what it would mean to lose him was sobering indeed. In a way, she could understand Jacob's reluctance to welcome his son home to his heart. More than anger, more than unforgiveness, she suspected, Jacob felt simple fear. By caring, he risked having to endure an incomprehensible degree of pain all over again.

Still, she and June-bug both hoped that the special peace of Christmas would draw father and son back together, once and for all.

Day after day, Olivia pressed on, cooking, cleaning, waiting on Miss Turnbull, conducting the ever more frantic pageant practices over at the church. Why, if Jamie hadn't been faithful about feeding the chickens night and morning, the poor contentious creatures would probably have starved to death.

Finally, finally, it was December 24, a clear, cold, blue-skied morning, spangled with golden light. Wes went to the mine early, whistling under his breath.

Last-minute preparations for the much-anticipated program would take up most of Olivia's day, and when the last hymn had been sung, when the candles had been put out and the shepherds and angels and Wise Men had gone home to their beds, Wes and Olivia planned to decorate the fragrant blue spruce hidden inside the woodshed. Olivia had bought a set of watercolors and a precious packet of paper for Jamie, and a new woolen shirt for Wesley, and intended to tuck the gifts amid the tree branches when everyone else was asleep.

She had always dreaded Christmas, a time that merely seemed to underscore the fact that she was alone, but this year was different. She had not only enjoyed looking forward to the pageant, she would always have the memory of it to warm her heart. She had friends, true ones, at long last, and, best of all, she had Jamie and Wesley. After so many years of loneliness and disappointment, she was actually going to be married.

She hummed under her breath as she supervised the installation of the community tree, taking a certain spiteful pleasure in telling Trey Hargreaves and Gage Calloway that it was leaning too far to the right, and then too far to the left, and then just a wee bit toward the front. The branches filled the small church with a luscious, festive scent, though, and the manger looked as fine as if it were part of some big-city production. Why, it even had straw, and though the pastor had drawn the line at bringing a real cow and donkey into the church, Miranda and Landry Kildare's two-week-old daughter, Nell, was to play the baby Jesus. The costumes were ready, neatly stitched by proud mothers in a friendly competition to outdo each other, and the little side room was already overflowing with cookies, cakes, and pies. Even Miss Turnbull had contributed to the cause by purchasing what looked like Cornucopia's entire stock of peppermint candy as a treat for the children.

It was all going to be perfect.

Emma Hargreaves hurried into the church at midmorning, pursued by an icy wind. Everyone expected more snow before nightfall. "I've got the foil stars and the candles," she cried, delighted. Her lovely face was flushed with excitement.

"Excellent," Olivia said, smiling. She was especially fond of Emma, who had proved to be even more helpful than expected.

"Mind you don't set the place on fire," Trey Hargreaves told his daughter, pulling on his coat as he spoke. Mr. Calloway had already fled, probably afraid that Olivia would decide the tree required more straightening.

"Oh, Papa," Emma said, with loving disdain.

Olivia laughed.

And in the next instant, the next heartbeat, it happened. A terrible rumbling sound rolled deep beneath the earth, shaking the floor and rattling the windows. A thunderous crash followed. For a moment, everyone was frozen in place.

Trey was the first to speak. "God in heaven," he rasped, bolting for the door, "the mine!"

CHAPTER

✖ 14 ✖

IT SEEMED TO Wes that an eternity yawned between the first roaring tremor undulating through the floor and walls of the mine and the collapse of the rafters overhead, although surely no more than a few moments could have passed. He lay still beneath a framework of fallen timbers, mentally reviewing the various parts of his anatomy until he was relatively sure everything was accounted for. That process, like the disaster itself, seemed to span an unreasonably long while.

"McLaughlin?" The voice, weak though it was, was at least proof that he wasn't alone in the vast pit that would probably become his grave. "You there?"

"Yup," Wes ground out. It hurt to talk, though he didn't think he'd broken any bones or managed to get himself punctured anyplace. Under the circumstances, he supposed he could overlook Ben's failure to address him by his given name. After all, they'd just been discussing the matter of his being a McCaffrey before the universe came down on their heads; Ben hadn't had much of a chance to get used to it. "You all right?"

"I think so," Ben said, but he sounded doubtful. "Lordy, what if we don't get out of here?"

Wes guessed by listening that his friend was somewhere under the same pile of beams and rafters, though of course it was hard to be sure. The darkness was so complete that they might have been tucked into the devil's hip pocket. "We'll get out," he said, though he wasn't at all convinced of the fact himself. The words had already left his mouth long before he could have taken their proper measure in his slow-moving mind.

"Tonight's Christmas Eve," Ben fretted.

Wes thought of Olivia, and of Jamie, and of his mother and father. A time or two in his life, he'd drunk himself stupid just to get past Christmas. Now, a sense of overwhelming sorrow swept over him, and just then those feelings seemed far more likely to crush him than the tons of earth and wood and rock creaking above their heads.

Damn, but he'd been a fool. If he'd had a lick of sense, he'd have dragged Olivia in front of a preacher days ago, when he first realized how deeply he cared for her. He would have found a way through his own stubbornness and pride, gotten his daddy by the shirt collar if necessary, and made him *listen*, made him understand. Made that cussed old man realize that he, too, had loved

Will—as much as anybody in the family, and maybe more. He'd been young and bullheaded and maybe even cowardly, all those years ago, when he went off to war and dragged his brother along with him, and he'd done some stupid things after that, too, but he'd paid for his mistakes time after time. Nobody knew better than he did that Will would probably still be alive, with a wife and a flock of kids, if it hadn't been for him.

I'm sorry, Daddy, he thought. *I'm so sorry.*

His father wasn't and had never been unreasonable. A man-to-man, honest-to-God apology would have been enough for Jacob; Wes knew that now. Now, when it was very likely too late to mend the breach between them.

A thousand times over the course of his life, Wes had wished he could go back to that day in September of 1863 and die in Will's place. Although he'd never put a gun to his head, he'd tempted death often enough, and denied himself the comforts of a home, friends, and a family.

Well, now it seemed the hour of reckoning had finally arrived. Will was probably waiting over on the other side of the beyond, ready to give him what-for and cuff his ears, provided they allowed such as that over yonder.

"You suppose we ought to holler for help?" Ben asked.

Wes was grateful for the distraction; it jerked him back from his woolgathering. "I reckon this place is about like a house of cards just now," he said, after some thought. Maybe his brain wasn't working as fast as it generally did, but his emotions were practically swamping him. If he'd been alone, he might have broken down and wept, though not because he was most likely about to meet his Maker and be forced to give an accounting for all his many sins. No, any tears he'd shed would be ones of regret for all the time he'd wasted, exiling himself the way he had. "I guess we ought to hold our peace for a while. They'll get us out of here if they can."

"I had a right pretty doll put by, over at the general store, for my Daisy and Rose to share," Ben went on. "A flower vase for Sally, too, made out of real china. You know, so she'd get a homey feeling whenever she looked at it. First Christmas since we got married that there's been a penny to spare for anything but seeds and grub and here I am, twenty feet underground."

Wes's eyes stung; he was glad his friend couldn't see his face. He'd done some present-buying himself, as it happened, bought a fancy silk bonnet for Olivia, a wooden sleigh for Jamie. A music box for his mama, and a pipe for the old man. For the next little while, he could hardly catch his breath, he wanted to be out of there so bad.

Ben went on, which was a good thing, given the state Wes was in. "They've all been looking forward to that Christmas pageant something fierce, you know. You suppose they'll go ahead with it, with all of us down here?"

Wes could see Olivia in the forefront of his mind, plain as day, standing up straight like she always did, her chin high and her cheeks pink with conviction. "Oh, yes," he answered, with a slight smile. "They'll go ahead all right."

"Good," Ben murmured, and he really did sound relieved.

"Hullo?" called Smiley Beckett, the foreman, from somewhere fairly close by. "McLaughlin? Is that you runnin' off at the mouth?"

"Yep," Wes answered. "Williams is here, too. You still smilin', Smiley?"

The other man laughed—it was a tired but long-standing joke in the mine, to josh the foreman about his name—and responded, "So far as I know, but I ain't so sure about old Gus, here. He's breathin', but it don't sound right to me. Rattly like."

Over the next twenty minutes or so, other voices came out of the darkness, scared and skittish voices, filled, nonetheless, with the joy of still being alive. Wes kept count, and worked out that there were only two people missing, an old man who'd complained of his rheumatism acting up, back at the beginning of the shift, and a half-grown boy who served as a sort of go-between, moving constantly up and down the shaft, shinnying like a monkey between the darkness and the light.

He prayed they were both safe aboveground.

It was Ben who first heard the sounds from overhead, faint and rhythmic, almost like music. "Listen," he hissed.

Wes strained his ears, which, like his mouth and his eyes, were full of dirt. Sure enough, he caught the vague *chings* and *clinks* of pickaxes and shovels. Rescuers. No doubt Jacob was up there, digging with the best of them. Trey Hargreaves, too, and every cowboy and drifter in the Brimstone Saloon. Gage Calloway, Landry Kildare, the whole outfit would turn out, because Springwater was that sort of town. A lot of the women would be there, too, working just as hard, contributing whatever they could to the effort.

He closed his eyes and tried to believe they'd get through before the air supply ran out, before the rest of the mine shaft gave way and silenced them all forever.

Somewhere, in the bleak, icy darkness, a man began to sing.

Silent night, holy night . . . all is calm . . . all is bright . . .

One by one, the others joined in, the voices quiet, the familiar words forming an invisible chain that linked them all together, like shipwreck survivors clinging to the same lifeline.

A light snow was drifting down as the townspeople began their frantic effort to reach the men entombed far, far beneath the ground. Olivia had run half the two miles to the mine before someone driving a wagon had stopped to pick her up, and the moment she arrived, she grabbed one of the shovels Cornucopia had sent over from the general store and began to dig wildly.

Jacob McCaffrey laid a strong hand on her arm, and when she looked up into his craggy face, she saw a despair to match her own. "He's down there, ain't he?"

Olivia's throat constricted and went dry as dirt. Sinking her teeth into her lower lip, she nodded.

Just then, June-bug came riding through the crowd, her hair trailing down her back. Like Olivia, she hadn't taken the time to put on a cloak. Reaching them, she jumped down off the back of an ancient white mule, and gripped her husband by the lapels of his plain black work coat.

"*Wesley?*" she demanded of her husband, ferocious as a she-cat seeking a lost cub. When Jacob didn't answer right away, but only moved his lips, she gave him a hard shake. "You!" she shouted. "You wouldn't forgive him—you wouldn't even *try* to understand—and now he could die believin'—"

Jacob bore the onslaught in silence, holding his head high and staring off into the distance. Olivia knew he was seeing his sons in his mind's eye, not just Will, not just Wesley, but the pair of them, young and whole and so certain, the way only young men can be, of their invincibility.

June-bug began to sob, pummeling Jacob's broad chest with her fists, and still he made no move to stop the blows. "Will died in his arms," she cried. "Do you hear me, Jacob McCaffrey? Our Will died in Wes's arms, out there on that battlefield, and Wes has had to live with that every moment of the day and night ever since!"

Tears welled in Jacob's dark eyes. He looked down at June-bug and, at last, took hold of her wrists. Her hands disappeared into his. "Hush, now," he said, in rough-hewn tones, full of love. "We're going to get him out of there. We're goin' to get them *all* out of there."

June-bug sagged against him, weeping inconsolably.

Over his wife's head, Jacob met Olivia's gaze. "See to her," he said softly, so softly that, ever after, Olivia wondered if he'd actually spoken the words, or simply thought them. "Please."

Olivia nodded and touched June-bug on one shoulder. "Mrs. McCaffrey," she murmured. "Come along. We'll ride back to the station and brew up some hot coffee to keep these men warm while they work."

June-bug turned into her arms, and Olivia embraced her tightly. Their cheeks touched, although Olivia was the taller by far, and their tears mingled. Then, lifting her head and drawing a deep breath, June-bug pulled herself together and dashed at her cheeks with quick, resolute motions of one hand. She sniffled and then, unbelievably, smiled.

"You're right, Olivia," she said. "We've got to make ourselves useful."

Olivia nodded. Her shovel had fallen to the hard ground at her feet; she stooped to recover the tool and surrender it to a cowboy who'd just ridden out from town at breakneck speed. Others would be arriving soon, she knew. Word traveled fast on the frontier when someone, anyone, needed help.

Jamie's eyes were enormous as she came into the station, crossed the large room, and leaned disconsolately against Olivia's side. "Is he gonna die down there?"

It was midafternoon, the snow was coming down thicker and faster than ever, and the men of Springwater had been digging for hours, without discernible progress. Still, Olivia refused to give up hope that Wesley and all the others were alive, that they *would* be rescued; any other conclusion was unthinkable.

She sat down in June-bug's rocking chair, next to the fire, and took Jamie's small shoulders into her hands. "Nobody's giving up, child," she said quietly. "Don't you be the first."

Jamie swallowed visibly. "I guess there won't be any Christmas program."

June-bug was stirring a big kettle of soup at the stove, and she and Olivia exchanged glances. Olivia hadn't given the pageant a thought since the catastrophe had struck; now, she bit her lower lip and considered the situation.

"I think we ought to go ahead with our play," she said, and met June-bug's gaze again.

June-bug nodded her agreement and offered a fragile smile.

"I don't reckon I can sing, knowin' they're all

down there," Jamie murmured. "Singin's a happy thing."

Olivia took the child's cold hands into her own, squeezed them slightly, in an effort to lend reassurance. "What do you think Mr. McCaffrey would want you to do, if he were able to talk to you right now?"

"Jacob?" Jamie asked.

"No, darling. Our own Mr. McCaffrey. Wesley."

Jamie studied the floor, as though expecting to find a message inscribed in the wide planks. They were smooth from the passing of many feet, those boards, and made pale by June-bug's regular scrubbing. Finally, the child looked up, and there were tears shining in her eyes. Her lower lip wobbled, and she sniffled inelegantly. "I reckon he'd say go ahead and sing," she answered.

Olivia took Jamie's chin gently between a thumb and index finger and lifted the little girl's head. "I reckon you're right about that," she said.

Presently, Trey Hargreaves came in, face red with cold, coat covered in snow. He paused just inside the door, as though unsure of his welcome. He took in both June-bug and Olivia, and his broad shoulders slumped slightly.

"This is my fault," he said.

June-bug immediately crossed the room and began helping Trey out of his coat. His motions were wooden with fatigue and shock. "No, it isn't," she protested, "and don't let me hear you say that again. Is there any word?"

"I wanted to tell you myself; we're down to the first layer of timber," he said, unable to hide the tinge of hope, of desparate hope, that laced his words.

Olivia had poured a mug of hot coffee just after Trey entered the station, and she took it to him without a word.

He sank onto one of the benches and rested his elbows on the tabletop. "Thanks," he said.

"Where's Rachel?" June-bug inquired. She stood beside Trey, resting one small hand on his shoulder. "You ought to be with your wife at a time like this."

"I don't think I could face Rachel," Trey muttered.

"Well, ain't that a fine howdy-do?" June-bug responded, with quiet spirit. "I never figured you for a coward, Trey Hargreaves!"

Trey covered his face with both hands. "I could have closed that mine long ago," he said, giving no sign that he'd heard anything June-bug said. "Lord knows, we've got money enough to last a lifetime—"

"There's been steady work in Springwater these past few years, because of the Jupiter and Zeus," June-bug insisted. "Why, look at Ben Williams and his family. I don't know what those folks would have done, if you hadn't given him that job."

"I gave him a job, all right," Trey said, staring straight ahead now, through the log walls of the station to something far, far beyond. "And a grave to go with it."

"Miss Rachel's across the road at the big house, lookin' after some of the wives and kids. I'll go fetch her." Jamie's voice startled everyone in the room; even Trey snapped back from wherever he'd been wandering.

"You do that, sweetheart," June-bug said. "I'm obliged."

Rachel arrived within five minutes, looking strong and competent and concerned. Trey stood up at the sight of her, his face anguished and pale, and she rushed into his arms. Watching the tender scene, Olivia felt a stab of envy so sharp that she nearly doubled over with the pain of it. Dear God, what would she do if Wesley never came back, if there were never another embrace, another kiss?

She blinked rapidly and looked away.

Rachel and Trey talked for a long time, in low voices, while June-bug and Olivia kept their distance, trying to stay busy. Finally, Trey finished his coffee, put on his coat again, and went back to help the others with the digging. Rachel embraced June-bug and Olivia, each in turn, and then returned to her grand house.

When the daylight began to fade, lanterns were brought to the mine site, and still the work went on. With every passing moment, deliverance became less and less likely, but not one man laid down his shovel to go home. Jacob McCaffrey, laboring as hard or harder than any of them, prayed silently all the while, making the same request over and over again. *Let me see my son again. Let me put my arms around him. Let me ask for his forgiveness, as I'm asking for Yours.*

Pres Parrish laid a hand on his arm. His dark hair was laced with snow, and his face reflected the worry and the weariness all of them felt. "That's enough, Jacob," he said, in that stern way of his. "Remember your heart."

Jacob leaned on his shovel, gasping for breath but determined to dig as long as digging was necessary. "He's down there. My boy. All I've got left."

Pres didn't flinch. But then, he never did; he was the steadiest man Jacob had ever known. "Nonsense. You've got June-bug and Toby and all the rest of us. We need you, Jacob. And when your son comes up out of that mine, he might need you, too."

"I don't believe I can abide standin' still," Jacob confessed hoarsely. He was as near to breaking down and weeping as he'd been since the day he heard the news of Will and Wesley's fall at Chattanooga. He turned and looked toward the distant station, where he and June-bug had made a life for themselves. "I've got to feel like I'm doin' something."

"I understand that," Pres answered. "Just rest a while. Go into town and see to June-bug. Have some coffee and warm yourself by the fire. We'll send word when the situation calls for it—"

Before he'd finished the sentence, there was a shout from the mouth of the shaft, and Jacob recognized the voice as Toby's. "I heard something," the boy insisted. "Somebody callin' out." He cupped his hands around his mouth as Jacob and Pres hurried to his side. "Hullo!" The word echoed, seeming to go on and on.

Faintly, so faintly that Jacob couldn't be sure he'd truly heard it, an answering cry rose from deep in the belly of the earth. Tears burned his eyes, and he made no effort to hide them. The men around him cheered; they were still a long way from reaching the trapped miners, everyone knew that, but someone down there was still alive. It was the first good luck they'd had since the whole nightmare began.

At six o'clock, right on time, the angels and shepherds and Wise Men lined up in the tiny side room of Springwater's one church, faces pale, eyes bright with determination. Olivia wanted to weep with pride, just looking at those children; many of them had a father, elder brother, or grandfather trapped in the mine, but here they were, ready to perform the pieces they'd practiced so carefully for weeks.

Jacob himself offered an eloquent opening prayer, all but dwarfing the large Christmas tree in one corner of the sanctuary, not so much by virtue of his considerable size as by the power of his very presence, his sturdy, unswerving faith. His wonderful voice echoed through the small, candlelit church as he asked the Lord's blessing on the men of the Jupiter and Zeus and upon their loved ones. He thanked his God for the support of friends and family in hard times, and allowed as how even though they all hoped to lay eyes on those men again, they'd leave the final decision to Him. His "amen" made the congregation, mostly women since the men were still working to save their friends and neighbors, sit up a little straighter on those hard, handmade pews. Tears glittered in more than a few pairs of eyes, but every backbone was straight and every chin high. Miss Turnbull was there with the rest, handkerchief in hand, dignified of countenance but obviously moved.

Olivia felt a sweet stirring in her heart, looking out over the gathering, come together to celebrate what they regarded as the most hopeful event in all of history. It was, in spite of looming tragedy, still Christmas.

The angels were the first to perform; they sang their chorus, voices tremulous and beautiful, announcing the Holy Birth. Jamie offered her solo, and the shepherds, guarding their flocks by night, were sore afraid, just as they'd rehearsed.

Mary and Joseph appeared, and Miranda Kildare stepped self-consciously into the tableau to place baby Nell in the manger. The infant immediately began to shriek, and a ripple of fond laughter moved through the small but intent audience. Miranda dashed back to claim her daughter and the play continued without a Baby Jesus, but nobody minded.

The Wise Men entered on cue, offering their gifts—a cigar box, someone's green glass vase, and a silver candy dish from Olivia's front parlor. Olivia, for her part, played the piano and prompted the actors, in a whisper that probably carried to every corner of the church, whenever someone forgot what they were supposed to say.

Little Clarissa Hargreaves, Trey and Rachel's four-year-old, a dark-haired child with striking silver eyes, seized with stage fright and surely sensing the undercurrent of tension coursing beneath the surface of the brave gathering, burst into tears in the middle of her Bible verse and Rachel had to come up and collect her. She smiled apologetically and held Clarissa very close as she carried her back to the front pew.

Everyone stood up to sing at the end of the pageant, and Olivia's own voice trembled as she joined in. She'd been able to keep busy ever since the disaster, but soon, she would have to sit still, waiting and thinking, hoping and being afraid. She wasn't sure she could bear being idle, when Wesley might be dead or dying, or very gravely injured.

The chorus of the final hymn rose from the congregation like a plea to Heaven.

Silent night, holy night, all is calm, all is bright . . .

Olivia, standing at the front of the church, with the children, raised her eyes when she felt the rush of cold air flood up the aisle, and then the first man walked in, covered in dirt but safe, blessedly safe. She recognized Ben Williams.

The singing stopped abruptly, and it really was, for those few infinitely sweet moments, a silent night. Daisy and Rose immediately broke ranks with the other angels and joined their mother in hugging Ben and sobbing for joy.

There were others, then, other miners come back from the grave, trailing in one after another, and the little church fairly shook with happiness, relief, and gratitude. Olivia stood rooted to the floor, staring at the opening, willing Wesley to be there, to be alive and unhurt. Jacob and June-bug McCaffrey stood still as well, and so did Jamie, watching the door.

And then they saw him. Wesley. Smiling, filthy, and unbearably beautiful.

He touched his father's shoulder as he passed along the aisle, squeezed his mother's extended hand, but he didn't look away from Olivia's face the whole time, nor did he come to a stop. Only when he was standing in front of the small dais, where the pulpit usually stood, and looking up at her, did he speak.

"I love you, Olivia," he said, for all to hear. "Will you marry me? Right away?"

She nodded, blinded by tears and too choked up to speak, and he gave a shout, reached up to grasp her by the waist, and spun her around twice, right there in front of the whole delighted town of Springwater. It wasn't proper church behavior, that went without saying, and neither was the cheer that went up from the congregation, but most folks probably figured the Lord would be inclined to overlook some indecorous behavior, given the special circumstances.

There was a grand celebration at the Springwater Station that Christmas Eve—miraculously, every man had come out of the shaft, conscious and breathing, though some had suffered broken bones and other injuries—and the townspeople were jubilant.

Young Toby McCaffrey, Olivia soon learned, was the hero of the day. He'd climbed down through a maze of rafters, once they'd been unearthed, and helped the others get out. When Jacob found out about it, he was obviously proud of his adopted son, but he gave him a hard knuckle-rub atop the head anyway, and told him he ought to be whupped for taking fool chances.

In time, people began to drift away, carrying sleeping children in their arms. Husbands and wives, reunited, left the station arm in arm, lost in each other's eyes, and Sally Williams put her daughters to bed, wearing their angel wings on top of their nightgowns, then retired to the room she and Ben shared to look after her exhausted, grubby, grinning man.

Finally, only Olivia, Wesley, Toby, and the McCaffreys remained; Jamie lay slumbering on one of the benches, covered with Jacob's coat. Like the Williams girls, she was still wearing her wings, and her tinsel halo lay askew over her forehead.

Toby, clothes as black as those of any of the men

he'd helped to rescue, was reticent, watching Wes thoughtfully as he sat next to the fire, talking with Jacob. Olivia settled herself on a stool next to Wesley's chair, and their fingers were interlocked, while June-bug stood behind them, her hands resting on her son's shoulders.

Wesley must have felt the boy's regard, for he turned, in the middle of a sentence, to look at him. Then he stood, crossed the room, and faced Toby squarely. His voice, though pitched low, carried to every ear in the room.

"I'm grateful for what you did today," Wesley said, "and I'd be proud if you and I could call ourselves brothers."

A tentative smile broke over Toby's handsome young face; no doubt he'd been thinking there would be no place for him at the Springwater Station, now that Jacob and June-bug had recovered one of their flesh-and-blood sons. "You mean it?"

Wes laid a hand on Toby's shoulder. "Of course I do."

June-bug sniffled and dashed at her cheeks with the heel of one palm. "I declare," she murmured, "I do declare."

Jacob rose from his chair and put an arm around her shoulders. "It's time we all called it a night," he said. "Tomorrow's Christmas, after all."

Wes turned, came back to Olivia and, taking her hand again, drew her to her feet. "There's one thing yet to be done," he said, and he was addressing his father, though his eyes were holding

Olivia's. "If you'll just marry us, Daddy, I'll be real obliged."

"I reckon I can stay awake long enough to do that," Jacob said and, fetching his Bible, took up his customary marrying place in front of the fireplace. There was a smile in his voice, though he and Wes still hadn't had a chance to talk, father to son, and begin settling their differences. No one doubted that the process might take a long time, and there would be bumpy stretches along the road to reconciliation, but each one loved the other, and that was enough for the moment.

Olivia felt as though a spell had been cast over her; she stood beside Wesley, light-headed with happiness, and repeated the proper phrases when Jacob indicated, with a kindly nod, that she ought to speak. The whole ceremony took no more than ten minutes, Olivia supposed, and yet in the space of that time, everything changed. When Wesley kissed her, her heart soared like a Chinese rocket, bursting against a dark winter sky, and she wasn't entirely certain that she would ever catch her breath again. Her bridegroom chuckled and steadied her when she swayed a little, his hands strong about her waist.

Alone for much of her life, Olivia was now part of a couple, a partnership. She was a McCaffrey now, she had a real family: Jacob and June-bug, Toby, and—please, God—Jamie, too.

She watched as Wesley—her *husband*—gathered Jamie up in an old quilt borrowed from his mother

and bid the small wedding party a good night
and a happy Christmas. They walked side by side
through the falling snow that Christmas Eve,
toward home.

Miss Priscilla Turnbull greeted them at the door
and even smiled at Wesley. "I'm pleased, young
man," she said stiffly, "to see that you've risen safely from the pit."

He gave the older woman a lopsided grin, and
she was obviously charmed. "Thank you," he said,
in a conspiratorial whisper, indicating Jamie with a
nod. "If you'll excuse me a moment, I've got a pretty tired angel here."

Olivia watched him with a full heart as he carried the child up the stairs.

"It is indeed a happy Christmas," Miss Turnbull
said.

Olivia turned to her boarder. "Yes," she agreed.
"Mr. McCaffrey and I are married now, Miss Turnbull. We can give Jamie—Martha Sue—a fine
home."

Miss Turnbull was silent for so long that Olivia
had long since steeled herself for a refusal when
the woman finally answered. "Yes," she said. "I
believe you can."

Olivia stared at Miss Turnbull, grasped the
woman's plump hands in her own. "Are you saying—?"

Miss Turnbull nodded. "You and your husband
can give the child a much better life than I ever
could." She paused, apparently searching for words.

Her eyes were bright when she met Olivia's gaze again. "It takes young folks like you to keep up with the likes of that little imp. And it's plain that you and that charming man of yours love each other very much." She sighed. "And this town, why, it's like a family." She looked into Olivia's eyes. "I—I would like a letter once in a while—just a word or two letting me know that Martha Sue—Jamie—is all right."

Olivia embraced the other woman gently. "Of course, Priscilla," she promised. "And thank you. Thank you so much. I promise, you'll never have cause to be sorry for trusting us."

"I'll need my cloak," Miss Turnbull announced, drawing herself up, full of pepper again. "My room is too drafty, and I can't get a good cup of tea in this house to save my life. I'm going to stay at the stagecoach station until I can leave this wilderness once and for all."

Olivia wasn't fooled in the least. Miss Turnbull was leaving because she did not want to intrude on the couple's wedding night. "Oh, but it's so dark out," she protested. It was a big house, after all. "And it's bitterly cold. You can move to the station in the morning."

Wes, standing on the stairs, put in his two cents. "We insist," he said.

Miss Turnbull, however, would not be moved. Wes ended up walking Olivia's former boarder up the road to the station.

When he returned, Olivia was at the stove,

cooking. After Wesley had taken a hot bath and consumed a plateful of eggs and salt pork, he curved an arm loosely around his bride, leaned down to blow out the kerosene lantern burning in the center of the kitchen table, and moved unerringly toward the darkened stairway.

Neither of them spoke; there was no need for words.

He was safe. They were married, they loved each other, and Jamie was theirs to raise. It was Christmas Eve. In the fullness of time, they would arrange their lives, make decisions and plans, ask and answer questions. For now, they need only think about the night ahead—their wedding night.

In the upstairs corridor, Wesley put his arms around Olivia and drew her close, close enough that she experienced his desire for her in no uncertain terms. Laying his forehead against hers, he asked, "My room or yours, Mrs. McCaffrey?"

She looked up at him, smiled. "Ours."

"Are you scared?"

She thought about it, then shook her head.

He kissed her, setting a familiar fire ablaze inside her. "Good," he said, and swept her off her feet to carry her over the threshold of the room they would share.

❧ Epilogue ❧

August 1883

THE LACE CURTAINS fluttered at the bedroom windows, and a cool, soothing breeze drifted across the bed. Wes laid a possessive hand on Olivia's bare and only slightly swollen belly; the pregnancy was their secret, for the moment—and Doc Parrish's, of course.

"When do you suppose she'll start moving around in there?" he asked.

Olivia laughed. Her heart was so full, she thought it would break wide open, and desire was stirring again, too. Wes could do that, make her want him at any hour of the day or night, just by lying down next to her, touching her, or even looking at her. "We've already got a daughter, Mr. McCaffrey," she said, snuggling against him and slipping her arms around his neck. "This is a boy I'm carrying. Wesley William Jacob McCaffrey."

He grinned and slipped down to kiss her stomach. "Boy or girl," he said gruffly, "it scares me to think how much I'm going to love this kid."

She moaned and arched her back slightly, aroused by the warmth of his breath on her skin and by the innocent kiss he'd planted there.

He laughed. "Hussy," he said. "Did I or did I not make love to you not half an hour ago?"

Olivia stretched. "I'm ready again," she mumured.

It wasn't often that they got to be alone together in the middle of the day, like they were then. Usually, Wes was busy at the blacksmith shop he and Jacob and Toby had built behind the barn at the station, but Jamie was gone to Choteau with Savannah Parrish and Rachel Hargreaves and their children, and the thought of having the house to themselves had simply been too great a temptation to resist. Olivia had been on her way to fetch Wes home by the ear, if it came to that, only to meet him in the road.

They'd spent a delightful interlude in the pantry, where she'd helped him with his bath. Or, perhaps, she'd hindered him.

"I love you, Mrs. McCaffrey," he said, and lingered where he was to run the tip of his tongue around her navel. "I reckon you're wanting some good old-fashioned proof of that, though."

A purring sound escaped Olivia; she was already half out of her mind with wanting.

He began nibbling at her. "Mind you, I'll make this one stick," he joked.

Olivia made a small, joyous, soblike sound and buried her fingers in his spun-honey hair. "Stop talking," she said, gasping a little.

He did as she'd asked, and occupied himself in a way that made her cry out in a ragged voice and arch her back high off the mattress. He stayed with her, driving her deeper and deeper into the fever of his loving, his hands, stronger than ever from tending the forge and shoeing horses, cradling her buttocks.

She began to toss her head from side to side on the pillow and to tug at him, wherever she could catch hold, trying to get him to mount her, make her completely and finally his, but he was bent on taking his time.

Sweat broke out all over her, but this time the breeze did nothing to cool her. She took fire, like dry grass under a shower of sparks, and began to buck in his hands, and still he enjoyed her, teased her, refused to let her go. Her breath turned to a rapid, shallow panting, and she pleaded shamelessly, in words that made no sense. He knew what she wanted, what she needed, but he continued to attend her in the way he chose, and when he began to work her even harder, even faster, even more thoroughly, white flames swept through her body and exploded, silver-white, in her mind. All her senses deserted her, with the exception of one; she was all feeling, as though her nerves lay outside her skin.

She jerked against him, helpless, and still he wasn't through with her. He made her climb to the top of the peak and tumble over the precipice twice more before he slid up as far as her breasts, and took his pleasure there until she was hot and needing yet again.

"I can't," she whimpered.

"You will," he said. And he was right.

When he finally, finally took her, she was so worked up that she found release instantaneously, and with a ferocious intensity. Wes murmured to her, nibbled at her jawline and her neck and her earlobe while she erupted beneath him, in slow, delicious fits and stages, and then his own climb began in earnest.

Olivia stroked his back while he moved upon her, raised and lowered her hips in the way instinct had taught her, months before, on their wedding night. She'd been nervous then—it seemed incredible now—but Wes had been infinitely patient, infinitely tender, and so skilled a lover that she'd honestly thought she would die, that her soul, soaring the way it was, would surely separate itself from her body and fly away. Until then, she'd believed, as many women did, that lovemaking was simply a wifely duty, designed for the benefit of the male gender and, of course, the conception of children. In Wes's arms, she'd discovered a degree of pleasure and fulfillment she had never dared imagine, never mind experience, and it frightened her sometimes, how much she loved him. How much she needed him.

Wes was a thorough man, and by the time his self-control was reaching its limits, at long, long last, Olivia was already moaning in the throes of a series of soft, sweet catches, taken quite by surprise. He stiffened upon her, and gave a hoarse, strangled cry of triumph and surrender, and she felt his warmth spilling into her, and received him gladly.

"Promise you'll never leave me," she said.

His eyes were still glazed, his arms still tense as he held himself poised over her, shuddering. "I— promise—" he ground out.

She drew him down to lie in her arms, and comforted him by stroking his love-rumpled hair and placing light kisses on his temples, his forehead, his mouth. In time, exhausted by joy, they fell asleep, entwined, and beyond the walls of that once lonely house, Springwater went on about its business.

Linda Lael Miller

SPRINGWATER SEASONS

Rachel

Savannah

Miranda

Jessica

The breathtaking new series....Discover the passion, the pride, and the glory of a magnificent frontier town!

Available now from Pocket Books   2043-01

LINDA LAEL MILLER

TWO BROTHERS

THE GUNSLINGER

THE LAWMAN

"Linda Lael Miller's talent knows no bounds...each story she creates is...superb."
—*Rendezvous*

**Available now
from Pocket Books**

2009-01